TO LOVE, HONOR, AND PERISH

SQUEAKY CLEAN MYSTERIES, BOOK 6

CHRISTY BARRITT

COPYRIGHT:

To Love, Honor, and Perish: A Novel
Copyright 2013 by Christy Barritt

Published by River Heights Press

Cover design by The Killion Group

The persons and events portrayed in this work are the creation of the author, and any resemblance to persons living or dead is purely coincidental.

CHAPTER
ONE

"GABBY, YOU LOOK STUNNING!" Teddi stepped away from the embankment of mirrors surrounding me and put her hand over her mouth.

I turned to look at my reflection and nearly gasped. "Mamma, mia . . ."

I was wearing a wedding dress. A real, certified wedding gown. It was sleeveless with a brocade around the corset and layers of white silky fabric and tulle flowing down to the floor and beyond.

"Riley's going to love it," Teddi said, circling me and taking in every angle. "Of course, I've seen the way he looks at you. He'd love it even if you were wearing a sackcloth."

"I think this is the one." I curtsied in the mirror, unable to take my eyes off the dress. I'd dreamed about this moment for so long. The day I'd find my

Prince Charming, he'd realize I was his soul mate, and we lived happily ever after.

Even though Riley and I had been engaged for more than a month, my wedding planning kept getting delayed for various reasons. That's why Riley and I had decided to have a small, private ceremony in a week. Yes, one week. A little less than that now, for that matter.

Today was Monday. Our wedding was on Sunday.

We were going to have the ceremony in Virginia Beach at the oceanfront. At sunset. I didn't care about the flowers or fancy invitations. But I did want a dress that would knock Riley's socks off. What's a fairytale without a gown worthy of a princess?

Teddi tugged at the back of my gown, right at the zipper, like a seamstress might. "I don't think you're going to need to have it altered even. It's like the dress was made for you."

Teddi was my dad's new girlfriend, and she was different from any of the other women who'd been in his life since my mom passed away. What the pint-sized woman lacked in stature, she made up for in hair. The former Texas beauty queen prided herself in having earned the title of Best Gown for three years in a row. In her mind, that made her a fashion expert, and I wasn't going to argue.

Her hands rested above my hips as she peered

behind me in the mirror. "Look at that tiny waist of yours. I used to have a waist like that."

I didn't mention that I'd probably dropped five to ten pounds from the stress of last week. Tracking down serial killers could do that to a girl. But that was all behind me now, and it was smooth sailing ahead.

She tugged at my red, curly hair, pulling it back away from my face. "Have you thought about your hair? How you'll wear it?"

"Probably down and curly. Riley likes it that way. No veil. Maybe a flower behind my ear."

"That sounds perfect." She grinned.

I looked in the mirror again and sighed. "I can't believe I'm getting married, Teddi."

I thought back on all the messes in my life. I remembered the moments when I thought nothing would work out. I reminisced the bad decisions, the broken paths, the train wreck that could have been. But somehow, someway, everything had worked out and had led me to this point in my life.

And now, in less than a week, I'd be marrying the man of my dreams. I knew that with Riley by my side, I could handle anything the world threw at me. Riley was my best friend, my partner in crime, the levelheaded one who balanced my brash impulsiveness.

"You are going to be one happy woman. I think

marriage will really suit you. My years with Jim were some of the best of my life."

"You were married before?" As soon as I asked the question, I wanted to take it back. It was nosy, and Teddi was dating my father. I had no idea what her story was, nor should I be inquisitive about it. I'd entered the land called "Awkward," and I had no one to blame but myself.

"I was married to Jim for twenty years, Sugar. Twenty of the best years of my life."

My throat tightened. "What happened?"

"Cancer. It can get the best of us, can't it? He held on for five years, but when the disease came back the second time, he was too weak to fight." Her eyes welled with tears a moment before she smiled sadly. "I find comfort that he's in a better place now."

I squeezed her hand. I couldn't imagine what it would be like to have found the love of your life and then lost him . . . what a tragic story. "I'm so sorry, Teddi."

She shook her head and pulled herself upright. "Don't be sorry. God brought your father into my life. He's been a blessing to me."

I had trouble seeing how my dad was a blessing, but I didn't say anything. My dad was trying to make some changes in his lifestyle. I had to give him credit for that.

Teddi motioned to the fresh-faced attendant who waited in the distance. "We'll take this dress."

"You really don't have to buy this," I started, gripping the skirt of the gown like my hands had taken on a mind of their own and might never loosen their clutch. "I'm perfectly capable of affording this myself."

She raised her hand, each finger a masterpiece from her golden, bejeweled rings to the manicured tips. "I'm not going to hear anything about it. I've decided this is how I want to help, and nothing you can say will stop me. I never had a daughter of my own, you know. And marriage is the last thing on my son's mind. He's too busy trying to make it as a country music star."

I could tell by the way she said "country music star" that Teddi didn't think too highly of his career choice. There was really so much that I didn't know about Teddi. I couldn't believe she'd stuck around for as long as she had.

"I appreciate your generosity," I finally said. If I was honest, I'd admit that money was really tight right now. I was back to crime scene cleaning, Riley was saving to buy a new car and trying to get his new law firm off the ground. Neither of us was at a place where we had a lot of disposable income.

Teddi clapped her hands together once and gave a confident nod. "Let's get this baby boxed up and paid for. Then we'll get some lunch at this little café down the street that I've been dying to try. I hear they have crepes that will blow your mind. Sound good?"

I nodded. "Sounds great."

Being with Teddi still felt a little surreal. My mom had died while I was in college, and I'd gotten used to doing things on my own. Having a mother figure to shop with and do lunch together seemed so foreign. But there was a part of me that loved it.

Maybe things were finally looking up for me. As soon as I figured out my whole career thing, I'd have absolutely nothing to complain about. You see, I'd landed my dream job with the State Medical Examiner's Office. But then budget cuts hit, so of course the new girl was the first one to go. No one else was hiring in my specialized field in the area, which brought me back to my original job as a crime scene cleaner.

I'd done an interview last week with the Medical Examiner's Office out in Kansas. I was supposed to hear any time now whether or not I got the job. It didn't really matter, though. I'd already decided that I wouldn't accept the position, mostly because I wanted to be near my family and friends here in Virginia.

The attendant knocked on the door behind us, appearing with a box in hand. Teddi nearly jumped out of her skin. She placed a hand over her heart and closed her eyes. From where I was standing, I could tell her breathing had quickened, that her muscles had tightened.

I didn't have to ask about her response. I knew exactly why she'd overreacted.

The Scum River Killer had abducted her. Thankfully, the man had been shot and fallen off the aptly-named High Rise Bridge—the structure easily stretched eight stories above the massive Elizabeth River below. Teddi and three other victims had been rescued.

I placed a hand on her arm. I'd been there in those final horrifying moments before Scum had been shot. I'd seen how terrified Teddi had been, and rightfully so. How many women had died at the hands of the man during his first terror spree out in California? I knew the answer. Thirteen.

"Are you okay?" I asked softly.

She nodded and pulled her eyes open. "Just jumpy."

"Are you sleeping any?"

The lines around her eyes tightened. "Not so much. I have too many bad memories. I keep thinking about . . ."

She didn't have to finish. I knew it would be a long time before she forgot about Milton Jones hiding in her closet and abducting her. Details of the things that had happened in that cabin in the woods were slowly coming out from the victims. I knew they'd been starved, threatened with a knife, and left in the dark. That had just been the start.

Teddi pulled me into a hug and kissed one cheek before backing up and patting the other side of my face in a way that made me feel eight. "I don't know what I would have done without you. You're one brave girl, Gabby."

I tried to smile but couldn't. "I didn't feel brave. My knees were shaking."

Flashbacks of being held by Jones at gunpoint, of being forced to drive, of being prodded out onto the catwalk of a massive bridge, flooded my own mind.

I'd encountered a lot of bad people in my life. Jones had been one of the worst, if not *the* worst. Riley had put him behind bars when he'd been a prosecutor out in California. When the man escaped custody, getting revenge on Riley had been his first priority.

As much as I hated to admit it, there was this small niggle of doubt in my mind when it came to Jones' death. I'd seen him shot. I'd watched him go over the bridge and hit the dark, black water below. If the bullet hadn't killed him, the impact of hitting the water should have. If the impact hadn't, then the river itself should have claimed him. There were a lot of layers there, which made it seem impossible that he could survive.

But I'd seen Jones do the impossible before. I knew that, against all odds, he'd escaped from prison and made it across country in less than forty-eight hours. I knew he had a little fan club. I knew he was without a heart.

The police never found his body. They all said there was no way he could have survived the bullet wound and the fall.

Part of me wouldn't rest until his body was recovered, though. I needed that closure and resolution.

"He's gone, Gabby." Teddi put a hand on my arm, almost as if she could read my thoughts and knew I was thinking about Jones.

I forced a smile and nodded, trying to reassure her and ease some of her anxiety. "Of course he is."

But I wasn't so sure he was gone.

I'd already been told that his remains might not ever be found. From the Elizabeth River, his body could have been swept out to the James River, then the Chesapeake Bay, and finally to the ocean. Marine life could be feeding on the man now.

It wouldn't surprise me if, even in his death, the man brought destruction. All those poor sea creatures would probably turn up dead in some kind of unprecedented fish kill. After all, it just wasn't the man's flesh that could rot. His soul was already rotten.

The attendant unzipped the gown, snapping me back to the present. I stepped out of my dress—feeling reluctant to do so, for some reason—and then pulled on my jeans and Bride-To-Be T-shirt.

Just as I grabbed my purse, my cellphone rang. I hoped it wasn't someone calling me with a crime scene cleaning job that couldn't wait. Chad, my business partner, should be able to handle things for a few hours. I couldn't afford to turn down work, but I really wanted a day just to feel normal, to be a woman out planning her wedding. I still had people to call and reservations to make in order for this ceremony to happen on Sunday.

I pulled my phone out and glanced at the number. When I saw the digits there, I blinked with surprise.

Detective Adams. The Norfolk detective had worked the case against Jones.

Maybe he was calling to tell me the killer's body had been found.

Wouldn't that be a great wedding present?

I excused myself for one minute, already anticipating sharing the good news about Jones with Teddi, as I put the phone to my ear. "I hope you found him in the swamp."

"Gabby?" Detective Adams said. His deep voice rumbled across the phone.

"The beach is too peaceful and pretty," I continued. "I hope Jones got washed up somewhere dank and dirty. Somewhere fitting." I paused. "That is why you're calling, right?"

"I wish that's why I was calling, Gabby."

Something in his voice caused me to stiffen. There were undertones of tension, of sorrow. If Adams wasn't calling about Jones, then why would he be calling? "What's wrong?"

"You need to get to the hospital, Gabby."

A million scenarios raced through my mind. Time seemed to stop for a moment. I leaned against the wall, bracing myself for whatever he had to say. Had something happened to one of Jones' other victims? Nichole or Clarice maybe? Had one of them had a mental breakdown? No one would blame them after what they'd been through.

"What . . . what do you mean? What are you saying?"

"Riley was shot this morning, Gabby. He's in critical condition. Come to the hospital. There's no time to waste."

IT WAS a good thing Teddi was with me, because I don't think I could have gotten myself to the hospital without an accident. My hands were shaking too badly. I could hardly breathe. My heart felt like it had been smashed into a thousand pieces.

Teddi pulled up to the Emergency Room entrance. Before the car completely stopped, I opened the door and ran through the gushing rain toward the automatic doors. I didn't bother to look back. To say anything.

My body seemed to take over, to know exactly what I needed to do—to find Riley. On autopilot, almost feeling outside of myself, I hurried into the hospital. I ran past the people milling around in the waiting room. Past the people with bloody, makeshift bandages. Past screaming children. Past those with pinched expressions.

I pressed myself against the reception desk. "Riley Thomas. I need to see Riley Thomas."

The middle-aged woman with an unnatural shade of red hair glanced at me, said nothing, and then took way too long to type something into the computer.

Each moment seemed suspended and urgent, like time had thickened, like each action had me moving through gel.

Finally, the woman peered up at me through her tiny turquoise glasses. "Are you family?"

"I'm his fiancée," I mumbled breathlessly.

She stared at me another moment, as if trying to figure out if I was telling the truth, before offering a slight nod. "He's in surgery."

"What floor?"

"The third, but you can't see him now."

I barely heard her. I took off in a slow jog down the hall, reached the elevator, and hit the UP button uncountable times until the door opened. A nurse pushed a man in a wheelchair out just as I slipped inside. I didn't bother to check for anyone behind me. I hit the "3" button and then the "Close Door." The elevator moved too slowly. Everything seemed to be in slow motion except me.

Riley? Shot? What had happened? Where? Was he okay?

My brain rushed a million different directions. Different scenarios. Different outcomes.

I was probably overreacting. Riley was fine. He'd have surgery. The bullet would come out. He'd recover. We'd go on with our lives.

So what if he was on crutches for our wedding. I could handle that. One day, we'd look back and laugh about it. We'd view our wedding pictures and remember how awkward it had been to try and stand on the sand with crutches and a cast.

Maybe we should move the wedding from the beach, for that matter. To somewhere more accessible. After all, it wasn't the ceremony that was as important as the commitment, as the vows.

Nausea welled in my gut as the elevator doors opened. I quickly followed the signs to the ICU. Before I reached the unit, I saw Detective Adams standing in the corridor. Something about his expression gave me pause, made a shudder run through me.

Okay, maybe we'd have to delay the wedding. Maybe Riley would need a little more time to recover. Maybe I was rushing things here. Being selfish.

As I stopped in front of Adams and saw his eyes, queasiness rose so strongly in me that I thought I would vomit. Something was wrong. Seriously wrong. More wrong than I wanted to accept.

My lips wanted to move but couldn't. I didn't know what to ask. What to say. What to think.

Adams placed a hand on my arm. "Let's sit."

I wanted to argue. Instead, I let the detective lead me to a gray padded chair against the wall. As I started to lower myself, my knees buckled. I grabbed the plastic gray armrests and caught myself.

Adams sat beside me. He stared at me a moment. "Riley's in surgery," he started.

"How . . . ? What . . . ?" Even as I asked the questions, warning bells were going off in my mind. Somehow, I realized this news, this conversation, would rock my world. I wouldn't be the same again.

"We're reviewing security footage right now, but it appears that a masked man walked into the law office at nine this morning. He pulled the trigger only once."

"And . . . ?"

"The bullet got Riley in the head."

I gasped. Cried out. My heart stopped. "The head? He was shot in the head?"

Adams nodded.

I bent forward until my face collided with my hands. This was even worse than I imagined.

His head? A brain injury . . . to say that was serious was an understatement.

Adams' hand went to my back. It was the first time the detective had ever touched me, had ever offered a moment of comfort.

That fact made another wave of reality wash over me. I wiped my cheeks, realizing they were wet. I wasn't sure when the tears had started to flow.

"Is he okay?"

"He's in surgery now. It's going to be a while before we know anything."

Two nurses hurried past. A family slipped into a room beside me. The sterile smell of Lysol and rubbing alcohol taunted me. Hospitals could be places of hope—of new life and healing. Or they could be places of life-changing tragedy and death. I had to hold on to hope.

I straightened, some of my clarity returning for at least a moment. "Who did this? It was Milton Jones, wasn't it?"

He shook his head solemnly. "We have every reason to believe that Jones is dead."

"But we don't know that for sure. He could have survived. He makes the most sense."

Adams' eyes held too much compassion for my comfort. "We're examining every possibility right now, Gabby. Jones is highly unlikely."

"If not Jones, then who?"

"I was hoping you might be able to help me answer that question."

I shook my head, trying to jostle my thoughts into place. "I have no idea. Riley's one of the kindest people I know. He helps people who are voiceless. He's . . . he's perfect."

"Certainly, in his line of work as an attorney, he's made some enemies. Not everyone likes a social justice crusader. Not the people he opposes. Has he mentioned anyone?"

I searched my memories but came up empty. "No, he hasn't said anything about anyone." Were there things Riley wasn't telling me? I just couldn't see it.

I had to push through my emotions for a moment, and asking questions seemed like the best way to do that. Asking questions and finding answers was what I did best. It was what I lived for. "Who found him?"

"One of the neighboring businesses—the accounting firm beside him, to be exact—heard the gunshot. They called 911. The first responders found him."

As the scenario played out in my mind, my thoughts came to a grinding halt. "What about Mary Lou?"

Adams tilted his head. "Who?"

"Riley's secretary. Is she okay? She's an older woman. A grandma. Retired. Sweet as apple pie."

"There was no one else at the office. Is today her day off maybe?"

I shook my head. "Not usually, but maybe she

took some personal time. Should I call her?"

Adams nodded. "Call her. Someone needs to call Riley's parents, also. Would you like me to do that?"

I swallowed, my throat raw and sore as I tried to restrain my tears. "No, I can do that. I should be the one to break the news. I'm going to be their daughter-in-law."

At that proclamation, my voice cracked. *Would* I be their daughter-in-law? What if . . . what if the wedding never took place? What if Riley didn't make it through the surgery?

A cry escaped from my lips. I had to think positive. I had to focus on what I could do, not on the "what ifs."

"I'm sorry, Gabby." The detective's voice sounded so soft and sympathetic that it nearly broke me. "You sure you can do this?"

I pushed aside my angst, nodded, and grabbed my phone just as Teddi appeared down the hallway. She sat beside me and placed her hand on my knee.

Didn't people know that every sign of compassion like that only made me weaker? I couldn't be weak. I had to be strong for Riley. He was going to get through this and be okay. All of this sympathy was for nothing. They'd see that. I just had to wait for the doctor to come out and give us an update. He'd tell us that, against all odds, Riley had come out of surgery okay and just needed some time to recover.

I stood and paced to the corner. Behind me, I saw Teddi and the detective talking. Teddi's hand went over her mouth as the detective no doubt filled her in.

I turned my back to them, unwilling to watch the scene. My hands trembled as I raised my phone and searched my contacts list. I could barely read the names, but finally I found the number I was looking for.

I hit CALL. I had to make sure that Mary Lou was okay, that some psycho hadn't abducted her in this whole process. The phone rang and rang again. With each jingle, my heart sped a little more.

Halfway through the fourth ring, the sound was cut short. A female said, "Hello?"

"Mary Lou?" I was breathless as I waited for her response.

"Yes? Who is this?" Her voice sounded soft and weak, like age had worn it down.

The tension in my chest eased for a moment, and my shoulders slumped with temporary relief. "Oh, Mary Lou. This is Gabby. I'm so glad you're all right."

"Gabby, what's wrong? You sound upset. Is everything okay?"

The tension returned as I braced myself to tell her the news. "Mary Lou, Riley was shot at work this morning."

It still seemed surreal having those words leave my lips. Surely this was a nightmare. Surely I'd wake up soon, and everything would be as it was supposed to be.

She gasped and let out a cry. "What? No . . ."

"I wanted to make sure you were okay."

"I had a dentist appointment, so I took the whole day off. Oh my . . . is he—is he . . . okay?"

I bit back tears. "He's in surgery now. We're still trying to piece together the details."

"Oh, Gabby. I'm so sorry. I just can't believe this. What can I do?"

"I'm sure the police will want to talk to you, to find out if anyone has threatened Riley recently. Anyone other than Milton Jones, that is." Even as I said the words, I realized that often the obvious answer was the right one.

The problem was, Milton Jones wasn't the type to walk into a building in the middle of the day with a mask on and shoot someone. No, he liked sneak attacks. He liked provoking fear. He liked his name to be known.

Besides, even if he had survived his fall off the bridge, he'd been shot in the shoulder. Could a man who'd been shot in the shoulder actually pull the trigger himself? That showdown had only happened a couple of days ago. He wouldn't have had time to recover.

"I'll go down to the station now. You call me if you need me. If you need *anything*. You hear?"

I nodded, though she couldn't see me, and hung up. The phone was still trembling in my hands as I searched for Riley's parents' number. I'd never called them before. I'd never had a reason to. Riley had called to tell them about our engagement, and then he'd called again yesterday when we'd decided to move up the date.

Riley had handed me the phone after he'd shared the news, and his parents had told me congratulations, that they'd see me soon.

I'd joked with Riley as I put their number in my Android.

"Just in case," I'd told him.

"Just in case what?" he'd asked.

"Just in case I ever need someone to set you straight."

The truth was, Riley hardly ever needed setting straight. No, that was me. I was the one who put myself in danger. I was the one who was impulsive, who didn't always think things through, whose mouth got her in trouble.

So why was Riley the one who'd been shot?

Using the back of my hand, I quickly brushed away a tear.

He was going to be all right. If only I could stay positive and think good thoughts. I couldn't let myself think about the worst-case scenarios here. I had to hold on to my faith.

Lord, please be with him. Be with the surgeon. Guide his or her hands. Heal Riley from this terrible wound.

I found Riley's parents' number and hit CALL before I realized I had no idea what to say. Before I could formulate anything, on the first ring, his mom answered. "Hello? Hello?" she repeated.

I cleared my throat, trying to pull myself together. "Mrs. Thomas? This is Gabby."

"Gabby!" Her voice changed from formal to warm. "What an unexpected surprise."

"Mrs. Thomas, I wish I was calling to talk about the wedding. But . . ." My throat burned. I sucked in a deep breath, willing my voice to remain even. It didn't cooperate. It squeaked up high as soon as the first word left my mouth. "Riley's in the hospital. I think you should come down."

I told her as much as I could. When I hung up, I turned around and saw everyone staring at me. My dad had shown up—Teddi had no doubt called him. He looked like he'd come straight from a construction site. Dust and paint splatters covered his work clothing.

My dad made no move toward me. Instead, he stood there with an arm around Teddi. But I could tell by the mist in his eyes as he glanced over at me that he was worried.

Detective Adams was still there, along with another police officer. The pastor from my church—I called him Pastor Shaggy because he resembled the character from the old Scooby Doo cartoons—sat in a chair, his head hanging down in prayer. I didn't know who'd called him.

I didn't want to be around anyone right now. I knew that one wrong hug could leave me as nothing more than a puddle on the ground. So, instead I nodded hello and crossed my arms as I approached them.

"No word still?" I asked.

Detective Adams shook his head. "Not yet."

"How about from investigators? Do they have any leads? Did they catch the person who did this?"

Adams lowered his voice. "Gabby, you just worry about Riley. We'll worry about finding the gunman."

But my mind was already racing. Why would someone have done this?

What if there was no logic? What if this was random, some crazy who just walked in off the street with an agenda to kill someone? Those random crimes were always the hardest to solve.

Nothing made sense.

And until I knew that Riley was okay, nothing would make sense.

That was the only thing I was certain about at the moment.

CHAPTER
THREE

AS THE MINUTES DRAGGED ON, I leaned against the wall, trying not to make eye contact with anyone in the hospital waiting room. Trying to ignore the tremble that had claimed my muscles. Trying to swallow any tears that fought to emerge.

Everyone seemed to read me well enough that they stayed away. Pastor Shaggy still had his head lowered in prayer. Teddi texted someone—she was probably starting a prayer chain. The detective and police officer mumbled to each other while exchanging glances down at the notepad in Adams' hands.

How long would this surgery last?

I glanced at my watch. Adams said that Riley had been shot around 9 a.m. It was already past noon.

Three hours had passed. Three hours. Shouldn't the doctors know something by now?

Finally, at 12:43, the door opened and a man in surgical attire stepped out. He lowered his facial mask and tugged his gloves off as his gaze searched the room.

I started toward him, then slowed a few steps, trying to read his expression. Hope had propelled me forward; fear caused me to stop.

His gaze fixed on me. "Are you the fiancée?"

I nodded, my insides like gelatin. "I'm Gabby St. Claire."

"The good news is that the bullet only skimmed the left side of Riley's brain," the doctor began. "A brain injury to only one side of the brain, and to one lobe, is much more survivable than an injury to both sides."

I wasn't sure if I was relieved or not. Conflicting emotions tattered my insides. "Is Riley going to be okay?"

He pulled his lips into a tight line. "The bad news is that the bullet caused an intracranial hematoma."

"What does that mean exactly?" I couldn't comprehend his words, but they didn't sound good.

"It means that a blood vessel has ruptured in his brain. The blood then compressed the brain tissue."

"Okay . . ." I tried to absorb the news. I hardly knew what to ask.

"Usually, when a person is injured—let's say, he hurts his ankle—then there's swelling and the skin expands to accommodate that. However, in a case where the swelling is in the brain, there's a different set of problems. The skull won't expand to allow for the swelling. So we had to go in and do an emergency craniotomy and clot evacuation."

My throat constricted. "That sounds serious."

"The good news is that his blood pressure is stable and his oxygen level is good."

I hardly heard what he said and, the little bit I did hear, I barely comprehended. "Can I see him? Can I talk to him?"

The surgeon grimaced. "Right now, we've put him into a medically induced coma. He was unconscious when he arrived. A brain injury like the one he's experienced can do that to a person."

"A medically induced coma?" I'd heard they were common after brain injuries, but I hadn't read up on it lately. Didn't think I'd need to. My chin trembled. "What does that mean?"

He lowered his voice. "It means that we wait and see."

I raised my head. "What does 'wait and see' mean? How long will he be in this coma?"

"It's anyone's guess, ma'am. There's no timetable for these things. It could be hours. It could be days. Weeks. Months. Or it could be . . ."

I squeezed the skin between my eyes before shaking my head and raising my shoulders with some type of false bravado. "He's going to come out of this. I know he will."

"I should tell you that the prognosis, even when we're able to wake him up and bring him out of this coma, may not be what you want. He may not be able to walk or talk. He may have memory issues. Brain injuries are unpredictable." He paused and locked gazes with me. "Most people don't survive them."

I rotated my shoulders back again. "He will. You'll see."

The doctor gawked at me as if trying to decide whether or not to pop my bubble of illusion. He must have decided not to because he offered a curt nod. "I hope you're right."

"Can I see him?"

"The nurses are getting him cleaned up. We'll let you know when visitors can come in. It will only be immediate family."

"I'm his fiancée!" I prepared myself for a fight.

"And you," the doctor obliged. "We'll let you know, Ms. St. Claire." With that, he used his card to unlock the door and stepped back down the hallway.

Every part of me wanted to fall apart. But I couldn't. Not now.

I turned around and drew on every ounce of

strength within me. "Pastor, I need you to call everyone we can think of. We need to get people praying. Now!"

He nodded. "Absolutely."

"Detective Adams, you need to be out there searching for the person who did this. I'll call you if anything changes. I deeply appreciate you being here for me. I know you didn't have to be."

He stared at me uncertainly for a moment. "You sure?"

"I'm positive. Mary Lou should be at the station by now giving her statement. Maybe she can offer something that I can't." *Because Riley sure didn't share anything with me about any threats on his life.* He wouldn't have kept that from me . . . would he?

"Teddi, would you pack up a few things for me at my apartment? Some clothes. A bottle of water. My toothbrush. I don't plan on leaving this hospital, not until I know something."

She stood and nodded. "Of course."

"And if you see Sierra or Chad, please let them know what's going on." I turned to my father. "Dad, take care of Teddi. She's been through a lot. And tell Tim what happened. He'll want to know."

My dad nodded stiffly. "You got it."

Teddi's worried gaze remained on me. "How about you? What are you going to do?"

"I need to wait for Riley's parents. They're

coming down from D.C., so it's still going to be a few hours. Besides, I want to see Riley as soon as I can."

Pastor Shaggy squeezed my arm before asking in that raspy voice of his, "Can I get you something to eat?"

My stomach ached in response to the question. "I won't be able to keep anything down. Not now."

"Someone should stay with you," Teddi insisted.

"I'll be fine. In fact, I could use some time alone."

She inspected me another moment before nodding and taking my dad's hand to walk back toward the elevators. As soon as everyone disappeared from sight, I sank into a chair and covered my face with my hands.

Finally, I didn't have to be strong anymore.

My first sob escaped.

My head bobbed up as the door to ICU opened forty minutes later. A young brunette nurse stuck her head out. "I'm looking for Riley Thomas' fiancée?"

I stood. "That's me."

I sucked in the tears that had been flowing down my cheeks, using a crumpled tissue to dab the remaining moisture around my eyes. I knew it would do no good. My entire face was wet, yet my mouth was dry. My soul felt as barren as the crumpled tissue in my fist.

"You can come see Riley now. I need to warn you that he doesn't look the same." Her voice was soft, cautious.

I stood and began following her at a slow pace. I'd been so anxious to see him. Why was I feeling reluctant now? "What do you mean?"

"His head has been shaved. It's bandaged. He's on a ventilator. Those will be the first things you notice."

I paused before I reached his curtained off room. "Can he hear me?"

She nodded. "Most experts say yes. The more you talk to him, the better."

I swallowed hard and then turned toward the hospital bed beyond the curtain. I sucked in a deep breath when I spotted Riley. Though the nurse had tried to prep me, he looked even worse than I'd anticipated.

Riley . . . the man who was so confident and strong and capable. Now he was being kept alive by machines that I couldn't identify, by fluids in little bags draped beside him, by prayers and by the grace of God.

After the nurse left, I dropped into a chair at his bedside and grabbed his hand. For a moment—and just a moment—I halfway expected to feel him squeeze my hand in return. But there was nothing.

I stared at the man I loved. I soaked in his hospital gown. Uncountable tubes and chords ran from him. He wore a neck brace.

I drew in a shaky breath and lifted another prayer. I stroked his hand. "Oh, Riley. We're going to get through this. I don't know how, but we're going to make it through. That's what you would tell me."

He said nothing. Of course.

I could only hear the beep of his heart monitor. Hear the suction from the machine that pushed air into his lungs. Hear the pitter patter of nurses as they did their jobs all around me.

Somewhere in the distance, someone laughed. Laughed? How could someone be laughing at a time like this? Didn't they know my world had been rocked? Didn't they know that the man I loved was on death's doorstep?

I lowered my head until my cheek touched Riley's hand. That was the closest I could get to him without hurting him. I left my head there, torn between fighting tears of loss and wallowing in hopelessness or digging into that stubborn determination that I was known for and holding on to hope that Riley would come out of this.

"I was going to buy your ring this week, you

know. I had it all planned out. I was going to tell you that we needed to buy some crime scene tape to use as decorations at our wedding. After all, wasn't it crime scenes that pulled us together? Of course, I'm not that tacky. I wouldn't have really decorated with yellow police tape draped across the backs of the chairs. Then I was going to take you to the jewelers. I pulled some money out of my savings account."

I raised my head and looked at him. "How about my ring? Did you have a plan?" He remained silent. "I know you did. You always have a plan. Just what was it, though?" My words choked at the end as I realized . . . what if I never found out?

I lifted my eyes and saw the heart monitor beating steadily.

As long as that heart kept beating, I wasn't giving up.

No matter what anyone said.

I'd been with Riley an hour. With each second that passed, my heart did a wild dance between acceptance of what had happened, mourning over the future, and hope that things would work out.

Most of all, I found myself praying that I would wake up. That I could simply call my business partner Chad and find out what jobs were lined up for the week. That I could look for restaurants to host our reception. That I was wearing that dazzling wedding dress and that Riley would see me in it and be blown away.

I wasn't going to wake up, though. This was reality.

Everything truly could change in the blink of an eye.

The nurse moved the curtain aside and metal slid across metal in a *slishing* sound. "Someone's in the waiting room for you."

It must be Riley's parents, I realized. I tried to pull myself together. I wished I had some makeup with me, so I could cover the blotches on my face. I knew my hair had frizzed since I'd raked my hands through it so many times. My clothes were rumpled, and I may have even wiped my eyes—even my nose—on my shirt a few times.

So much for good impressions. Just earlier, I'd been thinking about how much I wanted his mom and dad to like me. To think I was good enough for their son. To present myself in the best manner possible. I'd give anything for that to be my biggest worry right now.

I wiped my eyes again and tried to pull myself together. I stepped out the door and stopped in my tracks. Riley's parents weren't here. It was . . . Parker? My ex-boyfriend, a fresh-faced FBI agent, and a Brad Pitt lookalike, all rolled into one person.

His hands were shoved deep into his pockets. "I heard what happened."

"I wasn't expecting to see you here."

He reached out his arms for a hug. "I'm really sorry, Gabby."

Against my better instincts, I accepted his embrace. I didn't realize I needed one so badly. But I did. And I knew Parker wasn't here with ulterior motives. No, he was a father now and in a committed relationship with another cop, a woman named Charlie.

It had been a long time since I'd felt his touch. But there was only one man I wanted to hold me right now, and he wasn't able to do that. But still, I appreciated Parker's show of support.

I stepped back, ready to be away from his familiar scent. I crossed my arms over my chest, not sure what to say exactly.

"Have the police given you any updates?" He leaned against the wall, his hands tucked back into his pockets.

"All I know is that someone came into Riley's office this morning at around nine. They shot him point blank in the head, and Riley is lucky to be alive now." I shook my head in disbelief. "Who would do this, Parker?"

"That's what everyone is trying to figure out right now. You don't have any guesses?"

"Milton Jones?" Doubt filled my voice as I remembered my earlier conversation with Adams.

"He's dead, Gabby."

"Until there's a body, I don't feel really confident of that. I don't know who else would have done this. I really have no clue."

"Lawyers usually have their fair share of enemies. Riley never mentioned any?"

I rubbed my temples, realizing I probably needed some water. I'd cried so much that I was dehydrated. My head felt woozy. "No. He never brought up anyone."

Or had I just been so wrapped up in my own life that I never listened? I prayed that wasn't the case.

"Is there anyone *you* made mad who might want to go after Riley?"

His question felt like a slap in the face. I shook my head, unable to comprehend the implications. But I had to think about that possibility. Parker's inquiry was a good one, however painful it might be.

"There's any number of people who might not be very happy with me. There's that organized crime family."

"The Harrisons?" Parker asked.

I nodded. "Yep, they're the ones. Then there's the Cunninghams—remember them?"

"If it weren't for the Cunninghams, we would have never met."

Yeah, I tried to put that meeting out of my mind and stick to more important matters. Not just today —all the time. "There was that guy from Allendale Acres."

"You do have a long list of enemies, don't you?"

I half shrugged. "Those would be the obvious choices, I suppose."

"Something the police should look into, for sure."

I shifted, crossing my arms. "Is the FBI getting involved?"

He shook his head. "Not yet. There's no reason to right now. The local police should be able to handle this."

"What if they can't?" My voice cracked.

His expression softened. "They can, Gabby. Come on. What happened to that spitfire that everyone knows and loves?"

"My soul aches right now, Parker." The rawness of my words made me uncomfortable. They showed my vulnerability and made me look weak. At once, I realized I didn't care. Nothing else mattered right now except Riley.

Parker frowned. "I know, Gabby. And I'm sorry. I really am. If there's anything I can do . . . "

"I'll let you know."

If only there was something I could do . . . besides pray. All of this was in God's hands right now.

I looked up and saw Riley's parents step into the waiting room. I pulled myself together, bracing myself for another tough conversation.

CHAPTER
FOUR

ON SUNDAY, at six p.m., I sat beside Riley's bed with the bittersweet realization that we should be getting married right now. My heart still ached when I thought about what should have been. One moment could change the thousands of moments that followed.

Behind me, rain beat against the hospital window. Thunder shook the windowpanes and made the lights in the hospital flicker for a moment. Fitting, I mused, that it was storming outside at the very time my wedding should be taking place.

I stared at Riley's handsome face as he lay lifeless in the hospital bed beside me. He'd shown no signs of improvement in the past six days. The ventilator kept his lungs moving. An IV kept him hydrated. A feeding tube kept him nourished.

I'd stayed at the hospital as much as I could, but they wouldn't let me spend the night in his room on the uncomfortable little chair beside his bed. After the first day, the hospital staff had only let me stay with him in ten-minute increments. Then his mom and dad would go in. No one outside of the immediate family and myself were allowed into the ICU.

Every time I sat down beside Riley, my thoughts were flooded with the good times Riley and I had shared. I remembered meeting him in the apartment parking lot after I'd come from a crime scene turned fire. I'd looked like a mess with my singed clothes and hair. The smell of smoke had saturated my clothing. My hand was burnt, blistered, and bandaged.

I remembered how he'd looked amused when I'd introduced him as my male secretary while I was investigating a case once. I thought about how he hadn't even flinched before going out in public with me when I'd been dressed as a human pincushion. I remembered how he'd humor me by joining in when I would randomly burst into songs.

My smile faded when I remembered Riley saving me from the trunk of a running car when I'd been left to die of carbon monoxide poisoning. I remembered when he'd found me beaten and bruised in the entry of the apartment building. I reminisced when he almost took a bullet for me when a deranged Santa had me in the crosshairs.

Riley had rescued me on more than one occasion. Now it was my turn to rescue him, and I had no idea how to go about doing that very thing. I felt helpless as I sat at his bedside.

To say the past week had been tough would be an understatement. On Tuesday morning, Kansas had called. The medical examiner there told me I hadn't gotten the job. No, someone with a master's degree had been chosen over me, simply because he had more education. She'd apologized, told me the decision had been difficult, and encouraged me to go the extra mile with my schooling.

Even if she had offered me the job, I was going to tell her no anyway, but for some reason the rejection stung. I told myself that my overreaction was a combination of everything that had happened lately. But the idea that someone might have thought I was worthy enough to work in a professional capacity for the state would have felt nice. The idea that something in my life was going right definitely had its appeal.

Instead, it looked like crime scene cleaning would be in my future for a while yet. I wasn't even doing much of that since I'd been at the hospital. I'd worry about those bills later. Right now, I just wanted to worry about Riley.

Detective Adams kept me updated on his investigation. The police had no leads. It was like the man who'd popped into Riley's office had been a ghost. He'd left the law firm, walked down two streets, and then in a dead area between cameras, he'd disappeared.

The police searched the video feeds from blocks around Riley's law office, looking for a suspicious car or a suspicious figure. There was no one.

All they knew was that the handgun used had been a 1911 Colt .45 caliber. It had been fired from the doorway of Riley's office. Riley must have turned his head at the last minute, making the bullet only catch the side of his skull. Everyone agreed that the intended outcome was death.

Adams had been interviewing everyone who'd been in contact with Riley over the past few weeks.

But every lead came back to the same point. Every lead came back to nothing.

I rubbed Riley's hand. This was not the way my story was supposed to go. Today was supposed to be the happiest day of my life.

God, how could you let this happen? I know that believing in You doesn't promise us a life without trouble . . . but I can't help but feel like You've abandoned me. Like Your love isn't enough. Like my sacrifices have been in vain.

I was new in my faith, but I hadn't expected to feel so weak. This was my first real test, and it was a big one. Usually, I wanted to ace tests. Right now, a strange feeling of apathy was creeping in. I didn't take time to examine it now.

A drifting voice in the distance caught my ear. "You see that tattoo? You know what that means, right?"

"The Guardians," another woman whispered. "I've seen enough of those tats in my day."

"When I think about all the horrible things he's probably done . . . Do you know how many lives this man has probably taken?" the other woman whispered.

"It's not ours to judge. We just have to do our job."

Through the gap in the curtain, I saw someone being wheeled past on a gurney by two nurses. They came to a stop at the curtained off room beside Riley's.

The Guardians. I'd certainly ticked the street gang off. What did a street gang do to people who rubbed them the wrong way? Who exposed their deeds?

They got revenge.

I had a hard time seeing any connection between this case and The Guardians, though. I mean, sure, the hoodlums hated me. The fact that one of them would be Riley's neighbor while in the hospital was strange. But sometimes life was just like that.

I couldn't worry about them right now. There'd probably been some kind of gang fight, and now one of the members was here in the hospital fighting for his life. If someone came to visit him, I'd try to be careful, to not let my face be seen. That was all I could do.

That was all I could do . . .

Those sounded like words of defeat. Like the words of someone who'd given up.

Those words didn't sound like me. I was a fighter. An instigator. A person who got things done.

I looked back at Riley and sniffled. I'd been sitting here a week. I'd convinced myself to let the police do their job. I'd told myself that would be best for everyone.

But maybe the best way to help Riley was to find out who did this to him. To make them pay.

Vengeance is mine says the Lord.

I didn't feel vengeance. Did I?

No, this was justice. I couldn't sit around and do nothing, not when there was a deadly gunman out there. I was going to track every lead in this case. I was going to make sure the person who'd done this would pay.

And nothing anyone said would stop me.

Riley's parents stood as I stepped out from the ICU. Riley's father, Ron, looked just like Riley, only twenty-five years older. His hair was gray but full. His eyes were hazel blue. Father and son shared the same tall, lean build.

His mom, Evelyn, was tall and thin, with deep brown hair to her chin. In the past, she'd always seemed so confident and elegant. Right now, she seemed quiet and stately, but her grief had broken down some of her walls.

Both of them had been cordial and grieving and they'd tried, in their own way, to offer me some comfort. But I knew they were too distraught themselves.

I tried to smile as I approached them, just to be polite, but it didn't work. Instead, I nodded behind me. "You can go sit with Riley now. I'm going to rest for a bit. I'll be back to check on him."

Riley's mom nodded, as if that pleased her. "You need rest in order to keep up your strength. These days in the hospital can wear down a person."

Riley's mom looked like she'd aged ten years in the time since she'd been here. Today, her dark hair was frizzy, her makeup did nothing to cover up her pale cheeks, and her wrinkles, though few, seemed deeper.

I squeezed her arm. "You take that advice too, okay?"

"Oh, Gabby." She pulled me into a hug.

I froze for a moment with uncertainty before

wrapping my arms around Mrs. Thomas. I could feel her chest jerking with sobs. I held back my own sobs that wanted to escape.

"I know this has to be so hard for you," she murmured. "When Riley called last week, he sounded over the moon that you guys were moving up the wedding date. I just wanted to let you know that. My son truly loved you."

I didn't miss the past tense "loved." Did Riley's mom not think that he was going to come out of this? Our church had been holding prayer vigils ever since they got word about what had happened. Riley's story had been on the news. Organizations from across the country had called to say they were praying.

This wasn't the time I wanted to point out her wording, though. It was just a slip, an honest mistake brought about by not enough sleep, by too much grief.

"I appreciate that," I told her. "I'm not giving up yet, Mrs. Thomas."

"Call me Evelyn. Please."

I nodded. "Okay. Evelyn. I'm holding on to the hope that Riley's going to come out of this and that the police are going to catch the person responsible." *If the police don't catch him, I will.* I kept the last part silent.

"Riley always said you believed in him." Riley's

dad stepped forward with a grim smile on his face. "He believed in you too, Gabby."

Riley believed in me. Now I was going to do what I'd been trained to do. To track the evidence that would lead me to answers.

I forced a nod, my muscles tightening again, as they had been doing since I got this news. Grief did strange things to a body, I'd realized. Made you feel like you were outside of yourself. Made you feel like you were dying too.

I remembered some of those feelings from when my mother died. Those emotions were back again and stronger than ever, memories I didn't want to relive.

"I'll be back," I whispered.

I started down the hallway, trying to formulate my first plan of action.

CHAPTER
FIVE

MY FIRST STOP after I left the hospital was Mary Lou's house. She'd dropped by the waiting room a couple of times in the past week and even left a pot of chicken and dumplings outside my apartment. She'd been one in a slew of people who'd come by. Each of those faces was a bit of a blur.

She lived in a brick ranch house on Lake Whitehurst in Norfolk, not far from the Botanical Gardens there. Her back yard offered a beautiful view of the water. Apparently, her husband had been a lawyer, which had afforded them a nice life together. When he'd passed away five years ago, she'd gotten tired of sitting around and not doing anything. Two months ago, she'd gotten the job with Riley.

Her eyes widened when she opened the door and

saw me there. She didn't say anything, just pulled me into a hug. People were doing that a lot lately. I must look terrible because people just gave me one glance and had no words.

Mary Lou had a plump, matronly figure, kind eyes, and an infinite love for her grandchildren. She was a killer baker and her demeanor always screamed of southern hospitality and goodness. Riley loved having her work for him.

She ushered me inside, and I sat on a floral patterned couch. Before I realized what she was doing, I had a sweaty glass of sweet iced tea in my hands and a slice of lemon pound cake in front of me.

I'd lost weight this week. I didn't know how much. I didn't bother to check. But I knew my jeans were looser than before. I didn't have much of an appetite, but I did nibble on the cake. It was surprisingly tasty given that nothing sounded tasty.

"How are you holding up, Dear?" She sat across from me, her hands clasped in front of her. Rain beat against the wall of windows that usually presented a breathtaking view of the lake.

For a moment, the streams of raindrops flowing down the window made me think of God, made me wonder if He was crying with me.

I shrugged. "As well as to be expected, I suppose."

"No changes in Riley?"

I shook my head. "Nothing. So we just wait."

"And pray," she added.

I nodded, though I didn't feel confident, at the moment, that prayers would get me very far. I hated to feel so fragile in my faith this early on in my relationship with God. But I was wavering big time right now.

I set my tea onto the crocheted coaster on the table beside me. "I need to ask you some questions, Mary Lou."

She tilted her head. "About?"

"About Riley."

She smoothed the lacy doily on the arm of her chair. "I've already talked to the police, Gabby."

"Maybe they missed something."

"You're too close to this. That's what my husband would say."

"Maybe because I'm so close to this I have the passion to find the answers. The police aren't doing enough."

"They're working hard." She set her tea down on the coffee table, probably so she could offer me her full, undiluted sympathy.

"Please, Mary Lou. I need to do something." I didn't want to beg. I really didn't.

"What if doing something gets you killed?" Her

voice sounded soft, questioning, and compassionate. "Riley wouldn't want that."

But I already knew my answer. "Being killed while trying to find justice for my fiancé? I could think of worse reasons to go."

"Gabby . . ." She smoothed that doily again.

"Please, Mary Lou." I would beg if I had to.

She considered me a moment—a long, tension filled moment—and then nodded. "What do you want to know?"

My shoulders relaxed. "Who was mad at Riley? Certainly he made someone mad recently. Had anyone threatened him? Anyone other than Jones?"

She folded her hands together in her lap. "A lot of people get upset. But they don't mean it. Their threats are idle, said in the heat of the moment. You know how people can be."

"I promise. I won't jump to any conclusions. I just need a place to start."

She fidgeted again and let out a slow breath. "Garrett Mercer."

"Who's Garrett Mercer?" His name didn't even begin to ring any bells with me. I hated feeling clueless.

"Riley is working on behalf of a client to file a lawsuit against his company. Riley's client believes that she was unfairly targeted and eventually fired because of her religious beliefs. When Mr. Mercer heard about the lawsuit, as well as the negative publicity he may receive in return, he stormed into the office and demanded to speak with Riley."

Why hadn't Riley told me any of this? I mean sure, there was attorney-client privilege and all of that. But still. An angry man storming into the office seemed like something Riley would mention, if nothing else during one of those lulls in our conversations.

Mary Lou scrunched her eyes and wrinkles fanned across her face. "I can see you're hurt. Just know that Riley only wanted what was best for you. He knew you'd worry about him, and he figured you had enough on your mind."

That sounded like Riley. Always trying to protect me. "When did this happen?"

"Mr. Mercer came into the office on the Friday before you and Riley left for Allendale Acres."

Riley and I had an entire five-hour car ride to that resort when he could have mentioned the confrontation. So why hadn't he? "And have you heard from this Garrett Mercer since then?"

Mary Lou shook her head. "No, not a peep. That's why I didn't think much about it."

"Did you tell the police this information?"

"Of course."

So the police had talked to the Mercer man. Who

else had they talked to? What information did they walk away with?

Asking questions never hurt anything. Only I could think of a million exceptions to that reasoning. I could think of uncountable instances where asking questions had clued in the wrong people to what I was doing. Questions could drive people to fear, and fear could drive people to do things that they might later regret.

"Is there anything else you can think of?" I asked. "Anything at all?"

"Just be careful, Gabby. Whoever shot Riley did it without blinking an eye. If they did that once, they probably won't hesitate to do it again."

Her words were a chilling reminder about the person we were dealing with here.

That wasn't going to stop me, though.

My mind raced as I pulled up to my apartment building that evening.

I usually loved coming home. I anticipated catching up with Riley. I looked forward to running into my best friend Sierra. In my own way, I looked forward to hearing my neighbor and radio talk show host Bill McCormick's tangents on politics and his ex-wife. I anticipated when my upstairs neighbor Mrs.

Mystery, as I called her, might emerge from her writing cave.

Today I had to drag myself upstairs. I hoped no one would stick his or her head out. I just wanted to be alone.

At once, I wondered what it would be like if Riley never came home. I had a flash of what it would be like to pack Riley's stuff up. To plan his funeral.

I pictured what my life would be without Riley.

Tears tried to push their way out. Agony kept pressing closer, threatening to squeeze out any other emotions. I kept fighting, desperate to keep myself together.

If I fell apart, I feared I might never piece myself together again.

Disappointment bit at me. I was a Christian now. I was supposed to be stronger than this. Supposed to trust God that He worked through all things for our good.

Lord, I don't even know what to pray, except please bring Riley out of this. Please let him be okay.

Since I'd stopped by the hospital once more after visiting Mary Lou, I knew Riley's parents were still there. I didn't have to worry about running into them as I trudged upstairs. They were staying in Riley's apartment while they were in town. I didn't feel like making small talk with them again.

I unlocked my apartment and stepped inside. I

still shuddered every time I walked in here. Milton Jones, the notorious serial killer, had snuck into my place and not only threatened me but decorated my walls with blood. It made me sick to think about it.

There were other places I could stay. It only felt right to be here, though.

As soon as I'd pulled the chain across my door, someone knocked. "Gabby, it's me. Sierra. Can I come in?"

My best friend. We'd had so little time to talk since she'd returned from her honeymoon. She'd come home early after a hurricane in the Gulf shut down their resort. Hurricane season was now officially in effect here on the East Coast.

Sierra had sat with me at the hospital several times and we'd said almost nothing. Wasn't that the hallmark of every great friendship, the ability to communicate without saying a thing?

I unlocked the door, and Sierra stepped inside. Sierra was a second-generation Japanese girl, petite with plastic framed glasses, and a pierced eyebrow. She worked as an animal rights activist and had more passion for animals than most people had for life itself. The Yale graduate was known for doing whatever it took to save the lives of innocent animals both near and afar. Despite her obsession, I felt like she was the sister I never had.

Her gaze assessed me as she stood in the doorway with her hands on her tiny, nonexistent hips.

I hated that she'd returned from her honeymoon to this.

But I hated that Riley was in the hospital even more.

She continued to stare at me. "How are you?"

I lowered myself onto my couch. "Been better."

"I know. It was a stupid question."

"It wasn't. Not really." I looked off into the distance, searching for the right thing to say. I came up empty. "It's just that . . . you know."

She nodded and sat beside me. "I'm sorry, Gabby. I can't stop thinking about Riley. Any changes?"

I shook my head. "No. Nothing. It's just more of the same."

"Is there anything Chad and I can do?"

"If anything comes up, I'll let you know. But right now all we can do is pray." *And try to track down the person who did this.* I leaned forward, trying to clear my thoughts for a minute. "Tell me something to take my mind off of all this. What's new here?"

"We had an interesting visitor here today at the apartment building."

My curiosity piqued. "Who was that?"

"Mr. Sears' granddaughter."

Mr. Sears had been our landlord ever since we lived here. But he'd been found dead nearly two weeks ago. I hadn't even given much thought as to what would happen with this building now that he was gone. I'd had too many other things distracting me, I supposed. "What did his granddaughter say?"

"She's putting the building up for sale. She said she doesn't want to be a landlord, she lives too far away, she's not cut out to be a manager, etc."

My spine straightened. "Really? What's that mean for us?"

"Apparently, that all depends on who ends up purchasing the place. They could choose to keep it as an apartment building or they could make it into a private residence. That's what I've always been afraid would happen. This home has a lot of character. Someone who wants to preserve historic buildings might be interested in snatching it up and making it into their dream home."

My stomach sank farther. Despair threatened to bite deeper.

Riley was in a coma, and now my apartment building could be snatched away as well?

I knew people said the only thing constant in life was change. But why did the hard times keep raining down on me? Couldn't life cut me any slack?

"When will we know?"

"I guess all the papers are being signed this week, so we'll know something soon."

I cleared my throat, ready for yet another subject

change. "How are you and Chad? How's married life?" It still seemed weird to say those words.

Her face brightened. "We're good. I mean, driving each other a little crazy. I know people say we jumped into this whole marriage thing, but I think we did what was right for us. When you love someone, why waste time playing games?"

I smiled bittersweetly. "I'm happy for you. I really am. I never thought when I met Chad last year on that crime scene cleaning job that the two of you would end up married."

"Me neither. Life has a funny way of working out sometimes."

"If anyone deserves a happily ever after, it's you." Moisture filled my eyes.

Sierra scooted closer and put her arm around me. "You're going to get your happily ever after, Gabby. I know it may not seem like it, but you will. Everyone's praying for Riley. How could he not come out of this okay?"

I nodded, appreciating her faith in the situation, especially when I considered that she was an agnostic.

"I need to get my mind off of all this. Any chance you want to catch a movie?"

"Sure thing. Which one are you thinking about?"

"*The Princess Bride.*" Sierra gave me a questioning look, and I shrugged. A sappy romance with a wedding in it? I could see where it might not be the best idea. "It's got it all. Love, hate, revenge, fighting for what you believe in."

And I promise, I thought silently, *not to take any tips on revenge from Inigo Montoya.*

CHAPTER
SIX

THE NEXT MORNING, I stepped inside the headquarters of the Global Coffee Initiative, or GCI. I'd researched the company last night. Garrett Mercer owned the business, one that was known for being conservative with natural resources and liberal with values.

I'd read up on Garrett last night. He was quite the prodigy. He'd started his company at twenty-three-years-old and had grown it from a storage unit operation to a worldwide company that impacted people from all walks of life.

Today, he was thirty. From the pictures I'd seen online, I'd noted that he was a tall man with a shock of dark hair and broad shoulders. He had green eyes with a touch of mischief, loads of charisma, and enough passion to make people pause in curiosity.

I was hoping he could squeeze me into his schedule today.

GCI was located in an old warehouse. Stained, sealed cement floors met my feet. The space was wide open and airy. The ceiling had plenty of skylights and stretches of windows were carved out of the walls.

A toy plane circled on a string attached to the ceiling overhead. Statistics on world hunger flashed on a screen on the opposite wall. And there was an entire table of coffee of every sort—decaf, bold, breakfast blend, hazelnut, and even one called loco.

Most of the employees I saw wandering around in the distance wore trendy jeans, oversized glasses, and earth-toned clothing. My gaze paused at one employee. A man, probably in his mid-twenties, with light brown hair, a confident gait, and a trim figure, talked at a nearby desk. Where had I seen that man before? I put the thought aside for a moment, hoping who he was would come to me later.

I smiled as pleasantly as possible at the woman behind the front desk as I approached. She was a twenty-something black woman with a stylish Afro and a stunning profile. She screamed "hip" and "urban," which meant she fit in with the rest of the office space.

I tapped my fist on the wooden desk in front of me, feeling no-nonsense. I was usually up for being rascally at any given time. Not right now. "I'm here to see Garrett Mercer, please."

She paused from tapping at the computer in front of her. "Do you have an appointment?"

I shook my head. I hadn't concocted any type of cover story that would explain why I was here. I decided to go with the truth instead.

"I'm investigating the shooting of a local attorney named Riley Thomas. I believe Mr. Mercer may have some information that will be helpful in the search for the gunman."

The woman's eyes widened. "Let me see if he's available."

She picked up the phone, dialed a number, and a moment later she nodded me back toward a hallway.

I navigated the space. On one side of me, there was an open area full of desks, and on the other side were what I'd call the executive offices. I stopped by the one with "Garrett Mercer" on the nameplate beside the door.

The door was open, so I stepped into the office. Since the man's back was toward me, I took a minute to soak in the minimalist decorations. His desk was in the center of the room and had clean lines with lots of space between the drawers on either side. A modern red upholstered chair sat against one wall, and behind it were canvas photos of Garrett with children from across the globe. A bookcase stretched to the ceiling on the other side of the room. Bright windows spanned the outside wall.

Garrett spun around in his chair, his gaze falling on me with an inquisitiveness that had me sucking in my breath. I paused for a moment. I'd expected him to be cold, rigid, arrogant. Success had a way of doing that to people. I wasn't getting any of those vibes from him now. He held himself with an aura of confidence, yet a friendly easiness seemed to emanate from him.

He crossed around from behind his desk and approached me with an outstretched hand and a subdued smile.

"I'm Garrett." A British accent rolled off his tongue.

"Gabby," I mumbled, all of my mental preparation vanishing.

He straightened the sleeves of his pressed shirt and leaned against the back of his desk, comfortably crossing his ankles. "Did you help yourself to a cup of coffee?"

"I'm not thirsty." Actually, coffee sounded great. Why hadn't I grabbed a cup?

"Please, help yourself before you leave. Until then, what can I help you with, Gabby?"

"I'm investigating the shooting of Riley Thomas. I understand you had an altercation with him a couple of weeks ago."

His shoulder twitched upward, his demeanor not appearing ruffled in the least. "Altercation would be overstating it, I think."

"What would you call it then?"

"We had a discussion."

"I think 'discussion' would be *understating* it. I understand you were very upset. That you threatened him, for that matter."

He let out a slow breath and stared at me before nodding and rubbing his chin. "You're a P.I.?"

I raised my eyebrows, remaining noncommittal. "I'm investigating."

Half his lip curled in a smile. "Look, I don't know why you're here—"

"I think I made that clear. I'm investigating the shooting of Riley Thomas." I refused to break eye contact. I wanted this man to know I was serious.

Any hint of amusement disappeared, and he nodded. "Very well. What would you like to know?"

"I want to know why you were so upset with him instead of the person who filed a discrimination lawsuit against you."

He stood and walked over to a ten-gallon aquarium on his shelf. He picked up a container of food and dropped some flakes into the water. The fish scrambled to the top of the water to eat. When he was done, he glanced back over at me.

"I was upset because one frivolous lawsuit like

this can ruin a company, whether it be destroying the reputation of the business or causing financial ruin from overbearing legal fees. That money could be used to help starving people across the globe—or even here in our own backyard. Juliette wasn't listening when I tried to talk to her about it, so I thought I'd talk to her lawyer. It wasn't a smart move. I realize that in retrospect. But I was feeling desperate."

"Desperate enough to kill?"

His jaw hardened. "I'm not a killer. I like to help people. Every purchase that someone makes from us—"

"Helps to build a well for needy people across the globe." I nodded. "Yeah, I saw your website."

"I'm doing important work. Work that's bigger than myself. I didn't want one angry employee to ruin all of that."

"Then why did you fire Juliette?" Finally, I had a name. A first name, at least. "You have something against Christians?"

"Against Christians? No, I am a Christian. You can check any survey I've ever filled out. You'll see that's what I've marked. But it's one thing to be a Christian, and it's another thing to go over the top with that on the job."

"How did Juliette go over the top with it?"

He sighed again and leaned against his desk. "It's

one thing to talk about God to your coworkers. It's an entirely different thing to talk about God with our clients. There's a line, and she crossed it. I gave her plenty of warnings, and she didn't care. She wanted to do what she wanted to do. When I fired her, she threatened to sue. I got notice that she was going to take me to court a couple weeks later."

"That's when you started feeling desperate?"

He chuckled and shook his head. "Now you're playing with my words. I'm passionate about my company, Gabby. I fight for things I believe in, and I believe in helping others. I don't want to put those things in jeopardy."

"How far would you go in that quest? That's the question."

He sighed slowly again, grimness settling on his features. "If Juliette was a Christian, as she claimed to be, then she should have been respectful of the boundaries I placed on her here at work. She should have tried to work things out with me instead of filing a lawsuit. Look it up in the Bible. I think you'll see that God's Word agrees with me."

"I'll look that up. But, in the meantime, where were you last Monday morning?"

His face darkened. "I was out doing errands."

"If you're innocent, then you won't mind me asking where?"

He crossed his arms, that teasing grin returning.

"You'll just have to take my word that I was nowhere near that law practice."

"I don't take anyone's word."

He stared at me. "Then you're a smart woman."

I knew something was wrong when I arrived at the hospital and found Riley's parents both in the waiting room instead of with him. My suspicions were confirmed when they gave each other a nervous glance as I walked into the dimly lit room. Riley's father stood and nodded my way.

"Gabby," he mumbled.

I didn't waste any time. "What's wrong? What happened? How's Riley?"

They exchanged a glance again. "We need to talk to you, Gabby," Riley's mom started.

"Okay." Dread—impending doom was more like it—rose in my stomach.

"Maybe you should sit," Riley's dad started.

I dropped into the chair behind me. Riley must have taken a turn for the worse. That was the only conclusion I could come to.

Riley's dad sat across from me. He rubbed his hands against the top of his khaki pants before leaning toward me. "Riley's been in a medically induced coma for a week now. He's begun to stabilize, though ever so slightly."

Stabilize? He still wasn't speaking or reacting or talking. Machines were still keeping him alive. I tried to approach the subject with decorum, though. "He hasn't gotten worse, so I suppose that's positive."

"Of course he has a long way to go. But the swelling is starting to go down around his brain," Evelyn added.

"Okay . . ." Anxiety pinched my spine. Where was this going?

"Riley gave us durable power of attorney, Gabby," Ron continued.

"What's that have to do with anything right now? We all want the same thing. We all want Riley to recover."

Evelyn nodded. "Exactly." She clasped her hands in front of her. "As soon as we're able, we'd like to have Riley transferred to a hospital up in D.C., closer to where we live."

I forced myself to remain seated and to stay calm. "Why would you do that? I'm here."

"We're going to have to make some calls in terms of his health and what doctors can and can't do," Mr. Thomas said. "If Riley were in a hospital closer to us, we'd feel more comfortable."

"So you can get back to work and Riley won't be

an inconvenience to you?" Indignation laced my voice.

"It's not like that, Gabby," Ron started. "It's just that he could be in the hospital for months. It's not realistic to think that we can stay here that long."

"You don't need to. I can take care of him. I'm his fiancée." My emotions felt so strong that I could almost feel them materialize inside of me, as if they were a physical force.

"But we're the ones authorized to call the shots," Ron said quietly.

I swallowed, my throat burning as I tried to tamp down my feelings. "Are you sure?"

They glanced at each other. Finally, Mr. Thomas spoke. "We don't have the paperwork, Gabby, to be honest with you. But Riley told us . . ."

I stood up. "I beg you. Please don't move him. He's my fiancé. We're supposed to be married right now."

"Gabby, the doctor talked to us today," Ron started. His features looked strained, and he appeared to be aging with every breath.

I dropped back into my seat. "Okay."

"He's uncertain about the prognosis, at this point," he continued.

"With every day that goes past, it's a good sign, right?"

They glanced at each other again. "The swelling

isn't going down as quickly as they'd like, nor is Riley as responsive as they want him to be."

"He had a traumatic brain injury. It takes time." Even I knew that.

"None of us knows what Riley will be like whenever he comes out of this," Evelyn said. "He could be like a different person—personality wise, physically, intellectually. We don't know."

"I know that. I'm prepared to help him however I can."

"That's just it, Gabby. We have the time, the resources to really be there for him," Evelyn started. "That's why we think it's a good idea to move him up north as soon as we can. The hospital is one of the best in the country for traumatic brain injuries. Plus, there's a doctor there who's been doing some innovative things."

Innovative sounded like another word for experimental to me. "Define 'innovative.'"

"It's new," Ron said.

"New? New as in 'trial'? New as in 'we don't know what the outcome is'? New as in 'let's use Riley for a lab rat'?" The words came out harsher than I intended. But it needed to be said.

"It's not like that. The doctor goes to our church —" Evelyn started.

"Just because he goes to church with you doesn't mean he's not a whack job." I needed to keep my words more in check. I knew I did. But my emotions were bubbling up to the surface. This was my fiancé!

"Maybe you just need some time to sleep on this, Gabby," Ron started. "You've been through a lot. We all have."

I shook my head, not ready to back down yet. "What's this doctor's name?" I needed to do my own research here.

"Dr. Stephen Moreno," Ron responded.

"What kind of innovative therapy is he trying?"

"He combines hypothermia with electric impulses—"

I raised my hand, feeling a headache coming on. All I could see was Riley being electrocuted. "On second thought, don't tell me right now. I can't handle anymore. My brain is on overload." I squeezed the skin between my eyes, my head suddenly pounding. His parents wanted to take Riley away from me. "Don't I have any say in this?" My voice broke.

Riley's dad squeezed my arm, but I pulled away. The man felt like a traitor. Not like that father I never had. That's what I'd secretly hoped Riley's family might be. But no—they were just as selfish as my own family had been.

"We're not doing anything right now," Riley's dad said. "But we just want you to think about this. We want you to be prepared . . ."

I stood and shook my head. "I'll be prepared all right. I'll be prepared with a lawyer."

"Gabby . . ." Riley's mom started.

I didn't pay attention. I ran out the door, my mind racing. I had to figure out a way to stop them. I'd do whatever I could.

CHAPTER
SEVEN

IT WAS against my better instincts. But, as I thought back to Riley's lawyer friends, I realized the one who was easiest to locate was Derek Waters. He was sleazy in a womanizing, ambulance chasing kind of way. But he thought highly enough of himself that he had ads and commercials everywhere. That made him easy to find. A quick Internet search, and I had his number.

I sat in my van outside the hospital. My emotions fluctuated between mourning and anger, between intense sadness and intense rage.

How could his parents even be considering taking him away from me? If it was so he could receive better medical care, that would be one thing. I still wouldn't like it. But for their convenience? Moving him in his current state was risky. Then, on top of all of that, throw in some loopy doctor that they went to church with? No way.

I pulled back my tears, frustrated with myself that I kept giving in to the waterworks—into weakness. I was stronger than this.

At least, I'd thought I was.

I massaged my achy tear glands. I had to figure out some options here. With shaky fingers, I dialed Derek's number and listened to the phone ring. Finally, a woman answered. I asked to speak to Derek, she said he wasn't available, and I told her I was a friend of Riley Thomas and I was calling to discuss a highly-sensitive situation.

To my surprise, Derek picked up a couple of minutes later. I licked my lips, trying to collect myself. "Derek, this is Gabby St. Claire. We met at Allendale—"

"Gabby. Of course I remember you. You're Riley's girl. How's it going?"

"Not very well, I'm afraid. Riley was shot, Derek. He's in a medically induced coma right now. The doctors don't know what the future is going to hold . . ."

He was silent for a minute. "Man, I had no idea. I'm sorry to hear that."

"Derek, Riley's parents are talking about having him transferred to a hospital up where they live. I didn't know who else to ask. I . . . I just don't know—what to think, what to do."

"Did he write a Power of Attorney? A living will? An Advanced Health Care Directive, maybe?"

I searched my brain. "I don't know. We never really talked about it. Riley's parents claim they have durable power of attorney."

"Where would he have put a legal document like that?"

Frustration rose in me at my lack of answers. "I have no idea. Did he hire a lawyer? Do lawyers hire lawyers, for that matter? I'm just drawing a blank here."

"Don't panic, Gabby. You could still look for those documents."

"Where? A safety deposit box maybe?"

"No, probably not. Most people don't put them somewhere hard to access because then other people can't get to the documents when they're needed. They need to be easily available. Check his file drawers. His office maybe. Some people even put them in their freezers."

"Their freezers?" What other options might he suggest? A toilet bowl basin?

"I know it sounds weird, but if there's a fire or flood, usually the freezer will remain sealed and untouched." He paused a moment. "I don't know.

Riley just seems like the type who would have documents like that."

I nodded. Derek was right. Riley *was* that type. The question was: How did I get into his apartment while his parents were staying there in order to search for the documents? I'd have to think about that later.

"That's all I can do? There's nothing else?"

"If it came down to it, you could file a lawsuit to stop his parents from moving him. It would be time-consuming and costly, but it's worked before."

A lawsuit. Funny, this was the second time today that someone had brought up suing someone. Garrett didn't seem to think Christians should sue other Christians. I needed to do my own research and read the Bible to see what it said. It wasn't something I'd ever thought about before. Not really.

"Look for those documents, Gabby. If you don't find them and you need to take some action, let me know. I'll see what I can do to help. I'm actually licensed in Virginia and Massachusetts."

"Thanks, Derek. I appreciate it."

"I'm sorry about this, Gabby. Really sorry. Riley's a stand up guy. I know we're as different as night and day, but I don't want this for him."

Derek actually seemed like he had a heart. Maybe I'd been wrong about him. Probably not, but maybe.

"Thanks, Derek."

I hung up. I knew where I needed to go next.

I pulled up in front of Riley's law office. It was located on the outskirts of the downtown area, in a small one-story building that housed two different businesses—Riley's and an accounting office. A small parking lot with six spaces was out front and a dumpster peeked around the side of the building. Behind the space was a nice view of the high-rise towers of downtown Norfolk.

I hadn't been in here since the shooting. I really didn't want to see the place where my fiancé's life had nearly come to an end. My imagination was enough.

The crime scene had been released last week, and I'd gotten Chad to come in and clean it up for me. There were just some things a girl shouldn't have to do. I didn't want to see Riley's blood. I didn't want to picture the scene any more than I already saw it in my head.

I was pleasantly surprised to see Mary Lou's Lincoln Town Car in the parking space in front of the building. What was she doing here exactly? I was going to find out.

I climbed from my van and pulled at the front door. It was locked. Curious.

I tapped at one of the two glass doors at the front of the building. As I waited, I cupped my hands around the glass and peered inside. I spotted a peaceful picture of Jesus calming the water directly in front of me and a plaque with "Damascus Law" above that. A white door with "Welcome" was on the left and a regal looking armchair across from it.

A moment later, the interior door cracked and Mary Lou peered around the edge. She spotted me, lost the strained look on her face, and hurried toward the door to let me in.

"Gabby! I didn't expect to see you here." She pulled me inside and immediately locked the door again. "Call me paranoid, but I just can't leave this accessible for anyone to come in. Not now, not after what happened. Maybe after the person who did this is caught . . ."

I stepped into the office area, a bit unnerved myself. "I understand. What are you doing here?" I glanced at her desk, hoping I'd see a clue to her presence.

"I guess I should have mentioned it to you. I didn't even think about it. I knew you had other things on your mind." She ushered me toward a seat across from her desk.

I politely declined, insisting that I'd been sitting a lot lately.

She picked up a stack of papers and scurried toward the filing cabinets behind her. "I had to come in and let Riley's clients know what was going on. There were court dates and legal briefs due." She shook her head. "Riley wouldn't want people to think he'd forgotten about them. I've been on the phone and answering emails. I should have probably come earlier."

"Of course." How could I have not remembered that? Last week I'd been in a daze, it seemed. Everything was a blur. Everything except me sitting at Riley's bedside.

Mary Lou paused for long enough to hurry back toward me and feel my cheek with the back of her hand. "You're not looking too good, Dear. Why don't you sit down? Let me get you some tea?"

Before I could say no, she'd charged over to the single cup coffee maker and inserted a tea pod. The fancy machine had been a gift from Riley's parents when he'd opened the practice.

Just the thought of them made my muscles stretch tight under the weight of their betrayal.

"Any updates?" Mary Lou asked, grabbing a cup and putting it under the dispenser.

Yeah, Riley's parents are considering taking him away from me. I didn't say that. Instead, I shook my head. "No, not really."

"That's too bad. I'm still praying for a miracle.

The world just wouldn't be the same without the likes of Riley Thomas. He's a good man."

It hadn't been that long ago that I'd believed in miracles. For some reason, all of that felt like another lifetime ago. Right now . . . right now my emotions were wreaking havoc on me. They were making me doubt everything.

The water gurgled out from the coffee pot. Mary Lou grabbed the thick paper cup, added a packet of sugar, and stirred it with a little straw. Then she placed it in my hand and lowered herself across from me. "What brings you by here?"

"This may sound weird, but did Riley keep any personal documents here?"

"What do you mean?" She twisted her head.

"I don't know. His insurance policy or will or a living will maybe?"

Her eyes widened. "Sweetie, please don't tell me you're trying to figure out what you'll get if he dies? I thought more of you."

My hand squeezed the cup of tea so hard that scalding liquid poured over the edges. I jumped from my seat, tugging at the legs of my jeans to try and get the heat away from my skin. I was fanning my jeans as I looked up to finish the conversation.

"Mary Lou, I don't care about that stuff. I don't want anything from Riley, except Riley. Material possessions have never been a big draw for me. I need to know if Riley has a Power of Attorney document."

Her face softened. "I'm sorry. I just thought—" She shook her head, her cheeks flushing. "Please forgive me."

"It's okay, Mary Lou," I insisted. "But time is of the essence. If Riley has a power of attorney document, I need to find it."

She only stared at me.

I stared back before finally shaking my head. "His parents want to transfer him up to a hospital closer to their home. They want to try some kind of unproven treatment on him."

Mary Lou gasped, her hand flying over her heart. "That sounds scary."

I nodded. "They're already talking about when's the right time to move him, and they're not giving me any say in this. I'm not ready to face the possibility of Riley being someone's guinea pig, Mary Lou. I need to know who has the power to make these decisions while he can't. Riley can't tell me now, and I'm powerless to do anything without documentation."

"What can I do to help?"

"Can I get into his office?"

She stood. "Of course."

"His file drawers? Are they locked?"

"I've got the key." She paused. "Some information

is confidential, though. Attorney-client privilege, you know. You just can't look at everything."

I nodded. "I know."

She grabbed a key from her drawer and nodded toward the hallway. "Let's go."

My steps dragged. I wasn't sure I was ready to see Riley's office. I'd seen a lot of terrible things in my day. Truly. But seeing the place where a loved one had almost died . . . well, that seemed like the worst.

I paused at the doorway as Mary Lou jangled her keys near the lock. I sucked in a breath as the door swung open. My heart thudded in my ears.

Mary Lou stepped back, grief lining her face. "It's all yours."

I nodded a thank you as she went back to her desk. Then I stepped inside, trepidation claiming me.

I swallowed, trying to stay objective as I peered into Riley's office.

My first observation was that Chad had done a good job cleaning up after the crime. I could hardly tell anything had happened, other than a few stray objects being moved or removed.

All the blood was gone from the golden brown carpet. The rug had been high quality and soft under your feet—leftover from the previous building owner, who just happened to be a carpet supplier.

The only changes I saw were some books that had been moved from the bookshelf. Possibly blood had splattered there. Also, Riley's diploma was missing from the wall. I assumed that the glass around the frame had probably shattered because the document was on Riley's desk now.

His desk calendar was gone, I realized. It probably had blood on it, also. The police had most likely taken it for evidence.

As much as I tried to fight the images of what had happened here last week, I couldn't. They hit me with the impact of a speeding train.

At once, I pictured Riley here at his solid oak desk. I saw him looking over some documents, preparing for his day. Then he'd heard someone walk in. He'd probably stood.

Before he'd realized what was happening, a man appeared in his doorway. Wearing a mask. With a gun in his hand. Before Riley could react, the man fired. Riley turned, but not in time. The bullet still hit his skull.

From what I understood, the ambulance arrived ten minutes later. While the EMTs rushed him to the hospital, the police arrived and began their investigation.

And my life had been changed. Just like that.

Anger began growing inside me. Anger at the person who'd done this. Anger at Riley for not locking the front door, at Mary Lou for not being here that day, at me for not insisting he take some time off, at God for allowing it to happen.

I shook my head. I had to focus. I couldn't dwell on those things now. Pointing the finger at anyone other than the gunman would only waste my time and compromise my judgment.

Instead, I went to Riley's desk and sat down in his chair. I forced my mind not to go to the places where it wanted—places of grief and assumption. Places that formed haunting mental pictures of what might have been. Instead, I pulled open his first desk drawer.

I saw the expected—pens, highlighters, Post-Its, tape, scissors.

I opened the rest of his drawers but found nothing that was anything like a Power of Attorney document.

I looked behind me at the filing cabinets. There were six different cabinets, most with either four or five drawers. I knew that's where Riley kept his records, the paperwork I wasn't allowed to see.

I swiveled the chair behind me. A second desk was there. Normally, a computer sat atop it, but no doubt the police had taken that. Where might Riley keep his personal documents?

The obvious answer was: at home. But I wasn't sure how soon I'd be able to search there. I'd have to figure out a way. I wasn't above being sneaky.

I stood and walked to his bookcase. Mostly, there

were law books. Nothing exciting. I ran my finger down a shelf, pausing when I got to the end.

A devotional book we'd been doing together was there. I'd bought it for him a few weeks ago. A bittersweet smile came over my face as I pulled it off the shelf. I opened the book and read the inscription. "To Riley. It's you and me from here until eternity. Love always, Gabby."

I closed the book, fighting tears—again. As I rubbed the cover and started to put the book back, something fluttered out from its pages.

I bent down and grabbed a card. I studied the front. It was a picture of the sunset at the beach with a heart drawn in the sand.

I frowned. Where had this come from? I certainly hadn't given it to Riley.

My hands trembled as I opened it. A pretty, curvy scrawl etched the paper there. I squinted, trying to get the words to focus.

"Riley, I'm so glad we've reconnected. I hate to think about all the time we've lost in these last couple of years. I want you to know that I still care about you. Nothing will ever change that. I look forward to our meeting tomorrow. Love, Juliette."

I blinked. I couldn't have read that correctly. There was no way.

I read the note again. Certainly I was reading

something wrong because this note almost made it sound like . . .

I shook my head. Okay, I needed to think this through clearly.

Juliette was the name of the woman he was representing, the woman who wanted to sue Garrett Mercer.

Apparently, Riley knew Juliette before this case.

I'd only given him this book three weeks ago. That meant this note was recent.

But why hadn't Riley told me about the meeting with her? And what did Juliette mean when she said she cared about him still?

Just when I thought my unease couldn't grow anymore, it did.

Riley had been shot.

Riley's parents were considering making decisions I didn't agree with about his future.

And now . . . Riley was cheating on me?

I didn't want to assume anything, but my mind kept racing ahead of my desires.

I had to talk to this Juliette lady. And I had to talk to her now.

CHAPTER
EIGHT

BEFORE I COULD TALK to Juliette, I had to find out her last name. I sucked on my bottom lip as I considered my options.

I could ask Mary Lou. I had a feeling she wouldn't tell me. I could search the Internet. Maybe something had run in the newspaper about her being fired. I could search Riley's files but, since they were probably alphabetized by last name, that most likely wouldn't help me.

I sat back down at Riley's desk and pulled out my phone. Internet here would be slow, but it beat going back to my apartment. I quickly typed in "Juliette" and "Global Coffee Initiative."

Sure enough, an article about Juliette appeared in an online Christian magazine. Her last name was

Barnes. Juliette Barnes. There was no picture, only an image of the coffee logo from her previous employer.

I read the rest of the article, just so I could gather some more background information. Apparently, she'd worked for the company for almost a year. She was very vocal about her Christian beliefs and claimed she hadn't crossed any lines in the workplace. The end of the piece said that Damascus Law was representing her.

Riley had named the firm Damascus Law because of his own conversion. I'd only found out recently just how deeply his story ran. At first, I assumed Riley picked the name because of its Biblical reference. But after a friend had been killed in a drunk driving accident, his life had spiraled downhill. Eventually, Riley had realized he'd fallen off the straight and narrow. With the help of a friend, he'd turned his life around.

I checked the date of the article. It had just run nine days ago.

What I didn't find was Juliette's address.

For some reason unknown to me, I tucked Juliette's card into my purse. I was going to hold on to it, though I wasn't sure what purpose it would serve. Maybe it would only remind me of my doubts and fears and insecurities. Maybe it would provide answers. Maybe it would open up wounds, only add to my heartbreak.

I stepped out of Riley's office, locking the door behind me, and walked into the reception area. Mary Lou glanced up from her desk, where she was busy doing some paperwork. She offered a sad smile. "Hey there, Sweetie."

"Mary Lou, I know this is going to sound strange, but I need an address for one of Riley's clients."

"An address? I . . . I can't give out that information. It would be a breech of . . . something legal, I'm quite sure. Unethical, at best. Are you sure you can't find it online? I heard you could find anything and everything on that blasted Internet."

"I looked. It's not there."

"That's too bad." She frowned, her face wrinkling with the gesture.

I stepped closer. "Please, Mary Lou. It's important."

She licked her lips as she looked up at me. "Who is it you're looking for, Dear?"

"Juliette Barnes."

Mary Lou nodded slowly and tapped the envelopes in her hands against the desktop. "I wish I could help. I really do." She looked down and shuffled through the envelopes. "I don't know what to tell you."

I sighed. I'd figured that would be her response. Now I needed to think of another way to find the information.

Mary Lou stood. "I need to run to the little girl's room." She held up the envelopes, speaking very slowly and carefully. "I'm going to leave these billing statements right here on my desk. I'm about to mail them to all of Riley's most recent clients." She stared at me, as if silently asking, "Do you get my drift?"

I knew exactly what she was getting at. Gratitude filled me.

Mary Lou scurried off to the bathroom. I glanced down at the desk. Sure enough, the bill on top was addressed to a "Juliette Barnes." I grabbed a Post-It note and jotted down the information. She lived in Virginia Beach out by the oceanfront, so it would be a good thirty-minute drive from here in Norfolk.

There was no better time than now to see if I could find her.

I drove to the beach. It had taken me forever to find parking and, when I finally did, I'd had to pay ten dollars. The oceanfront was busy with tourists taking last minute vacations before the school year started again. Everything was more expensive down here at this time of the year.

I stopped in front of the condo complex listed as her address. The building was four stories high and right on the water—in other words, it was really expensive to live here. Who would have thought that Global Coffee paid this well?

I knew I should go and find Juliette's place, pound on the door, and demand some answers.

Instead, I stood out front, staring up at the pastel-colored building. What if Juliette told me something I didn't want to know? What if she revealed something that changed my entire view of Riley—for the worst? Riley was in a coma. He couldn't explain anything himself.

But my need for answers had brought me here. I needed to do what I'd come to do, despite whatever the outcome might be. I had to stop being wimpy.

I pulled open the front door, took the elevator to the third floor, and found Condo #3021. I practiced some yoga breathing before knocking on the door. Then I waited, the butterflies in my stomach feeling more like bats that were growing more ferocious with each second.

Nothing.

I pounded at the door again.

Still, nothing.

It appeared I'd just wasted ten dollars. I was going to have to come back again some other time.

Just as I turned, I saw a twenty-something guy headed my way, a towel around his neck and sand on the tops of his flip-flop clad feet. I offered my best smile. "Excuse me, I'm looking for Juliette

Barnes. Do you know when the best time to catch her is?"

"Juliette?" He shook his head. "I couldn't tell you. I haven't seen her in a while."

"Really? I wonder if she's out of town or something."

"Couldn't say. I couldn't tell you much about her except she looks great in a bathing suit and she loves Jesus." He rolled his eyes at the last part.

"She always did like to talk about Jesus, didn't she?" I took a stab at it.

"Favorite topic of conversation. All about how He'd changed her life." He paused and gave me a better look. "Probably shouldn't be giving out a lot of information about people. It's always the innocent ones you have to look out for. You're not going to break into her place tonight or something, are you?"

I pointed to myself. "Me? No. I just knew her way back when, and I heard she'd moved back to the area. I wanted to catch up, but I don't have her cellphone."

"Where'd you know her from?" I had a feeling he was testing me.

"Up in D.C." I took another guess. The D.C. area is where Riley grew up and went to law school.

He nodded, as if I'd passed. "Nice area up there. But too much traffic."

I leaned against the wall, trying to look casual.

"Listen, she didn't have a roommate, did she? I'd love to leave her a message, but I don't want to drive back down here again."

"I don't think she had a roommate. Maybe a boyfriend? I saw a guy come up here with her a few times."

"Blond hair? I wonder if it's Tony from up in Arlington. I always thought the two of them would get married."

"No, he had dark hair. He was tall, fit, blue eyes." He shrugged. "I don't know. They seemed really into each other. Talked the whole time, all quiet though, like they had secrets."

Tall, fit with blue eyes?

Riley?

Had Riley been up to her apartment?

I remembered the guy was waiting for me to respond. "I bet Tony's heartbroken then." I pulled my purse tighter. "I'll have to try again some other time."

"All I Ask of You" from *Phantom of the Opera* echoed in my head. Such a beautiful song. A song about someone who thought they'd found their true love, only to find out that love loved another.

Yeah, Tony and I could both relate to that one.

I called Sierra on my way home and asked if she'd come up to my apartment when I got back. I really needed to talk to someone, and Sierra was a great listener.

As soon as I walked in the front door, she stepped out from her first floor abode, gave me a quick hug, and then we walked upstairs arm in arm without saying a word. At my door, I picked up a casserole dish from the floor, unlocked my apartment, and ushered Sierra inside.

Thankfully, Riley's parents didn't stick their heads out from his apartment. I knew they were here. I'd seen their SUV outside. I didn't feel like seeing them now.

"Do you want something to eat?" I asked her, putting the casserole dish on the counter.

She stood with her hands on her hips beside the breakfast bar. "What do you have? Anything vegan?"

I opened my refrigerator door and tons of uneaten food stared back at me. "Maybe. I think there are some beans in here somewhere."

She peered over my shoulder. "Where in the world did you get all of that food?"

"The church has been bringing by meals for me every night." I pulled out a salad and checked another bowl to see if they were green beans inside. Bingo.

"It doesn't look like you've eaten a thing." She

raised her eyebrows until they peeked above the rim of her plastic framed glasses.

"I've nibbled on this and that. I gave a few things to Riley's parents. Do you want to take something to Chad?"

"He'd love that. Even though he knew I was a vegan before we got married, I still think he envisioned me cooking him meat and potatoes every night. Men. I don't know what they're thinking sometimes."

I pointed to the food on the counter as I pulled some white plates out of the cabinet. "Help yourself." I pulled out some kind of chicken pasta for myself, plopped a glob of it on a plate, and stuck it in the microwave. "I feel terrible that I haven't been able to help Chad out lately with Trauma Care. I know he's slammed."

"Yeah, he's been busy. But your friend Clarice is helping him."

I raised my eyebrows. "Clarice? I had no idea." Clarice had helped me the week while Chad was on his honeymoon. That was until Milton Jones had abducted her. I'd underestimated the girl. I'd give her that.

"Yeah, I guess she's driving him crazy. She talks a lot. About clothes and TV and boys."

I smiled for the first time all day as I pictured that

playing out. I could see it perfectly. "I'm glad she could help."

Sierra ignored the green beans, mumbling something about them being seasoned with bacon fat, and instead fixed herself a salad and put some bottled lemon juice and olive oil on top. Then she plopped at my small kitchen table. "So, what's new?"

I thought about being polite or hemming and hawing. Instead, I jumped right in. "Do you think Riley would ever cheat on me?"

Sierra looked at me, dumbfounded for a minute. "Riley? No way. Never. Why would you ask that?"

I told her what I'd discovered today, ending with the trip to Juliette's condo.

"Maybe there's a reasonable explanation," Sierra offered, taking a bite of her salad and chewing slowly.

I grabbed my food and sat across from her. "I've been trying to think of one all day. There's absolutely nothing I can come up with that would make this make sense. This woman seems to have some connection with his past."

"If you can figure out what the link is, maybe you'll find some answers." She took another bite of her salad. "Why were you looking around in Riley's office anyway?"

"That's my other crisis of the day. Riley's parents are talking about trying to get him transferred up north, closer to where they live. They said they have power of attorney and can make those decisions."

She nearly dropped her fork. "You're kidding? It seems like it would be dangerous to move him right now."

"I wish I were kidding, and I agree. It seems too risky. His parents claim the move would be better for him all around."

"You mean, better for them."

I let out a disgruntled laugh. "Tell me about it. In other words, I'm not enough for him. They made it sound like I didn't have the time or the resources to really be there for him."

"That's terrible. You look out for the people you love. If Riley's parents knew you, they'd know that."

"Thanks, Sierra." I pushed my pasta away. I wasn't even that hungry anymore. "Unfortunately, they don't know me. At this point, I'm not sure if I want to truly know them."

"I'd think the same thing if I were in your shoes. They sound horrible."

"I had all of these happy dreams about fitting in with them, about his family becoming the family I never had."

"Chad and I will be your family."

I looked up and smiled. "Thanks, Sierra." The smile quickly faded. "When Riley wakes up from this coma—and he will wake up—the relationship between his parents and me is going to be strained. What a way to start a marriage."

If there was a marriage.

Sierra stabbed some lettuce and studied it for a moment. "What happens if you don't find his Power of Attorney?"

"Then I can take legal action." I still needed to look up that Bible verse. Part of me didn't want to. Part of me just wanted to take matters into my own hands without consulting the Good Book.

"You mean, like, suing them?" The way her eyebrows arched together I could tell she was surprised.

I cocked my head to the side, trying to look nonplussed. "Something like that. What's the big deal? Your company has sued plenty of people."

Sierra worked for an animal rights organization that liked to ruffle feathers in the community, using whatever means necessary. Most of them were legal. Nearly all were provocative.

She raised her hands. "I'm not judging. You just took me off guard. I mean, in-laws are scary. But in-laws that you've sued?" She shuddered. "I don't even want to think about that. But you have to do what you have to do."

I sighed. "I hope it doesn't come down to that, though."

"What a mess."

I began stabbing at pieces of chicken on my plate. "What do you know about GCI?"

"Global Coffee Initiative?"

I nodded. Sierra knew about all things green and "save the planet" campaigns. That world was her realm.

"They're a great company. All of their coffee is eco-friendly, chemical free, and falls under Fair Trade. They even use biodegradable packaging. Even better, for every bag they sell, they donate money to make the lives of people in third world countries better."

They were a case study for do-gooders who paved the way for other companies to move beyond selfish gain and reach out globally. I couldn't argue that.

"You heard of Garrett Mercer?"

"Sure I have. He's quite the prodigy. Very innovative and dynamic."

"And flirty?"

She shrugged. "Maybe. I don't know. Why are you asking?"

I explained the lawsuit, ending with my visit to Juliette's apartment.

Another terrible thought slammed into my mind. "Sierra, Juliette's neighbor said he hadn't seen her in a while."

"Okay . . ."

"What if Juliette was the one who pulled the trigger and shot Riley? What if that neighbor hasn't seen her because she skipped town?"

Sierra's face paled. "It's a possibility."

I picked up my cellphone. "It's worth mentioning to Detective Adams."

CHAPTER
NINE

THAT EVENING, after Sierra left and after I'd placed my call to Detective Adams—who'd promised to follow my lead—I sat at my computer and did an Internet search on Juliette Barnes.

Earlier when I was at Riley's office, I'd searched for "Juliette" with "Global Coffee Initiative." Searching for "Juliette Barnes" opened up all kinds of new possibilities and leads.

I scrutinized the picture in front of me. Juliette Barnes had bright brown eyes—not bright with color, but bright with life. Her hair was a light brown with blonde highlights. She had a smattering of freckles, a slim build, and an infectious smile.

She hardly looked like a killer. Of course, in my day I'd been surprised more than once.

The first mention of Juliette that I could find

online was of this lawsuit. Before that, there were no articles about her. I couldn't find her name on any social media sites. Nothing.

Which I thought was weird.

Was Juliette Barnes a fabrication? Had she made up the name for some devious purpose? Or was there a logical explanation in all of this?

I had none of those answers. I wasn't a hundred percent sure where I'd find them either.

I leaned back in my computer chair and shook my head. "Oh, Riley, just what were you up to?"

If my life were a movie, there would be some incredible twist where it turned out that Juliette secretly designed award-winning wedding rings and Riley had hired her to design mine. Or they would secretly be long-lost cousins who'd reunited after years apart. But stuff like that only happened in the movies, and my life was no movie.

On another whim, I typed in the name of "Dr. Stephen Moreno" into my search engine. Pages of results came up.

Most of them weren't good. My eyes widened as I read the stories of patients who'd suffered at the hands of his experimental treatments. I did not want that for Riley. Not at all. How could his parents? Were they so desperate to have their son back that they wanted to torture him while he was incapable of making decisions on his own? Because that's what the doctor's treatments sounded like.

Dr. Moreno alternately dropped the body temperature of those with brain injuries, and then shocked them. Somehow, he said this helped to preserve the brain. He had no proven results but, to me, it looked like desperate people had given him a chance. Two people had started websites, sharing their stories of how a loved one had died because of his treatments.

My heart felt even heavier. Why couldn't I find that Power of Attorney document? If I was listed, then I'd be able to stop this madness.

I wasn't ready to give Riley's parents free reign to do whatever they thought best with his life. But did that mean I should take legal action? Was that the only way to save Riley?

Out of curiosity, I did one more Internet search, this one to find some Scriptures about Christians taking other Christians to court. I then looked up 1 Corinthians 6:1-7.

"If any of you has a dispute with another, do you dare to take it before the ungodly for judgment instead of before the Lord's people? . . . Therefore, if you have disputes about such matters, do you ask for a ruling from those whose way of life is scorned in the church? I say this to shame you. Is it possible that there is nobody among you wise enough to judge a dispute between believers? But instead, one brother takes another to court—and this in front of unbelievers! The very fact that you have lawsuits among you means you have been completely defeated already. Why not rather be wronged? Why not rather be cheated?"

What did that mean exactly? That I should go before the church and plead my case? What good would that do when I went to a different congregation than Riley's parents? Perhaps I should ask Pastor Shaggy to intervene? Was that a better stance to take?

I had no idea. Truly. I could see where having a Christian sue another Christian would only lessen the church's credibility in the world's eyes. But . . . I shook my head and closed my Bible.

Exhaustion pulled at every part of me. Perhaps the best thing I could do for myself was to get some rest. Sleep somehow helped to work out the problems floating in my brain and helped them to fall into place.

I went into my bedroom. There on the nightstand was the devotional book Riley and I were supposed to be reading simultaneously. This was my copy, not the one where Juliette's note had been found. I picked it up and flipped through the pages. Then I closed it.

No, not tonight. Tonight I wasn't in the mood to be reminded of my doubts—both about my relationship with Riley and my relationship with God.

The next morning, I squeezed Riley's hand and stared at his unmoving form in the hospital bed. I watched his chest rise and fall, thanks to the help of a machine. I inspected the tubes and the wires and the IV solutions.

And it hit me just how totally unfair life was.

Why had God given me Riley and now practically snatched him away? If I prayed hard enough that Riley would be healed, if my faith was strong enough, would Riley come out of this? Was God punishing me for the sins of my past?

I had no idea. Riley was always the one I'd turned to when I had questions like that. Now I was wondering if my faith was my own at all. Maybe my baptism had just been a whim.

I rubbed Riley's fingers and leaned closer. "Who is Juliette Barnes?" I whispered.

I waited. Of course I had no hope that Riley would respond. I knew better than that. But I really wished he could. I wished he could give me some answers.

It felt like it had been weeks since I'd slept. Having Riley in a coma was bad enough . . . but questioning his commitment to me made it even worse. I had too many questions and hardly any answers.

I stayed for twenty minutes, until the nurse told me I had to leave.

Then I braced myself. I knew who'd be waiting in the next room.

Riley's parents.

I'd woken up early this morning in an effort to beat them to the hospital. I wasn't unrealistic. I knew eventually I'd see Ron and Evelyn and we'd have to talk again. I just wanted to avoid that for the time being.

I had no idea what to say or how to act. I had no idea what *they* would say or how *they* would act.

I kissed Riley's forehead, promised him I'd come again soon, and then I took the dreaded walk toward the waiting room. I was aware of each step closer I got to the moment of impending doom. I was never one to shy away from confrontation. But right now I felt weak and tired . . . and I could really use Riley's advice on how to handle this whole situation, which only made everything even harder.

I froze when I stepped out of the ICU. Sure enough, Mr. and Mrs. Thomas were there. My gaze shifted. My dad and Teddi were here also.

My stomach dropped. I'd imagined all of them meeting at the wedding where my dad would be at his finest. In the very least, he'd be clean and wearing khakis and a button up shirt. Worst case scenario, he'd be wearing his best jeans and an unstained T-shirt.

Right now, he wore work pants that were splattered with plaster and paint. His hair was a mess. He hadn't shaved. Teddi sat beside him, all pretty looking and sweet in her typical overblown way.

I could only imagine the conversations they'd had. I could only imagine what Riley's parents were thinking about my family. This visit with them in the waiting room had probably confirmed that I'd never fit in with Riley's family, that I wasn't good enough for their precious son.

They all stood when they saw me, and awkwardness shifted between us.

"Gabby," Mr. Thomas said. "We were hoping you might be here."

And I'd really been hoping that they *wouldn't* be here.

I gave my dad and Teddi a quick hug before nodding toward Riley's parents. "I see you've all met."

Riley's dad nodded. "Your father was telling us all about your family."

Dread pooled in the pit of my stomach. "Entertaining, I'm sure." If you defined entertaining as humiliating and nightmare inducing.

"We just wanted to check on you," Teddi said,

putting her hand on my arm. "You didn't return our calls, so we got worried."

"Sorry. I've been distracted, but I'm hanging in. Thanks for checking on me."

"Is there anything we can do?" my dad asked.

I shook my head. "Just keep praying."

They both stared at me a moment before nodding. "Do you have time to do lunch?"

I glanced at my watch. "I've got a meeting, unfortunately. Can I take a rain check?" I should have grabbed the meal invitation as an excuse not to talk to Riley's parents. But, however hard the conversation was, I knew we had to have it.

Teddi nodded. "Of course."

Teddi squeezed my dad's hand, they said goodbye, and disappeared from the waiting room.

Then I had to face Riley's parents.

"We feel terrible about the way things ended between us yesterday," Mrs. Thomas started. "We wanted to talk to you again and explain ourselves a little better."

I swallowed, my throat tight and achy. "I don't know what there is to explain."

"Please, would you sit down a moment?" Mrs. Thomas asked.

Against my desires, I nodded and sat across from them.

They exchanged that worried look before Mr.

Thomas started. "Gabby, you need to know that doctors are still uncertain about Riley's outcome. We talked to Riley's neurosurgeon yesterday, and there's a good chance that Riley isn't going to come out of this and be like he was before. I don't want to lose my son any more than you want to lose your fiancé. But there comes a time when you must ask the difficult questions. None of us want to do that, but we have to. We have to plan for the future."

"In his heart a man plans his future, but the Lord determines his steps," I whispered. I'd said that a lot, but that was still the main point I wanted to come back to. "Why don't we just take this day by day? I feel like you're jumping the gun." I winced. "Bad choice of words."

"Perhaps we should have waited a little longer to broach the subject of moving Riley," Ron said. "But we wanted to give you time to prepare yourself emotionally."

"I'm not ready to give up hope on Riley. I'm not ready to release him into the hands of a quack."

"We're not giving up hope," Evelyn explained. "Dr. Moreno isn't a quack. Some people—most people—think he's brilliant. We're trying to do what's best for our son."

I jabbed my finger into my chest. "I'm what's best for Riley! You're taking him away so some Dr. Kevorkian can experiment on him."

"Sometimes it's hard to understand God's ways." Mrs. Thomas blotted beneath her eyes with a tissue. "This is hard for all of us, Gabby."

"Not giving Riley a voice in all of this isn't fair either," I interjected.

"Gabby, please understand our point of view," Mr. Thomas said. His eyes pleaded with me. He had Riley's blue eyes. I wished he didn't. "Dr. Moreno has some good results."

"Do you understand my point of view?" I stood and shook my head. "I don't care what the doctor says. There's still hope. Without hope . . . there's nothing. If we let this other doctor get his hands on Riley, we might as well sign his death certificate."

"I don't think that's true. Besides, Riley would never want you to put all of your hope in him," Mrs. Thomas said.

"Please don't lecture me right now." I stood and started toward the door before I said something else I might regret. "I need to go."

"Gabby, please—" Mrs. Thomas stepped forward.

I kept walking. Enough was enough.

I stormed to my van. I needed to pay Garrett a visit again. Maybe he could give me some answers on Juliette.

Garrett was surprisingly receptive to seeing me. I'd expected him to be in a meeting or to have excuses as to why he was busy. Instead, the receptionist called him, and I was ushered right into his office.

I was again taken by how much the man's presence could fill a room. He greeted me with a smile and a handshake. Then he leaned back in his chair, looking at ease and laid-back.

"Gabby . . ." He tapped his fingers together. "I never did catch your last name."

I lowered myself into the seat across from him. "St. Claire."

He lowered his chin in approval. "Pretty name."

"Thank you." I couldn't care less about if my name was pretty or not at the moment.

"What brings you by again? Did you think of something new to accuse me of?" Amusement tinged his voice and his eyes sparkled.

"I have more questions."

"Shoot. I'll answer as many as my lawyer has given me permission."

"Can you tell me about Juliette Barnes?"

He raised his eyebrows. "Juliette? What do you want to know?"

"Was she a good employee?"

"When she wasn't breaking the company's code of conduct, she was great. Outgoing, friendly, warm. I hated to fire her. But I couldn't have my employees blatantly going against my orders. It makes me look weak as a boss."

"How long did she work here?"

"Less than a year."

"She was from D.C., correct?"

He pursed his lips and looked in the distance for a moment. "I believe so."

"Did she come down here just for this job?"

"I believe she told me one other time that she had some unfinished business in the area."

My throat burned. "Did she have a boyfriend?"

His lips pulled back in thought. "Someone did meet her here for lunch a few times. I don't know if he was a boyfriend or not."

Riley? The very idea caused numbness to spread across my chest. "Any idea what she's been doing since you fired her?"

"Besides causing me trouble?" He shrugged and leaned forward, resting his elbows on his desk. "No idea. Can't say I care."

"What exactly did she do for you here at Global Coffee?"

"She worked sales." He leaned closer. "Why all the interest in this case, Ms. St. Claire? I'm still not sure how you're connected with this investigation. You're not with the police, and you're not claiming to be a P.I."

"I have a personal stake."

He stared at me another moment before nodding. "I see. How's Mr. Thomas doing?"

"Still in a coma," I responded.

"I'm sorry to hear that."

I nodded. "Me too."

His phone buzzed. He pressed a button and his secretary's voice sounded in the room, informing him his next appointment was here. He thanked her and then turned back to me. "I'm afraid we're going to have to cut this short. I'll answer more questions," his twinkling gaze caught mine, "but only if you get drinks with me."

I licked my lips, flattered yet not. "I don't drink."

"A soda then."

I held up my hand. "I'm engaged."

"Purely professional, of course. You know, not on work hours so I don't muddy the waters."

I stared at him, trying to size him up. A player? Maybe. Sincerely willing to talk about Juliette? I couldn't be sure.

I stood. "I'll think about it." I plucked a business card from the holder on his desk. "I'll be in touch."

ON MY WAY OUT, I spotted the same employee I'd seen last time in the distance, the one who looked familiar. Spontaneously, I leaned against the receptionist's desk. "I know this is totally inappropriate," I whispered. "But who is that guy over there? He's gorgeous."

The receptionist smiled. "Him?" She nodded toward the man.

"He's the one." I added a grin.

"Get in line, Honey. There's a long waiting list of women who'd like to get a piece of him. Name is Todd Harrison."

"Harrison? As in, James Harrison?" Things began clicking in my mind.

"You mean, the Lord of Crime Ring?" She chuckled. "He's the one."

Great. I could add one more person to my suspect list now. I'd made *that* family mad as well. Now Todd was working for Garrett. Garrett hated Riley. Juliette worked for Garrett, and Juliette apparently loved Riley.

How were all of these people connected?

I thanked the receptionist, went outside, climbed in my van, and shoved my keys into the ignition. As soon as the engine rumbled to life, I flipped on the AC so the fans blew at full strength. My entire body felt hot from the heat and humidity outside, hot enough that I stuck my face right in front of the vents and let cold air sweep over me.

I didn't really have a lot more information on the case, except that Juliette seemed to be an outstanding person who loved God so much that she couldn't stop talking about Him. She was willing to lose her job for her faith. I couldn't help but compare myself to her.

I did talk about my faith, just not to everyone I met on the street corner. I felt it was more of a personal thing that I talked to my friends about. Maybe one way wasn't right and the other wrong. I didn't know any more.

Nor did I know why Riley was meeting with her. Was he the man who'd met her for lunch at work? Who'd been to her condo? If so, why hadn't he mentioned it? Why would Riley sneak around behind my back?

In the back of my mind, I wondered about Juliette's judgment in sharing her faith even when her job requirements forbade her. Had she done the right thing? Or was the right thing to respect her boss's wishes and share her faith when she wasn't on company hours?

Part of me was surprised that Riley had agreed to represent her. He was pretty by the book. He liked to stand up for people who were voiceless, but it sounded like Juliette's problem was that she had too much of a voice.

I put the van in drive and headed down the interstate toward Virginia Beach. I was going to stop by Juliette's condo one more time. If she'd found another job, there was a chance she was at work right now. I was going to take the risk. I needed more information on her before drawing any conclusions.

I parked in the same lot I did yesterday, paid my ten bucks, and made my way up to Juliette's condo. I pounded on the door and waited.

Nothing.

I knocked again and waited.

Nothing.

I glanced around. Was there anything I was missing here? Any other way I could find out some more information?

There was no one else around. No neighbors that I could be inquisitive with. If I were more skilled at picking locks, I might be tempted to do just that. But I wasn't.

It looked like another waste of time.

I went back downstairs and stood on the boardwalk and turned my phone off, not in the mood to talk to anyone. I needed some time alone, so I decided to wander down the beach for a moment.

I shoved my hands down into the pockets of my jeans and enjoyed the smell of salty ocean water as it rolled over the sand. Seagulls squawked overhead. Tourists lolled past on bicycles or ate ice cream or used one of the city's showers to rinse off before heading home.

I remembered Riley and I being here while investigating a dead Elvis impersonator. I remembered eating at a restaurant on the strip where Sierra had freed some crabs and nearly gotten us arrested. I remembered getting baptized in the middle of winter in this water.

Now here I was questioning everything. Not even a musical could cheer me up from this.

I sat on a bench for several minutes, staring blankly at everything around me. In the distance, someone blared "Time of Your Life" by Green Day from his radio. The song reminded me of life's uncertainties and crossroads. The haunting lyrics nearly did me in. Were the best days of my life behind me? It was a possibility I didn't want to think about.

Finally, I turned my phone back on and checked my emails, trying to distract myself from the melancholy that threatened to squeeze the life out of me. There were plenty of notes from friends, church members, and even some from clients I'd worked with in the past.

I paused by one for Trauma Care. I read the email, read Chad's response, and then I knew exactly what I needed to do to sort out my thoughts.

I stepped into the small bungalow of a house with faded beige paint on the wood trim outside. Azaleas, long past their blooming season, were browning in the beds out front. The windows to the house were opened, and I could hear the roar of the air scrub inside the home. I stepped over some extension cords, not bothering to knock at the front door.

Instead, I paused in the living room where pea green carpet met my feet. I stared at my business partner as he worked a piece of the floor. Chad was a former mortician who'd left behind the demands of the funeral world and turned to crime scene cleaning instead.

He was a surfer in the summer and loved skiing

in the winter. He had the lean build of someone who worked hard, the tanned skin of someone who loved the sun, and the scraggly hair of someone who just didn't care about what people thought.

I didn't say anything, but when Chad caught a glimpse of me out of the corner of his eye he did a double take. He nearly dropped his saw.

"Gabby?" Chad paused from cutting out a section of subfloor and gawked at me. "What are you doing here?"

I grabbed a Hazmat suit. "I need to do something else, to feel normal for a moment. I thought you could use a hand."

I heard movement in the adjacent room. The next moment, Clarice burst out of the doorway and came running toward me. The girl was the epitome of a high-maintenance female with perfectly manicured glossy brown hair, fingernails that were always polished and pretty, and she wore designer clothes like some people wore deodorant—all the time. She had never been someone I'd pictured as a crime scene cleaner, but here she was.

"Gabby!" The college girl threw her arms around me.

"Hey, girl. How are you?"

"I'm taking some time off from college this semester." She shrugged. "Because . . . you know."

Because a madman had snatched her. She was probably going through therapy. Maybe on some heavy medication. Definitely having nightmares. "You're going back to school, though, right? You'll finish your degree?"

She nodded, a new somberness about her. "Yeah, this is just temporary."

I tapped her glasses. "And those are real glasses?"

She blushed. "Totally. No hidden cameras this time."

"Good girl."

"Chad has me scrubbing baseboards again. I think I've found my calling." She frowned comically.

"Speaking of which," Chad tapped his watch. "We've got another job to do before the end of the day. As much as I hate to break up this little reunion . . ."

Clarice nodded. "Got it. I'll talk to you later, Gabby."

I continued to suit up, my gaze soaking in the house. A suicide had taken place here, and it wasn't pretty. Apparently, the man had flown into a rage before taking his own life. He'd had a couple of failed attempts that made the whole scene even more gruesome.

"You sure you want to be here, Gabby?" Chad asked. "You don't want to be at the hospital?"

I let out a slow breath. "It's complicated."

"Any updates?"

I shook my head. "No, not really."

"I still can't wrap my mind around why anyone would do this to Riley." He stroked his soul patch and shook his head. "It's messed up."

"Messed up is right. That's the question of the week. The year. Of my life, for that matter."

"Any leads?"

"No good ones." I snapped my gloves on and pulled some goggles over my eyes. Then I grabbed some cleaner and began scrubbing the walls. The splatter on this plaster could almost pass for modern wall art. But only if you were sick and twisted. Or Gabby St. Claire.

Chad began to spackle some stray bullet holes. "I know you really wanted to keep working for the medical examiner, but I'm really glad to have you back here, Gabby. When all of this settles down, I have a proposition for you."

I continued to scrub, curious but deciding to wait on Chad's timing to learn about this "proposition" of his. The rhythmic motion of wiping and scrubbing somehow brought me a certain measure of comfort. "This is the first scene we've worked together since my career at the medical examiner came crashing down, isn't it?"

"Crashing down is a slight exaggeration. They

would have kept you there if it hadn't been for those money issues."

I shrugged. "It doesn't matter. We make a good team."

"Don't forget me!" Clarice yelled from the next room.

Chad and I shared a smile.

"You too, Clarice," I yelled back.

Chad took measurements so he could replace the section of floor. He was much better at stuff like that than I was, which was just one more reason we worked well together. I was not exactly a handyman, but I was pretty amazing when it came to getting bloodstains out of carpet.

"You hear from Kansas yet?"

I grimaced. "I didn't get the job."

He paused. "What? Are they crazy?"

"They chose someone with more education."

"Education over experience? I'm not sure I agree."

I wiped a hair from my eye, using my forearm. "It's weird. I mean, I knew I wasn't going to take the job, even if they did offer it to me. But still, it would have been a nice little *attaboy* for my self-confidence to at least have the opportunity to turn it down, you know?"

"Maybe the Big Guy Upstairs knew you'd have your hands full here, you know?"

I resisted a sigh. "Yeah, I guess you're right."

"So, moving on to another subject. Who are your suspects? I know you have some. I know the way your mind works." He jotted down some numbers using his hand for a notebook.

"All I have are a lot of guesses." Too many guesses. Nothing concrete. Nothing even close to being a real lead.

"Tell me about your guesses then."

I rocked back and rested on my heels for a moment. With the windows open and the humidity outside, on top of wearing the Hazmat suit, it was hot in the house. I could feel the sweat beading on my forehead.

"Originally, I thought this could be tied in to a client Riley was representing," I started. "Apparently, there's this woman who used to work for Global Coffee, and she's suing her boss for firing her. The boss came storming into Riley's office a couple of weeks ago, trying to convince Riley to drop the case."

"I think I heard about that lady on the news!" Clarice yelled. "She sounded dogmatic. That's my word of the week, by the way."

I couldn't help but smile. Clarice tried to learn a new word every week. The girl came across as an airhead—okay, she acted like an airhead most of the time—but deep down inside, she was likable and funny and smart.

"Why was she fired?" Chad asked.

"She kept trying to convert people while she was on the job, even though she was asked to stop. She's claiming discrimination and a violation of her First Amendment rights."

Chad squeezed his shoulders up. "I don't know. I might be on the side of the boss in this one. It's kind of like if your boss says you can't smoke or cuss on the job. You have to respect those wishes."

I grabbed a clean rag and wiped my forehead. "I agree. I mean, there's nothing wrong with sharing your faith, but the time has to be right. I'm sure this woman—her name is Juliette—would probably say that her boss is a Jewish carpenter and she doesn't have any time to waste in sharing the good news. I can appreciate her passion. It even makes me feel a little guilty, truth be told."

"I don't know, shouldn't your actions speak louder than your words?" Chad asked. "I mean, what good is it if you're talking about Jesus, but you're never acting in obedience?"

I tilted my head. "I'm impressed. I take you to church a few Sundays, and you already know that much?"

He chuckled. "Yeah, something like that. Anyway, we're getting off topic. Tell me about your suspects."

I rewound my thoughts until they got back to the case. I quickly reviewed the people I'd already either questioned or considered. "At first, I thought maybe the person who shot Riley was this guy who'd stormed into his office. His name is Garrett Mercer. I talked to Garrett, and I honestly don't think he'd pull the trigger. He's too slick."

"Slick people can be killers. Slipping into an office, pulling the trigger and disappearing without a trace is pretty slick." Chad wiped his forehead with the edge of his T-shirt.

"I can't argue that. I also considered maybe his client, Juliette, was guilty."

His hands went to his hips. "Why would you think that? Why would she shoot her own lawyer?"

Tension pulled at my shoulders. "Apparently, Riley and Juliette knew each other before all of this happened. I don't know how. Riley never mentioned it."

Chad's eyes widened. "Uh oh. He's going to be in trouble when he gets out of this coma, isn't he?"

I smiled again, and I knew it was a good choice to come here. Chad could always get my mind off of life's burdens. So could crime scene cleaning. "Yeah, he's going to have some explaining to do."

He grabbed a piece of wood, ready to patch the house. That meant we needed to wrap up this conversation because it was really hard to talk with a saw screaming between us. "But there's still the question of why this woman would shoot her own lawyer?"

"It's like this. I can find no history of this woman before the past two months. No one has seen her for the past week, so she's either on vacation or she skipped town."

He started toward the front door, where his table saw was set up. "Okay, it sounds like you need more information before you can draw any conclusions."

I stood and followed him, ready to get out of the house for a moment. The place seemed to be trapping heat. "Exactly. But it's been a lot harder to find that information than I thought it would."

"My Auntie Sharon says the best things in life are the things that don't always come easy!" Clarice added her wisdom from out the front window. Apparently, she could hear everything we were saying, even with the air scrub on.

I paused by the front door. "Sharon's a wise woman." Except when it came to men. Then Sharon was totally wrong.

"Who else?" Chad asked from the lawn.

I leaned against the porch railing, trying to settle in for the conversation. Any other time, I would push myself to work. But today I needed to cut myself some slack. "The person who did this was either a.) a random freak who walked in off the street. I have a hard time thinking that's the case, though. If this person isn't random, then that means that b.) it's someone who's mad at Riley or c.) someone who's possibly mad at me."

Chad set up the wood on his saw and began making measurements. "But no one has claimed anything? No one has left any notes or hints of who they are or why they did it?"

"No. Nothing."

He shook his head, pulling his safety goggles on. "Who could want to make Riley pay?"

"Besides Milton Jones?" I kept my voice even, knowing I might sound crazy.

"Jones is dead."

"What if he's not?" My voice trembled, as it usually did when I mentioned my theory.

"Then he's injured. Even if he survived, I doubt he could prance into Riley's office and pull the trigger." I'd given Chad and Sierra the run down of everything that had happened with Milton Jones when they'd returned from their honeymoon. Riley had been with me. We'd gone to get Mexican food and had lots of laughs that night.

It seemed like another lifetime ago.

"Maybe he has another accomplice," Clarice yelled.

I looked over and saw her peering from the bedroom window. We hadn't really invited her to be a part of this conversation, but I didn't really care.

The way she kept inserting herself amused me, so I had to give her points for that.

But, when my amusement faded, dread filled me. An accomplice was a possibility I'd considered as well. There were so many what ifs in this case.

"Is there anyone you've made mad?" Chad asked, pausing and leaning on the sawhorse.

"A whole list. But, of all of those, The Guardians have popped into my mind quite a few times lately." I tried to sound casual, not uptight or paranoid. I wasn't sure if it worked, though.

Chad pulled his lip up in something close to a snarl. "The Guardians? They haven't bothered you since that confrontation a few months ago . . . right?"

"I know. They pretty much forgot about me, which is surprising considering I really made them mad." I fully expected retaliation. All I'd gotten was silence.

"You injured their pride when you sprayed them with cleaning solution. Then you led the FBI and DEA right into their lair. Wasn't their ringleader arrested? Is there anything worse for macho members of a street gang?"

"You seriously messed with The Guardians? They're some bad dudes," Clarice added. "Even I know that. You shame them; they'll shame you."

"I didn't intend on messing with them. It just sort of happened," I explained. "Anyway, no, I haven't heard from them in forever. But I was interviewed for the news a couple of weeks ago, back when," I lowered my voice, "Clarice was snatched."

"I heard that! Auntie Sharon said you did a great job! She said the camera loves you. I knew it would." Clarice grinned.

"I wonder if one of The Guardians saw that interview, remembered how I'd wronged them, and decided to finally get their revenge," I continued.

"They seem like the types who would let you know they were responsible," Chad said.

I nodded. "Exactly. Six days after Riley was admitted into the hospital, a member of the gang was also admitted into ICU."

"Coincidence?"

I shrugged. "Probably. I guess if he'd been admitted on the same day, it would be more alarming. Six days later? Not necessarily. He apparently has gangrene, which isn't exactly a battle wound."

"I'm not following."

I shook my head. "There's nothing to follow. I'm just trying to put the pieces together. Unfortunately, a good chunk of the pieces probably aren't going to fit, and no amount of forcing them to will help anything."

Chad pulled his safety goggles down. "Anything I can do?"

I shook my head. "Nothing that I can think of."

"How about me?" Clarice asked.

"If I can think of anything, I'll let you know."

Right now, the best thing I could do was work and let Chad get finished here at this scene, especially since I was the reason he was overworked right now.

I went back inside and began scrubbing again.

CHAPTER
ELEVEN

THAT AFTERNOON, I was determined to sit with Riley for a little while—at least until the nurses kicked me out. I liked to think that Riley could hear everything I said to him.

I successfully managed to sneak in to the ICU without seeing Riley's parents. I didn't want to argue with them anymore, nor did I want to be reminded that they were trying to take my fiancé away from me. Maybe that was a selfish way to look at it, but that's how I felt. It was like they were saying I was incompetent—both financially and with life in general—and that they could do a better job than I could in helping him heal.

As I sat at Riley's bedside, staring at the man I loved, I suddenly didn't know what to say. I stared at all the tubes and wires that kept him alive. Without those machines, his brain would have swelled, and he probably wouldn't have survived.

I knew the prognosis might not be good for him, but I couldn't think like that now. Right now, I just wanted him to get better. Slowly. Step by step. I'd take whatever I could get.

I squeezed his hand, but I didn't know what to say. There was a part of me that wanted to keep my distance, that felt like I couldn't trust him. Then I reminded myself that Riley and I would have time to talk these things out later. Right now, I had to send positive vibes. I had to let him know, even in his drug-induced comatose state, that I was here for him.

I stood, deciding to make the nurse's job easy today by leaving on my own instead of being kicked out. As soon as my foot stepped around the edge of the curtain, I saw a familiar figure walk into the ICU. I quickly ducked back before he saw me.

It was T-Bone. At least, that's what I called him.

He was a member of The Guardians.

I'd made him especially mad. In fact, I was surprised he wasn't in prison since I'd practically led him right into the hands of the feds. They'd probably given him some type of plea deal. That seemed like something they would do.

I held my breath as he walked past. I heard him walk into the curtained off area beside me. "Hey, hey Iceman. Wassup?"

"I don't know man," Iceman slurred back. He was the one admitted for gangrene. From what I'd overheard, he'd nearly lost his leg.

"How are they treating you here at the torture chamber?"

"It's a'ight. I gotta get out of here, though. Got to get my foot working right."

"If you ain't been crashing the car on that last job, this wouldn't be no problem."

"You know I did what was best for the brotherhood. I tried to stay low key. Then my foot started turning black."

"Anyone asked any questions?" T-Bone asked. He'd lowered his voice.

"Nah, they just been doing their jobs here," Iceman replied. "They have no idea what went down."

I couldn't make out the rest of the conversation. These guys were no good. Just what had they done to some poor innocent soul, all for the sake of loyalty or drugs or power?

"Ms. St. Claire, I'm sorry, but your time is up. I wish you could stay longer." A nurse appeared in front of me, and I nearly jumped out of my skin.

Her name was Kellie Miller, I'd learned through my frequent visits. She was in her mid-thirties with a sharp wedge hair cut and a matronly figure. She wasn't overly friendly, nor was she rude. I seemed to see her more frequently than the rest of the nursing staff.

Panicked, I looked from Kellie to the room beside me. The conversation on the other side of the curtain had halted. I wondered if they'd heard? I wondered if they'd recognized my name?

"Are you okay, Ms. St. Claire?" She watched me quizzically.

I nodded and backed into the curtain more. My throat felt raw as I looked over at Riley. What if The Guardians knew Riley was stationed beside one of their gang members? Would they remember him? Would they use this as an excuse to get that revenge they'd promised?

"Ms. St. Claire?" Nurse Kellie stared at me.

She had to stop saying my name. I put a finger over my lips and silently begged her to be quiet. I nodded toward the adjacent room, hoping she'd get the hint.

"What's going on?" Her hand went to her hip.

I really wanted to hand her a sign reading, "Clueless."

Some people just couldn't take hints.

I leaned toward her. "Please be quiet," I whispered.

"Why?" Her voice was anything but a whisper.

I scowled at her, which didn't seem to win me any more favor in her eyes. Didn't she understand that if

The Guardians found out Riley was a neighbor of one of their members . . . I couldn't imagine what they might do.

A shadow went past the curtain. I couldn't be certain, but I thought it was T-Bone. Had he heard all of that? Had he made the connection?

"Please, keep your voice down," I whispered. "Will you stay here with Riley while I go to make a phone call? It's of vital importance."

She studied me a minute and then nodded. "Just remember. I have other patients here too."

I sighed and then hurried out into the waiting room. I pulled out my phone and dialed Adams' number. I twirled around and searched the people in the area as the phone rang.

I didn't spot T-Bone anywhere. Thank goodness.

"Gabby?"

Was it sad that the detective recognized my number? I quickly explained everything to him.

"We can't arrest this Iceman guy for being a gang member, Gabby. You know that. There's no crime in being part of a gang. We can only arrest them if we can prove they've done something illegal."

"But what if they try to hurt Riley?" I tried to tamp down the panic rising in me.

"Have they made any threats?"

"Not in a while."

"Then we've got nothing right now."

"Can't you station an officer outside his door?"

"We don't have the manpower to do that. Besides, the ICU is a very secure area. I'll get the nurses to keep an eye on him. I know they already are. Fact is, I doubt they'll recognize Riley right now."

My heart squeezed. It was true. With all the machines hooked up to him, I hardly recognized him.

"It's going to be okay, Gabby," Adams said.

Didn't he know that nothing would be okay? My whole life had been turned upside down. And there was nothing I could do about it.

I hung up the phone, slipped back inside the ICU, and motioned Nurse Kellie over. She cautiously approached me, her eyebrows knitted together on her forehead, as if she suspected I might be up to something.

"I need you to keep an eye on Riley," I whispered.

"That's my job," she started, saying the words slowly, as if my comprehension skills were in question. "I monitor everything about him."

"Listen, his neighbor—Iceman, as his friend called him—is a part of a gang that has a grudge against him."

Her eyes widened with alarm. "Did you tell the police?"

I nodded. "Of course. They claim there's nothing they can do right now. There's been no direct threat."

"I monitor everyone who comes and goes from Riley's room."

Another thought hit me. "I thought only family was allowed in?"

"Usually, that's the case. This guy beside Riley, he has no family. No one has wanted to see him until today when this guy stopped by."

Maybe, just maybe, T-Bone wouldn't be back. Gangs only seemed loyal to each other when it worked to their advantage. T-Bone probably didn't want to show his face around here too much. Not after everything he'd done.

"Listen, I'll make sure no one gets in who's not supposed to," Nurse Kellie said. "I promise you that."

I patted her arm. "Thanks, Kellie."

I went and told Riley goodbye. Then it was my time to leave. I had to trust that Kellie would do as she said. Besides, Iceman might not have any idea who Riley was. T-Bone may have even forgotten him. I was the one who'd had the encounter with the gang. I had to be careful, so I didn't trigger them that I had a loved one here.

Just as I started to leave the hospital and head outside toward my van, I ran into Riley's parents. Wonderful. Could my day get any better?

"Gabby . . ." Riley's dad started. He reached out, but then his hands dropped to his side.

"You should know there's a gang member who's Riley's neighbor," I blurted. "I'm only telling you this because I'm afraid they'll try to do something to Riley if they discover he's their neighbor."

Riley's mom's hand flew over her mouth. "A gang member?"

"It turns out a member of The Guardians has a bed right beside Riley."

"The Guardians?" Evelyn asked.

"Street gang. Riley and I aren't their favorite people. I just wanted you to know so you can keep an eye on him also. I've already told the police and they'll be monitoring the situation." I glanced at my watch. "Speaking of which, I really should be going."

"Can't we talk . . .?" Riley's dad asked.

My heart thudded with compassion. I knew they loved their son. But would we ever see eye to eye? "Could we save it for another time? I'm beat right now. Exhausted. I really just need to get home. I'm afraid I'll say something I'll regret."

Mr. Thomas stared at me a moment before nodding. "I understand."

I smiled, though it was tight and strained. "Thank you."

"Get some rest, Gabby."

I waved goodbye and started walking. I kept

walking until I reached the parking garage. As soon as I took the first step inside the dark cement structure, my cellphone rang. I checked the number, but it was a Boston area code. Could this be Derek Waters calling me? Had he found out anything?

I took a chance and answered. "This is Gabby."

"Gabby, it's Derek."

"What's going on, Derek?" The shadows filled the parking garage. I'd never been a fan of the structures, but I especially wasn't a fan at the moment. My gaze wandered to my surroundings as I talked, T-Bone still on my mind.

"Did you find that Power of Attorney?"

"No. I haven't had any luck." A sound in the distance made me jump. I let out an airy breath when I realized it was just a motorcycle roaring to life.

"Do you want me to file an injunction for you?"

I frowned at his words. That wasn't what I wanted at all. I didn't want any of this, for that matter. Plus, I remembered that Scripture I'd read about Christians suing other Christians. All of this was so complicated. "I still have more time. I'm hoping to avoid all of that legal stuff."

"I'm telling you, sometimes you have to use the legal system to your advantage. This might be one of those times."

Said the person who made a living on malpractice lawsuits.

I tugged my purse closer, quickening my pace as I entered the grungy stairway that would take me to the third floor and, therefore, my van. "I'm keeping it in the back of my mind."

"Smart girl."

I didn't know. I really just wanted to find that Power of Attorney. I knew Riley. He liked to dot every "i" and cross every "t." He was the type who would have a Power of Attorney document for times like this.

My breaths were coming out more quickly than I would like as I hurried upward. My thighs burned and lungs strained. But I refused to slow down. "Listen, Derek, while I have you on the phone . . . did you go to law school with anyone named Juliette?"

"Juliette?" His voice lilted in thought. "Hm . . . no, I don't think so. The name doesn't ring any bells. Why?"

"Just wondering." I sucked in another breath as I reached the top of the staircase. I wanted to stop, to continue sucking in deep gulps of air until I could breathe normally. But my instincts—or my paranoia—wouldn't allow me to do that. Why hadn't I thought to ask Adams to have someone escort me home? That would have made a lot of sense, looking back.

"Whatever floats your boat. Okay, I've gotta run,

but let me know if you need any legal help. I'm here for you."

I thanked him and hung up. I kept the phone in my hands, my fingers poised on the "9" button. That was what I'd programmed for 911. If I saw trouble, I'd hold that down. The police could use my GPS to track the location of my phone.

Of course, by that time, my phone would probably be sprawled on the sweltering concrete beneath me and I'd either be lying dead beside it or I'd be abducted. Neither choice sounded that great.

A footfall sounded in the distance.

My pulse quickened as I pictured T-Bone. Maybe he had heard my name in the ICU. Maybe he'd waited for me out here. That seemed like something a member of The Guardians might do. And I'd practically walked right into his plan, making it entirely too easy for him to get his payback.

I was nearly jogging toward my van now. I'd spotted it in the distance. But so much could happen in the dark recesses between here and there.

Where were the other car owners? Why wasn't anyone else in the garage right now? And why couldn't they have brighter overhead lights in here?

I heard another footfall. I burst into a run. I fished through my purse and found my keys. But I kept moving.

I kept picturing T-Bone hiding around a corner.

Ducking behind a car, just waiting to make his move. Poised with a gun in hand, ready to make a statement.

Something moved. I saw it out of the corner of my eye. Someone was approaching me.

The footsteps quickened, coming closer, closer.

I made a split-second decision. I stopped, held up my keys like weapons, and faced down the person following me.

I KEPT MY KEYS RAISED, holding them out like Wolverine raising the blades between his knuckles. My weapons weren't nearly as impressive or cool, but I had to use what I had. I prepared myself to fight, drawing on every last ounce of energy in me. I fully expected to see T-Bone with his gold teeth and tattoos.

But I didn't see T-Bone.

No, I saw a middle-aged security guard with sagging jaws and sad eyes.

He squinted at my outstretched keys, and a wrinkle formed between his eyes. "You okay, ma'am? You looked a little frightened."

I let out a quick laugh and hung my head for a moment. I lowered my keys, feeling foolish at my overreaction. "No, I'm fine. Just too tightly wound, I suppose."

He nodded. "You can never be too careful."

I thanked him and hurried to my van. I climbed inside, locked my doors, and let silence absorb me for a moment.

My life was spiraling out of my control, wasn't it? Everything that had felt so certain now felt unstable. No matter how hard I tried to fix things, nothing seemed to be better.

I wasn't going to let that stop me in my quest for finding answers, though. Because finding answers was the only thing keeping me going right now.

The next morning, I waited until I heard the door to Riley's apartment open. I listened as footsteps plunked down the steps. I watched from my apartment window as his parents climbed into their SUV and drove away.

Then I stepped into the hallway, unlocked Riley's door, and slid inside his apartment. I paused in his living room and let my gaze wander the space. Funny how I'd been in here hundreds of times before, but right now I felt like a foreigner in a strange land.

Riley's parents' things were everywhere. Mrs.

Thomas had brought dainty teacups for her morning brew. The newspaper was spread over the dining room table. It smelled like someone else had been here too. The odor in the air wasn't Riley's leathery cologne. No, it smelled like roses and Old Spice and clogged up toilets.

I pushed myself from the wall. I checked his bookshelves. I even checked his freezer and the toilet bowl basin. Nothing.

Then I hurried toward Riley's desk. I looked through the drawers there and inside books stacked on the shelf and underneath his Bible. Nothing.

Quickly, I turned on his computer.

Why did I feel guilty being here? Riley had given me a key to his place, in case I ever needed it. We were supposed to get married. Yet I felt like I shouldn't be here, like I shouldn't be looking through his stuff.

Despite my misgivings, I searched his emails looking for something, anything, that would give me a clue as to what was going on in his life.

My eyes stopped at one name. Juliette Barnes. My heart froze for a moment.

My fingers trembled as I clicked on the email.

My eyes could barely focus on the words, but finally the cloudiness cleared and the letters came into focus. "Thanks for lunch today. It was fun. I look forward to putting the past behind us and embracing the future. You're an incredible man. Love, Juliette."

I leaned back, feeling like I'd been hit by a truck. So the man people had seen Juliette with *had* been Riley. He'd been seeing her, and he hadn't mentioned it to me. Why would he do that?

I'd given up a lot for Riley. I'd been fully prepared to turn down that stupid job in Kansas—if I'd gotten it—just to be with him. I hadn't been working since he'd been shot, so I was going to run out of money. Those were sacrifices I was willing to make. But now I felt like I should have never trusted him.

Maybe I should be ashamed of myself, but I just couldn't bring myself to go visit him now. No, I feared that even in his comatose state he'd pick up on the bad vibes I was feeling. Maybe it would only delay his recovery.

Instead, I was going to keep looking for the person who'd shot him.

Just for the sake of being well balanced and fair, I decided to look at people other than Juliette Barnes. I needed to let her simmer for a while, and maybe then I would figure out a way to track her or make sense of how she and Riley were connected.

Until then, I had to keep my eyes open for other possibilities.

That's why I was sitting in my van, wearing a baseball cap pulled low over my eyes. I was outside of GCI, waiting for an opportunity to talk to Todd Harrison. As much as I'd like to charge inside and ask the kind receptionist if I could speak to him, I didn't want to press my luck.

So, I sat there. I watched people come and go. I saw nothing and no one interesting. No Garrett. Not the trendy receptionist. No familiar faces.

Until lunchtime. That's when I saw Todd Harrison leave the office. By himself.

He climbed into an expensive looking BMW and started down the road. I, of course, followed him. I had no idea where this would lead. But I was desperate for answers.

He pulled to a stop in front of a diner located on the outskirts of an old working class neighborhood. Not exactly the hangout I'd imagined him frequenting.

I quickly pulled behind him, put my van in park, and chased him down in the parking lot. I didn't know who he was meeting inside, and I didn't want to take any chances that more members of his crime family would be there.

"Excuse me!"

The man slowed his gait. He was tall—really tall

—and thin. He had light brown hair and spiked bangs. His face was perfectly balanced and portioned. He wore faded khakis and a well-worn plaid shirt. His leather shoes were scuffed and he had a man purse strapped over his chest.

If I hadn't known he came from a rich family and if I hadn't seen his BMW, I wouldn't have guessed that he was loaded.

He scrunched his eyebrows together as he glanced back at me. "Can I help you?" He looked behind me, as if afraid I was a woman with a nefarious plan.

I jogged to reach him, not wanting this moment to slip by. "I'm hoping you can help me."

He continued to look behind me. Being in a family full of smart criminals had probably taught him that. "Did you follow me here?"

I nodded, hoping honesty would prove to be the best policy. "I did."

His eyes held a mix of confusion and wariness. "I'm sorry. I don't have much time."

"Please. I'm desperate." I almost reached out to grab him, but I stopped myself.

His gaze did another scan. "Who sent you here?"

"Sent me here? No one. Just me." I paused, wondering how much he knew about my involvement in his past. "Do you know who I am?"

Finally, his eyes met mine. "Should I?"

Would it work to my advantage to remind him that I'd put away members of his family? I doubted it. I'd wait on sharing that information. "I'm investigating a friend of mine who was shot."

His stance loosened for a moment. "I don't know how I can help you with that."

"Does the name Riley Thomas ring any bells with you?" I watched his expression carefully.

He shook his head. "No, none. Why?"

I stared another moment. He gave no indication that he was lying. He looked relatively relaxed, had good eye contact, and didn't flinch at my fiancé's name. I needed a new approach. "It's like this. How do you feel about the people who helped put members of your family behind bars?"

"I applaud them."

I blinked. That was not the answer I'd expected. "Say again?"

"You heard me right. I applaud them. What my family was doing was completely unethical."

"I can only imagine what Thanksgiving is like around your place."

His jaw flexed. "I've disavowed myself of my family. I'm my own person. I don't have their money. I don't want it."

"Just their cars?" I nodded toward his.

"That was a gift to me. I'm okay with keeping it. But that's as far as it goes. I've made my own way. I don't even like people to know I'm related to *those* Harrisons, truth be told."

He glanced behind me once more. He wasn't really a trusting guy, was he? I guess I wouldn't be either if I'd turned my back on my family, and my family just happened to not give a second thought to murdering people who got in their way.

"What's all this about?"

I decided to come clean with him. "I helped bring down your family, and now someone has shot my fiancé."

"And you're wondering if I did it?"

"That's right." Why lie?

"Look, I'm sorry about your fiancé. But, even before that whole showdown between the feds and my family a few months ago, I was done with them. As far as I'm concerned, you did us all a favor."

"Do you think there's someone in your family who might have pulled the trigger?"

He shook his head. "Honestly, if they wanted revenge, they'd come after you, not your fiancé."

I considered what he said for a moment before nodding. His words made sense. The Harrison mafia wasn't the type to beat around the bush or play games. They would have come right for me. "Thanks for your time."

And with that, I let the man enjoy the remaining fifteen minutes of his lunch break.

"You're Riley's fiancée, correct?"

I looked up from Riley's bedside and spotted the doctor standing at the entrance to Riley's room.

I'd changed my mind and decided to swing by the hospital after all. I couldn't live with myself if I wasn't there for Riley now, despite whatever secrets he might have been keeping. So, here I sat, my mind loaded with questions and doubts and fear.

Dr. Grayson, a name that fit the gray haired man, waited for me to say something.

I stood and rubbed my hands against my jeans. "Yes, I'm Gabby."

The doctor moved toward Riley and checked a machine by his bedside. He typed in some notes on an electronic tablet, looking down the end of his nose at his bifocals.

"Riley's parents said I shouldn't have hope," I blurted. "Do you agree?"

He paused, pushed his glasses up, and sat down across from me. The doctor could handle the hard questions. I knew that. I just wasn't sure I could handle his answers.

"It's very difficult to know what to do in these situations," he started. "There are people with brain injuries who make a full recovery. Then there are others who are never the same. Two people with the same injury could have two totally different recoveries."

"The majority of the time, what happens?"

The doctor pressed his lips together, calm and professional. I could only imagine the strain of conversations like this on him. I hoped he could understand my strain as well.

"The majority of the time, people don't make it," he said. "But Riley has already come a long way. He's responding well to the tests we do on him. The pressure in his brain is still dangerous, but it's low enough that we have hope."

My heart lifted but only for a moment. "How much longer will you leave him in this coma?"

"I'd like to see the swelling go down some more first. I'm afraid I can't give you a deadline. There are numerous factors we have to pay attention to."

"When you stop giving him the medicine to keep him in this state, will he wake right up? Could he still be vegetative? What should I expect?"

He pressed his lips together in a tight line, but his voice remained even and reasoned. "Brain injuries are unpredictable, Gabby. I know you want answers and that you don't want to hear, 'Wait and see.' Sometimes, that's all we can do, though. The CT imaging shows us that the brain bleeding is healing right on schedule. Now we just hope for the best."

"He's in no state to be moved right now, though.

Right? That would be dangerous. He's much better off here."

The doctor looked down at the tablet in his hands quickly before nodding slowly. "I understand his parents would like to move him closer to their home."

"They want some quack doctor to do experimental treatments on him." I practically spit the words out. Voicing the words aloud made me feel sick to my stomach. How had things gotten this crazy?

The doctor pushed his glasses up on his nose and said nothing for a minute. "The next of kin is the one to call these shots, or the person with Power of Attorney. Unfortunately, that can make medical situations like this even more difficult, especially when there's a disagreement."

"I feel like I should have some say in this."

He grimaced again. "I know this is hard, Gabby. I wish I had an easy solution for you. The hospital up in D.C. is a good one, and I know he'll be in good hands."

I wasn't ready to let it go at that. I softened my voice, though, trying to remain respectful. "What would you do if this was your loved one, doctor? His parents want to use the services of some Dr. Moreno. The man has had limited good results, but nothing is proven. And for every good result, I fear there's been several more devastating ones."

He released his breath to such an extent that I wondered if he was buying time. "I'm more comfortable with the tried and true. However, I haven't done any research on this doctor they'd like for Riley to see. I'm afraid I can't give much of an opinion. I can only treat Riley while he's here under my care."

"Is there anything I can do to stop this?" I hated feeling helpless. I wasn't good at it. Maybe I was too much of a fighter for my own good.

"You can hire a lawyer, Gabby. That might slow the process down." He pulled his lips into a thin line again. "We just want to do what's best for our patient. The good news is that, if they move him, the hospital they're looking at has one of the best programs for brain injury in the country."

I wanted to sneer at his advice. But I didn't. Instead, I patted Riley's hand and grabbed my purse. My time was up. "Thank you for the chat."

The doctor nodded goodbye.

Now I had to face Riley's parents again. What would our confrontation hold this time? I didn't want to find out. But there was only one approved exit from this unit and, on the other side of that exit was the waiting room. It was kind of hard to avoid them.

I hesitated a moment before pushing the door

open. When I stepped into the dimly lit room, my steps faltered. I saw Riley's dad sitting in a chair. His head was bowed and his shoulders hunched as if in pain.

Mrs. Thomas wasn't with him.

An unknown emotion began hovering around me, tinged in shades of black and gray. What was going on?

Part of me wanted to slip past without Mr. Thomas seeing me. With his head lowered, I might be able to escape without notice. I couldn't do that, though. I knew that something was wrong—even more wrong than usual.

"Mr. Thomas?"

He raised his head. His eyes were filled with tears. They were red, blood shot, and haggard.

I'd never seen the even-keeled man look like this before, not even after he got the news about Riley. And where was Mrs. Thomas? In the bathroom? Not feeling well? Maybe she'd returned to D.C . for the day to take care of some business.

"Gabby," he started. His voice cracked when he said my name.

"What's wrong?" The worst-case scenarios that rushed through my mind were like tornadoes that destroyed everything in their paths.

He let out a soft moan. "It's Evelyn. She . . . she

had a heart attack at the hospital last night. She's in critical condition."

"What?" My own heart felt like it stopped beating for a moment. Had I just heard him correctly?

He nodded. "All the stress . . . it was too much on her. Her blood pressure was through the roof. The doctor said he was surprised the heart attack didn't kill her outright."

"Oh, Mr. Thomas. I'm so sorry." Guilt pounded at me, rapidly and full of high-stakes pressure. I knew we were on different sides of the fence concerning Riley's future, but I would have never wished this on anyone. Especially not them.

I pushed aside any other thoughts and pulled Mr. Thomas into a hug. He held me tighter than I expected for longer than I expected. I waited until he was ready to let go.

When he stepped back, I kept my hand on his arm and squeezed it. "What can I do?"

"Just pray, Gabby." If the eyes were windows to the soul, then Mr. Thomas' soul was devastated right now. The hurt I saw in the depths of his gaze were enough to send a jolt of heartbreak through me.

"I will," I whispered.

"Praying is all any of us can do at this point."

My thoughts turned over and over on the way home. A heart attack. I couldn't believe it.

Poor Mr. Thomas. Dealing with a son and wife being in the hospital was more than I could imagine. I wished I could somehow help, that I could make things better. But maybe the best thing was for me to stay away.

I didn't know.

As soon as I arrived back at my apartment, Sierra met me at the door. "You're back!"

I couldn't even bring myself to smile. My heart felt heavy and burdened as I remembered my conversation with Mr. Thomas. "Yep. I'm here."

"Let's go over to The Grounds for a minute." The Grounds was a coffeehouse and one of my favorite hangouts. But even the thought of going there couldn't cheer me up at the moment.

I raised my hands to say "no." "I'm not really in the mood. It's been a rotten day. Even more rotten than some of the other bad ones I've had."

"I know that life has been treating you awful lately, but . . ." She tilted her head. "Just for a minute? Please."

I'd never known Sierra to beg for anything. I glanced across the street and figured a cup of coffee and some time with my best friend could be just the medicine I needed right now. "Just for a minute," I finally conceded.

I didn't even bother to bring up anything that had happened in the short walk from our apartments to the coffeehouse. No, the discussion was too heavy for such a short jaunt. I needed a walkathon to get everything out.

As soon as I walked into The Grounds, people jumped out from every corner and shadow and yelled, "Surprise!"

I stepped back and gawked at everyone for a moment.

This wasn't coffee with my best friend. No, this was a full-fledged social gathering. I wanted to run, to escape, to not be here. As kind as the sentiment was, I wasn't sure if I could fake my way through this.

But Sierra's hand was on my back, and, for a petite little Asian girl, she had an iron grip that wouldn't let me go.

"Happy birthday, Gabby!" Sierra exclaimed.

I blinked and stared at my best friend's smiling face. My birthday. Was that really today?

It took me a moment to concede that it actually was. I felt like I was 29 going on 79.

"You didn't forget, did you?" Sierra said with a laugh.

"Of course not," I muttered.

I glanced around and saw my dad, Teddi, Chad, Sierra, and even Clarice.

"We just threw this together at the last minute. We didn't want to plan something big, not with everything that happened. Just a few of your closest friends." Sierra leaned closer. "And Clarice, but only because she overheard our plans."

I forced a smile, not wanting to hurt the feelings of those closest to me. Apparently, being offensive was only reserved for everyone else in my life. And I did mean everyone lately. "It's fine. It's great. Thank you."

"Your brother apparently is up doing some kind of rally in D.C. or he would have been here," Sierra added.

That was my brother for you. I hadn't seen him in a couple of weeks, but he disappeared and reappeared like that. As long as he was happy, I was happy.

Clarice approached me with a latte in hand. "For you!"

My brain seemed to perk at the idea of coffee. Coffee always made things better. I reached for it, but Clarice pulled it back.

Her eyebrows shot up as she grinned. "Do you realize what you just said?"

I just stared at her. I had no clue what she was talking about.

"You said, 'My Precious,' just like that freaky little

dude from *The Lord of the Rings* when you reached for this drink."

"Gollum?" I questioned.

"Yes! Him. You sounded just like him."

I wasn't sure if I actually said these things or if Clarice just heard what she wanted to hear. This wasn't the first time she'd said something like that. In fact, sometimes she insisted when I said, "Hello, Clarice," that I sounded just like Hannibal from *The Silence of the Lambs*.

She handed me my latte—finally. Then she rambled on about her favorite coffee, which led to more ramblings about her favorite pastries, which then led to her favorite diet plans.

After about five minutes, Sierra and Chad swooped in and saved me. I liked Clarice. I really did. But I was in a rotten mood right now.

Maybe I'd ask Sharon, the coffeehouse owner, if she could blare, "It's My Party and I'll Cry If I Want To" on the overhead. The song seemed fitting at the moment.

"You doing okay?" Sierra asked.

Would this be a rotten time to tell her about Riley's mom? Probably. She'd gone through the trouble to plan this party after all. I didn't want to seem ungrateful. "Hanging in."

I mingled at the party for another hour, making sure I talked to everyone. Thankfully, everyone kept the conversation light. They tried to make it seem as normal as possible.

But what would they say if they heard the awful truth? The truth that words I'd spoken had almost done Riley's mom in?

Could my life get any worse?

CHAPTER
THIRTEEN

I SAT in my van the next morning, the AC blowing on me, drops of rain hitting the windshield. My mind was anywhere but the ghetto-like neighborhood around me.

Instead, in my mind, I was at the hospital. I pictured Riley waking up from this mess and resuming normal life—because I still had hope that he would.

Then I pictured myself telling him that I'd filed a lawsuit against his parents—my future in-laws—and that his mother had a heart attack because of the added stress I'd placed upon her.

This was not a great way to start my happily ever after.

In fact, if Riley knew, this would probably break his heart, and I couldn't stand that thought.

I'd stopped by the hospital this morning to check on him. He was the same.

I'd started down the hallway with flowers in hand to check on Evelyn, but then I'd stopped. Seeing me might only cause her more stress. For that reason, I'd asked a nurse to deliver the flowers for me. Maybe the most merciful and compassionate thing I could do was to stay away.

I hadn't even run into Riley's dad, a fact which would normally relieve some of my stress. Today, all I felt was guilt. I felt responsible. I felt like I should have been more diplomatic when arguing with Ron and Evelyn. I had no idea how to fix this or how to make things better.

I just had no idea about anything right now. Too little sleep, too little food, too much stress. All of those had come together to form the perfect emotional storm in my life.

As I reflected on my interactions with Evelyn, I remembered that I'd been arguing for what I thought was best for my fiancé. I was only trying to look out for him, to keep him away from some crazy doctor. What was I supposed to do when presented with a situation like this?

I shook my head. What a mess. One thing was for sure: If anyone could make a mess of things, it was me.

Back in the present, I glanced across the street at

The Guardians. They were playing basketball on a court set up in what was affectionately known as "the projects." I had a basic idea of where they liked to hang out. But I also knew that a big white van in the middle of their neighborhood wasn't the norm, so I had to be careful.

I watched closely. T-Bone was there. He was pushing around a couple of other guys. Yep, that's what he was. A bully. I didn't quite understand gang culture, but I did understand the need to belong.

I also didn't fully understand why I was sitting here watching them. Maybe I was hoping for a clue as to what they were up to or if they had any clue Riley was in the hospital. Right now, I had nothing except that T-Bone had a mean slam-dunk.

I slunk down in my seat and looked at my phone again. I'd missed another call from Pastor Shaggy. He'd been trying to reach me for the past few days, but I hadn't returned his calls. I didn't even know why. It was just that I couldn't bring myself to talk to him. I'd feel like I had to be strong and pretend that I was doing a great job trusting God throughout the storm.

I knew the truth. I knew I was sinking in the waves instead of walking on water right now. And I didn't want to own up to that fact. I'd thought I'd be stronger than this. But, every time I let my thoughts wander, their destination seemed to be the place where doubts tarried and lingered. I let my so-called faith mingle there as well.

Suddenly, someone tapped on my window. I nearly jumped out of my skin. My phone tumbled to the floor.

My first thought was that The Guardians had seen me and had come to finish me off. I needed a weapon. Something to defend myself with. If all else failed, maybe I'd burst into a Broadway song. That should sufficiently scare away any gangbanger, right? If not from the Broadway effect, then maybe they'd simply think I was crazy. Who wanted to mess with crazy?

When I looked over, I saw Parker standing there instead. My jaw dropped in agitation. "What are you doing?"

He motioned for me to unlock my passenger door. I looked over at The Guardians, hoping we hadn't drawn attention to ourselves, and then let Parker into the van.

"What are you doing?" I repeated.

He made himself comfortable in the passenger seat, one arm leaning on the cushioned rest and the other against the nook of the door. "The question is: What are you doing? Staking out The Guardians? Not a good idea."

I couldn't even argue. Why bother anyway? "No

one's coming forward to claim they shot Riley. Speaking of which, how did you find me?"

He scowled. "I tried to catch you at the hospital. I saw you leaving and followed you."

The timing wasn't computing in my head, no matter how I tried to figure it. "But I've been here fifteen minutes."

He shrugged. "I stopped to get some coffee."

It didn't sound like talking to me was that urgent, which was strange considering he'd followed me. I'd never understand men. Especially not Parker. "Okay . . . why are you here?" How many times would I have to ask before I got an answer?

He shifted his arms, tugging at his slacks as if to get out any wrinkles. Then he looked from left to right and back again before meeting my gaze. "You didn't hear any of this from me."

"Hear what from you?" Why was Parker making absolutely no sense today? Was the newborn baby at home affecting his sleep so much that he'd lost all common sense?

He shifted to face me and lowered his voice, as if someone else might hear us in the van. "Someone was abducted. They found a picture of her at the crime scene. Her eyes were Xed out."

Alarm washed through me, making my skin tingle with sudden awareness. I only had one question . . . "Milton Jones?"

He looked from side to side again. "That's what someone made it look like. I'm not saying it's him, though. It could be a copycat. That's the most likely scenario."

My gaze didn't leave him. I wanted to study his every expression and gesture until I saw the truth. "Is that what you think?"

He tugged at his collar a moment and looked out the windshield. He paused for three seconds before saying, "I haven't seen enough evidence to have an opinion."

Oh no. That answer was not going to cut it. "Parker, do you think Jones is dead?"

His gaze still didn't meet mine. "If he's not dead, then he's Superman surviving what he did."

"People have survived some crazy situations before. I wouldn't put it past him."

His chest slowly filled with air until he finally turned to me. "All along, we thought he had an accomplice last time—and we were right. He was working with someone."

"What if he was working with two people?" I could fill in the blanks . . . even though I didn't like the information that filling in the blanks required.

Parker nodded grimly. "And what if another person is continuing his work now? It may not matter if Jones is dead or alive, not if he has minions trying to finish what he started."

"Maybe that same person shot Riley." The answers filled me with a strange satisfaction—a satisfaction that I finally had a real lead. At the same time, anger rose in me that someone would be as mindless as to pull the trigger just because someone else wanted them to.

Parker nodded. "My thoughts exactly."

I took a few breaths, trying to calm my racing heart—and my racing thoughts. I had to cling to my logic here. My emotions would only pull me over the edge. "Tell me about the woman who was snatched."

"She lived in Virginia Beach. Same basic personality as the other women. She was young, enthusiastic, the oldest sibling by default—her older brother died, I guess. Some would call her bossy."

"She does fit the profile. Anything else you can tell me about her?"

"We're still gathering all the preliminary data."

"Are you part of this investigation?"

"I stopped by the scene for just a few minutes, for long enough to get the basics, just in case I'm called in later. I think I will be."

"What about her name? Did you get that, at least?"

"Name was . . ." He checked his notepad. ". . . Juliette Barnes."

The blood drained from my face. "Juliette Barnes?"

Parker narrowed his eyes. "You know her?"

I nodded, my head suddenly pounding uncontrollably. "In a manner of speaking."

Parker left, and I grabbed my cellphone. After I fished the business card from the bottom of my purse, I quickly dialed Garrett Mercer's number. The receptionist put me through. That woman was a saint.

I knew I didn't have much time if I was going to talk to Garrett again without interfering with a police investigation. Soon, the police would be all over GCI, asking questions of Garrett Mercer and all of Juliette's coworkers. That's why I had to strike now.

"Ms. St. Claire. I was hoping you'd call again." Garrett's rumbling, irksome British accent flowed over the line.

I didn't even ask why he was hoping I'd call again. I didn't have time to play any games. "I have more questions."

"I thought you might. I was just getting ready to take my lunch break. Care to meet me?"

"On purely professional terms? Yes. Name the time and place."

He listed the name of an organic, farm-to-table restaurant called The Farm Girl that Sierra liked to frequent. I couldn't care less about the organic or farm fresh aspect, but I said yes. I had just enough time to get there and put a fresh coat of powder on my face so my skin wouldn't look quite as pale.

I shuddered as I pulled into the parking garage. I continued to shudder as I stepped out of my van and hurried toward the exit. I was nearly jogging down the sidewalk in an effort to reach Garrett in time.

The day was still gloomy and more rain threatened to spill from the sky. I'd heard murmurings about an approaching hurricane. Right now, I just hoped I made it inside before the sky burst.

Finally, I walked into the restaurant, practically panting but dry. I wanted to take a moment to compose myself, but when I looked up, Garrett was standing there, a twinkle in his eyes. "Ms. St. Claire. Breathless to see me again, I see."

I scowled. "Something like that."

He smirked. "I have a table waiting for us." He extended his hand, showing me which direction to head.

I took in one last breath and then weaved between the country-style tables. His hand went to my back, and shivers went through me. Though I was sure he was just being polite and guiding me in the right direction, the last thing I wanted was for him to touch me. No, he was way too flirty as it was.

And the fact that my body was actually responding was even more disturbing.

If I didn't need information from him so badly, I might have swatted his hand away. But I maintained a polite façade. I needed to stay on good terms with him.

We sat at a chunky wooden table. Butcher paper covered the top, and crayons—for adult and child's use—were in a bowl in the middle, right beside a jar of dried wildflowers. The restaurant cut out the best tabletop drawings and displayed them on a board by the waiting area.

"The sweet potato cakes are fabulous here," he offered, not even bothering to pick up the menu. Instead, he stared at me, an amused expression on his face.

The thought of eating sweet potato cakes made me want to hurl. Instead, I flipped open the menu in an effort to distract myself from his obvious curiosity about me. I held the menu up high so he couldn't see my face and I couldn't see his. I kept the menu there until the waitress came, then I ordered a salad. I doubted I'd eat much of it. Garrett ordered his sweet potato cakes and a cup of coffee. I'd glanced at the menu and noticed GCI was the brand served here. Convenient.

He laced his fingers together and leaned toward me. "So, for what do I owe this honor? I'm assuming this meeting isn't because you simply couldn't wait to see me again. I've heard my impeccable good looks have that effect on women."

"Don't flatter yourself. No, I'm here because of Juliette Barnes."

He didn't flinch. "Okay. I thought I'd told you nearly all of what you'd need to know. I don't know what else I can share."

"Was she friends with Todd Harrison?"

"Harrison? No, not really."

"What do you know about him?"

"He's a good employee. A hard worker. Smart." He raised his palms, as if at a loss for words. "I don't know. What else do you want to know?"

"His father was involved in something close to the mob."

He shrugged. "I wouldn't want him to suffer for the sins of his father."

"So, you think he's a stand up guy?"

"I wouldn't have hired him if I didn't. And, no, I don't think he's capable of murder, just in case that was your next question." His eyes sparkled.

"Okay, let me turn this conversation back to Juliette then. Did she have any friends at work?" I figured if Garrett couldn't answer all of my questions, he could lead me to someone who did.

He leaned back and stared into space a moment.

"There was one lady Juliette seemed particularly fond of. Her name is Sutton Emerson."

Sutton? With a name like that I had images of someone spoiled, who'd been doted on by wealthy parents who thought the world revolved around her. "Is Sutton still with your company?"

He nodded. "Of course she is. She's one of our best sales representatives. Personable, attractive and passionate—three qualities we look for in our employees."

"Attractive? One of your top qualities is attractiveness? That's just another lawsuit waiting to—" A diatribe started in my head, but I squelched it. I had to stay on task. "Do you think I could speak with this Sutton?"

"That's up to Sutton." He tilted his head, still amused.

He wasn't even the slightest bit flustered over his admission about liking his employees to look good. The man was confident; I'd give him that. He raised his coffee mug. A waitress scurried over, giggled, and refilled it. He was obviously a regular here.

I fought the urge to roll my eyes.

"You seem to have a personal stake in this case, Ms. St. Claire."

I kept my gaze fastened on his. "Maybe. It doesn't matter."

It actually mattered more than anything, but Garrett didn't need to know that.

He took a sip of his coffee and kept his mug suspended in the air as he addressed me. "You think Sutton is responsible for shooting that lawyer?"

I shook my head. "No, I don't."

"Then you think Juliette is responsible?"

I shook my head again. "Not really."

"Then why all of the interest?"

Before I could respond, Garrett's cellphone rang. He held up a finger, as if to say hold that thought, before answering. His brows furrowed together as he spoke with the person on the other end. "Okay. I understand. Absolutely. I'll be right there."

He hung up and scrutinized me for a moment. "That was the police."

"Oh?" I tried to sound neutral.

Garrett watched me carefully. "Juliette appears to be missing."

"That's terrible." And it was. Even if she had a secret relationship of some sort with Riley.

"Why do I have a feeling that you knew that?" The skin at the corner of his eyes crinkled with a mix of intelligent observation and unbridled curiosity.

I swallowed. "How would I have known that?"

His eyebrows flinched upward. "That's a good question." He stood and placed his napkin on the table. "Rain check?"

"Perhaps." I didn't want to commit, especially not until I knew what the man's intentions were. At the same time, I didn't want to burn any bridges, not when this man could be the link to finding the person who shot my fiancé.

He dropped some bills on the table, started to walk away, and then paused. He backed up and leaned down until his lips were practically on my ear. "Sutton's favorite restaurant is the deli down the street. She's probably there now. Look for a blonde with short hair. Like a pixie. Probably by herself. Don't tell her where you got the information."

He didn't bother to look back. He walked away, calling goodbye to several of the restaurant's employees. I wiped my ear, still aware of the man's breath on my skin. What was up with him? Did he not understand that I was engaged? Or was it simply that he didn't care?

I stood.

I had to talk to Sutton before the police got to her.

I DIDN'T EVEN BOTHER to wait for my salad. Instead, I darted from the restaurant and into the rain. Of *course* it had started raining. And of *course* I didn't bring an umbrella.

The rain came down in sheets. I'd only taken a few steps when thunder rumbled through the air, shaking the tall buildings of downtown Norfolk. I kept running, going the entire two blocks until I reached the deli.

I spotted Sutton as soon as I walked in. Sure enough, she not only looked like Tinker Bell, but she sat alone in the corner, reading a newspaper while sipping on some water. A half-eaten sandwich was shoved to the side of the table.

I slowed my steps as I approached her. I didn't bother to ask if I could sit down; I simply slid into the plastic red chair across from her and waited for her to speak. As the AC tangoed with my wet clothing, I tried to resist the shivers that wanted to claim my muscles.

She lowered the paper, her eyes widening when she saw me there. "Can I help you?"

"My name is Gabby St. Claire, I'm investigating the shooting of attorney Riley Thomas, and I think you might be able to help me." I laid it all out.

She blinked her big green eyes several times. Maybe I should have slowed down some. What I'd told her was enough to overwhelm anyone. Finally, she shook her head. "I don't know how I can help."

"You're friends with Juliette Barnes?"

She shrugged. "We weren't BFFs or anything. We talked at work. Hung out a couple of times on the weekends. You know, casual stuff . . . you said your name was Gabby?"

I nodded. "Gabby St. Claire. I'm investigating. When was the last time you talked to Juliette?"

"It's probably been a couple of weeks. She was fired and then she got all weird. After she filed that lawsuit, I decided maybe I should keep my distance if I wanted to keep my job—and I do want to keep my position at the company. This is the best job I've ever had. Garrett is innovative, passionate about helping others, and brilliant. But he's also firm, he has high standards, and he doesn't like people to question his authority."

"Do you think it was right that she was fired for her beliefs?"

"Garrett was very nice when he asked her to stop talking about her faith with our clients. I thought his request was reasonable. Juliette was very in your face about the topic of religion—relationship, as she called it. She really rubbed some people the wrong way. She would flat out tell people what she thought of their views. She said there was no time to waste. Jesus could come any day."

I half admired the woman and half thought she'd been too pushy for her own good. But I didn't have time to ponder that now. "Did you guys share the same viewpoint?"

Sutton stared out the window at the rain for a moment. "Look, I'm way more liberal than she is. But I'm not going to tell people how to live their lives. I let them figure it out themselves."

"Yet, you were still friends with her?"

"When she wasn't talking about religion, she was a fun girl. She had lots of innovative ideas, she loved being outside and hiking and biking and running. She said she'd been given a new start and that she wanted to make the most of it." She shrugged. "Besides, I kind of like it when people aren't afraid to be who they are, you know? That was Juliette.

Whether you loved her or hated her, she didn't back down from her beliefs or being the person she was created to be, as she said. You have to admire that."

I supposed you did. That wasn't what I was here about, however. "Did she ever say where she went to church?"

"Like every week. When she invited me to go with her." Sutton rolled her eyes. "It was Lafayette Community. She always used words like 'On fire,' 'Lit up,' 'World changing.' She apparently loved the place."

I made a mental note of that. Maybe I'd talk to her pastor. "Any other community affiliations?"

"Not that I can think of." She picked up her water, swirled it, and then took a sip.

My throat burned. This next question didn't have to do with her disappearance. But I had to know. "Did she ever mention a boyfriend?"

Her face scrunched up in thought. "I don't know if he was a boyfriend or not. There was this guy she was always talking about. How he was just great and they had some kind of history. They met for lunch a few times."

"No names?"

She shook her head. "No names. I just know her face flushed every time she talked about him."

I didn't bother to run back to the parking garage. No, I took my time. I let the rain soak me. I listened to the cars zoom past on the street. I didn't even get mad when one driver splashed water all over me.

I felt like my life had been turned upside down. Maybe I'd been operating under the illusion that things were going to finally get better for me. Maybe I'd thought that for once in my life, maybe things would go my way, that tragedies could be held at bay for a while, that God had realized my need for a little peace.

Instead, things seemed worse than ever. I didn't want to feel sorry for myself, but I did. I should be married right now. On my honeymoon. Working at the Medical Examiner's Office. Getting my life on track.

I tried to think of even one aspect of my life that was going right, and I couldn't come up with a single thing. Still, I had to stop whining about it. Why was it so hard?

I reached the parking garage and shook myself off. Water droplets flew everywhere. I paused for a minute, listening to the roar of the rain as it cascaded outside.

I started to my van when, all at once, a chill came over me.

I paused and glanced around me. I saw no one. No businessmen or women. No college students. No one out shopping or construction workers going to or from a job. Then why were my internal alarms blaring?

I reached into my purse and grabbed my keys. I'd parked on the first level, so at least there were no staircases for me to battle. And it was the middle of the day . . . usually daylight offered a certain measure of protection.

Then I remembered that Riley had been shot in broad daylight.

That's when I heard the first gunshot fire in the parking garage.

I ducked to the ground, crawling behind the first car I saw. Grit from the floor coated my fingers. The smell of motor oil rose in waves from the concrete. A straw from a fast food restaurant and a piece of gum socialized near a tire.

My lungs froze. I listened. Waited.

Nothing.

No retreating footsteps.

No guns cocking.

No ammunition being fired.

Exactly what was going on here?

I hadn't imagined that bullet, had I? I knew I hadn't.

I also knew that I couldn't stay here hiding all day. On my hands and knees, I slowly crawled forward. A puddle of water that had crept in from the sidewalk outside soaked my jeans, but I didn't care about the grimy liquid.

Instead, I peered around the edge of a black Mercedes beside me. No sooner had I peeked around the corner than another bullet flew my way. The headlight exploded into thousands of pieces, showering me with plastic.

I had to think, and quick.

Just then, I heard sirens in the distance. Were they coming my way? Had the gunshot been reported? I doubted anyone but me had heard the noise over the pounding of the rain.

Footsteps echoed in the distance. Running away from me.

I chanced it and peeked my head up once more. A figure dressed all in black disappeared around the corner.

And, against all common sense, I started chasing after him.

I wasn't sure what I was doing. The only thing I was sure about was that the person who'd shot at me was the same person who'd put my fiancé in a coma. This was the closest I'd gotten to the shooter, and I didn't want him to get away.

My muscles burned as I pushed myself as fast as I could go. The man disappeared behind a car.

I paused. Waiting. Anticipating. Bracing myself.

The barrel of his gun appeared from the edge of a

concrete column. Pointed at me. I threw myself on the ground just as a bullet pierced the cement behind me.

I waited again, my breath heavy in my own ears. I heard the footsteps again. I pulled myself up, ignoring my torn jeans. Ignoring the blood from my scraped knee. I pushed myself from the ground, ignoring the tremble in my muscles. Then I stood, remaining stooped and on alert.

I rounded the corner and paused behind a massive column.

Slowly, I peered around. There was nothing. No one. Only cars and silence and a time bomb ticking away in my head—a time bomb that reminded me that this whole situation could blow up at any time.

If I walked between those rows of cars, I'd be a sitting duck, an open target . . . an idiot.

Instead, I hid behind an SUV and dialed 911. My fingers trembled against my phone. The dispatcher answered and said help was on the way.

Until then, I'd wait.

Jolly voices rang out behind me.

I turned and saw two women emerging from the staircase, shopping bags in hand. One had a phone to her ear. The other held coffee.

"Get down!" I yelled. "There's a shooter."

One of the women screamed. One dropped a bag. Both ran.

Better scared than dead.

I stayed where I was.

Suddenly, an engine revved in the distance. Tires squealed. A black sedan came flying through the parking garage.

The smell of burning rubber filled the space.

I looked up. The car headed right for me.

CHAPTER
FIFTEEN

WITHOUT THINKING, I threw myself over the hood of the SUV. I landed on the other side just as the sedan swiped the vehicle.

The dark, tinted windows of my assailant's car didn't afford me a view of the driver. I quickly memorized the license plate, the make and model.

Then the car was gone. I took a few steps after it before realizing the futility of trying to chase it.

Five minutes later, the police showed up.

One shot of espresso short from being a latte.

I gave them my statement. The shoppers who'd ducked out of the way also offered their accounts of what had happened.

The CSI team came, collected bullet casings, took pictures of skid marks, and looked for footprints or other evidence that might give a clue as to who this shooter was.

The paramedics showed up. They checked me over, even though I said I was fine, despite my scraped knee and bruised ego.

Adams eventually showed up. He said he'd been delayed by another case and had gotten here as soon as he could. He still didn't mention Juliette or the fact that someone had copied Jones' M.O. when they snatched her.

As all of this was happening, a thought began to swirl in the back of my mind.

Riley had been shot, and now Juliette was gone. There was one person who'd most want those people to be silenced. One person who had the most at stake, things like his company, his reputation, and his mission to help the less fortunate.

There was also one very busy businessman who kept finding time for me in his schedule. Who'd tried to charm—or maybe it was distract—me. One person who'd willingly told me how I could locate one of his employees. Maybe so he could buy himself some time?

Garrett Mercer.

Had he sent me to talk to Sutton so he'd have a chance to get ready? Had he gone to change into the black shooter outfit and waited for me to return to the garage? Did he fear I was getting too close to the answers?

I wasn't sure. But it was a theory worth exploring.

I waited for Adams to fess up that Juliette Barnes had been snatched. After all, we were tight, right? We'd worked together a lot in the past. He'd helped me get my job with the medical examiner.

But there was nothing but silence on his part. He took notes, asked questions about the shooter, even asked how I was doing with the whole Riley situation.

But Milton Jones was never mentioned, nor was Juliette.

From that, I concluded this was all hush-hush, at least until something was confirmed. After I gave a report to the police and was cleared to leave, I realized that I had a whole list of people I needed to talk to. But before I could do any of that, I had to get out of these wet, dirty clothes.

I pulled up to my apartment building. The first thing I noticed was the "For Sale" sign in the small patch of grass by our parking lot. I stopped and stared at it.

"You've got to be kidding me."

But I knew this was no joke. My apartment

building was up for sale. I might have to find a new place to live soon.

Which made me think of my mantra to never think things couldn't get worse. As soon as that thought entered my mind, things certainly got worse. In my experience, at least.

I dragged myself up the stairs and into my apartment. I locked all the doors before trudging to the bathroom, turning on the water, and letting my wet clothes drop onto the bathroom floor. I climbed into the shower, relishing the steamy water as I tried to wash away the reminders of all that had happened. An impossible task.

As I got out and pulled on some clean clothes, my cellphone rang. It was Parker.

"I heard you were shot at. I'm in the neighborhood. I'm coming by."

He hung up before I could argue.

Ten minutes later, he knocked at my door. I checked through the peephole just to make sure it was Parker. I had enough people after me that I didn't want to take any chances.

Sure enough, I saw the Brad Pitt lookalike standing outside my door. I quickly let him inside.

He closed the door behind him and stared at me. I saw him glance at my still wet locks of curly hair, my makeup-less face, and my bare feet. Finally, he asked, "Are you okay?"

I nodded and crossed my arms, wishing I'd had more notice so I could look more presentable. "You mean, aside from the fact that my fiancé is in a coma, I threatened to sue my future in-laws, Riley's mom had a heart attack, I was shot at and nearly run over, I discovered Riley may have been cheating on me, and my apartment building is up for sale? Other than that, I'm great. Swell. Couldn't be better."

He blinked at me, silent for a moment, before muttering, "Wow."

I nodded and walked over to the couch. I plopped down there, exhausted. "Yeah, wow is right."

He sat across from me. Instead of sitting upright and professional, he slouched. His posture reminded me that he'd been here many times before, usually not as a professional.

I counted to three, trying to pull myself—and my thoughts—together. I glared—I mean, glanced—at Parker. "Why are you here?"

He plucked some lint from his pants. "Can't I just check on a friend?"

"It sounds like you have a busy case to work on. Plus, you have a newborn at home."

He shrugged. "Yeah, it's a madhouse there."

"A madhouse how?"

"Charlie's parents are there. George keeps crying. Charlie's all hormonal." He waved his hands in the air near his head in what I was pretty sure was the internationally known sign for "crazy." "I'd rather be working. I'll take terrorist-induced stress to hormone-induced stress any day."

"Parker!" I didn't like to judge, but really? "Charlie just had a baby. She needs you. Your baby needs you."

"We need space right now. Believe me." He shook his head. "This isn't what I wanted to talk about. Things between Charlie and me are fine. I'm just going to let her do her thing. I have enough to keep me busy with work."

"So, are you officially investigating now?"

"Not officially. The FBI is on standby, donating our resources and knowledge. It won't surprise me if they get us involved. I mean, if this is Milton Jones, it's huge. They want to be certain before they sound any alarms."

"Any updates?"

He shook his head. "Everything matches right now with Jones' previous crimes. Authorities are still collecting evidence, though. Still questioning people. Still finding out information about the victim. You know the drill."

What would they find? Jones? One of his followers?

Or had Garrett Mercer read up on Jones? Had he known that Jones always left photos of his victims with the eyes Xed out? Had he planted a brilliant distraction that would point the finger away from him?

Maybe Todd Harrison was just as devious as his father. Maybe the whole "I despise my family" was just a front. Todd was smart enough to arrange a murder and make it look like someone else was guilty. He had the best to learn from.

But even the smartest killers sometimes made mistakes. Bundy was discovered when his teeth marks were found on a victim. The BTK killer tooted his own horn one too many times. David Berkowitz, the "Son of Sam" killer, was caught after he parked his car illegally and got a ticket.

Parker stepped closer. "Gabby, I didn't tell you all of this so you could go out chasing answers. You know that, right?"

I stared back defiantly. "I don't want to chase down anyone. I just want whoever shot Riley to pay."

"If Jones did somehow survive—and I'm not saying that he did—I'm worried that he might come after you again. For some reason, he's fascinated by you."

"Who wouldn't be? I'm pretty fabulous." My joke fell flat, even to my own ears.

"I'm serious, Gabby." Parker sat upright now, all signs of being laid-back and relaxed gone.

"What do you want me to do? Have plastic

surgery, radically alter my appearance, get a new name, and move to a foreign country?"

"No, I want you to do something a little simpler. I want you to be careful."

"I'm always careful. Being careful gets me nowhere—it leaves me with no answers and with a death threat anyway." My thoughts were already turning. How could I find answers without trying to track down Jones and potentially walking into any traps he set for me?

"The country's best are going to be working on this."

I barely heard him. My thoughts continued to turn. What would be the best way to either track down Jones or figure out if he was working with someone else? An idea began brewing . . .

"What are you thinking about, Gabby?"

"I'm thinking about talking to someone."

"Who?"

I remembered Parker's caution about being careful. "I'll tell you . . . if you come along for the ride."

CHAPTER
SIXTEEN

I LET PARKER DRIVE. He had a fancy sports car —a Viper. I couldn't believe Charlie hadn't convinced him to give it up. It would be really hard to get a baby seat in this sucker.

I placed a quick phone call to Clarice, just to make sure she was okay with us stopping by. She said she was. I ran through the best approaches to ask her my burning questions as the urban miles rolled past.

Parker stole a glance at me. "Did you say that you threatened to sue Riley's parents?"

I nodded, remembering and replaying the entire conversation I'd had with them in my head. Heaviness pressed down on me again. "They're talking about making some decisions about Riley that I don't agree with."

"Like pulling the plug?"

"No, not pulling the plug. We're not there. Thank goodness. But it's other stuff. Some serious decisions that could affect Riley's recovery. I told them I'd take them to court if I had to."

"And Riley's mom had a heart attack afterward?"

I nodded, my heart squeezing with guilt. I rubbed my forehead, trying to relieve some of the pressure there. "I'm sure I didn't help that situation."

"You were just fighting to keep the man you love alive. There's nothing to be ashamed of there. I'd like to think Charlie would do the same for me." He glanced over at me as streetlights illuminated the car's interior for just a moment. "Why would you think Riley is cheating on you? He doesn't seem like the type."

"Isn't every man the type?" As soon as I said the words, I clamped my mouth shut. I'd been burned one too many times in the past. I thought I'd moved forward, but maybe not. Maybe all of that old baggage would always be there. "I don't mean that. It's just the stress talking."

"That sounds like the old Gabby, the one I used to know."

"I'm trying to put the old Gabby behind me." I thought I'd done a good job. I thought I'd changed. Maybe change wasn't possible.

"The old Gabby was kind of fun too, you know." He raised his eyebrows playfully.

What exactly was he saying? I assumed I didn't want to know, and left it at that.

Besides, the basics about me were still the same. I was still spunky and sarcastic. I was still headstrong and determined and stubborn. But I'd like to think I'd matured. I'd like to think I'd learned to treat people better, to think before acting, to reflect before speaking. At least, I *was* doing better until Riley had been shot.

I wasn't going to get into all of that with Parker now. Instead, I filled him in on the note I found from Juliette to Riley. Talking with my ex about my fiancé who was in a coma wasn't ideal. But I was doing it anyway.

Parker threw a glance my way. "There could be an explanation for that note, Gabby. Don't get tunnel vision."

"Tunnel vision? Is that what you think I have? Not only about the investigation, but about Riley?"

"Detectives get it all the time. They draw a conclusion and they're so set on their solution being the correct one, that they miss other clues around them. The biases in our lives are strong. They can lead us astray. Keep that in mind. Not just with the cases you work on, but with life in general. Assumptions can be brutal."

"Those might be the wisest words I've ever heard come out of your mouth."

He shrugged. "The FBI usually doesn't take dummies."

I started to joke, but Parker beat me to the punch line.

"Usually." He grinned.

Any playfulness disappeared. "I really don't understand why this is all happening, Parker." My ex wasn't exactly the one I wanted to discuss life's problems with. Not by a long shot. But he was here, and the questions were on my mind. "Things seemed to be going so well. Now all of this . . ."

"You're a strong woman, Gabby. You're going to get through this. It might be hard at times. Really hard. But you'll be stronger at the end. You always have been."

Was that admiration in his voice? I couldn't be certain, but there was a distinct possibility. Finally, I nodded. "Thanks for the vote of confidence. Sometimes I don't care about being stronger, though. Sometimes, I think I'd be perfectly content to skip all of the bad stuff and settle for staying right where I am."

"Wouldn't we all? Unfortunately, that's not life. We can conquer it or we can let it conquer us."

"When'd you get so smart?"

He rubbed his chin. "I like to think I'm pretty brilliant all the time."

There was no doubt about that in my mind.

He pulled to a stop in front of the address I'd rattled off to him. "This it?"

I stared at the apartment building in front of me. It was nothing extraordinary, just a square, boxy complex finished in red brick. I'd actually expected something a little more refined for my prissy friend.

The address was close to one of the local universities where Clarice had been a student. She was taking some time off, but she'd already signed this lease with two roommates, so she was still living here until they could find someone else. "Sure is. Let's get this done."

We walked through the soggy evening. Puddles dotted the landscape, the air felt murky, and even the nighttime hadn't cooled the atmosphere.

I walked up the stairs to Apartment 231 and pounded on the door. A moment later, Clarice answered.

Her normal perkiness was gone. In fact, she looked downright tense. That fact made me feel bad about being here.

I'd seen her at the crime scene . . . had that just been yesterday? She'd seemed like herself. But I had a feeling Clarice was the master of covering up how she was really feeling. She'd admitted to me not long ago that she often acted like an airhead, just because that's how people had come to think of her. People put on fronts all the time just to be accepted or to convey an image.

"Clarice, you remember Parker? He's with the FBI."

She nodded and pushed a hair behind her ear. "I think. It's kind of all blurry."

"Thanks for letting us come," Parker said.

He sounded so polite. Maybe he *had* matured. Having a baby could do that. So could getting a job with the FBI.

She waved behind her. "Have a seat."

I looked around and saw boxes. "Moving?"

She nodded. "I'm moving in with Auntie Sharon. I'm just going to keep paying the rent here until they find someone else. I can't keep living here, though."

"Your roommates gone tonight?" Parker asked.

"Yeah, they all went out to a party." She drew her lips into a line. I could see the trepidation in her eyes. "I'm just not into that kind of thing right now. I'd rather stay home."

Post traumatic stress. That's what I'd bet she had. The poor girl had been through a lot. I still felt partially responsible. If Clarice hadn't been working for me, she would have never been targeted by Jones.

"You sure you're okay with crime scene cleaning, especially after everything that happened?" I asked, worry about my new friend setting in.

She nodded. "Yeah, I actually think it helps me

feel like I'm doing something to make the world a little better. Strange, huh?"

I shook my head. "Not at all."

"This might sound crazy, but I'm thinking about changing my major to criminal justice."

"I could totally see you doing that, Clarice. I think it's worth looking into." A strange satisfaction filled me. I wasn't happy about what had happened to Clarice, but I was happy that she was making some good changes in her life. The road wasn't going to be an easy one, but she'd be stronger in the end.

Kind of like what Parker had just told me. It was easier for me to believe it about other people than to let that truth saturate my own life, though.

"If you ever need any pointers about your schooling, let me know," Parker offered. "My degree was in criminal justice."

Something about his offer left something unsettled in my mind. I knew Parker, and I knew how he operated. I didn't want to see him turning to a pretty girl like Clarice just because he was suddenly feeling lonely at home. I was probably reading too much into this but, just in case, I'd keep my eye on the two of them.

Parker and I sat on the couch, while Clarice lowered herself into a wicker chair across from us. Even though the apartment wasn't all that cool, she wore a sweatshirt and had the sleeves pulled over her hands.

"Can I get you a drink?" Clarice asked.

Both Parker and I shook our heads no.

Clarice swallowed hard and nodded. "So, what's going on?"

"I have a couple of questions for you," I started. "I don't want to upset you, and I know you've already told a million-and-one people the details of what happened to you after Milton Jones abducted you."

"I keep thinking it was all a nightmare, then I remember that it was real." She nibbled on her bottom lip, a far off look in her eyes.

"Have you gotten any help for it?" Parker asked. "There are resources we can provide for you. Therapy. Counseling—"

Clarice nodded. "I'm seeing a counselor. She told me it's going to take a long time. I shouldn't put pressure on myself to heal too quickly. That fear is normal."

Parker nodded. "She's right. You should listen to her."

Whew. I'd thought for a minute that Parker was going to offer her his shoulder to cry on. Maybe Parker really was a family man now instead of a cheating, no good, arrogant player.

Clarice stared at us. "So what do you want to know about Jones? Is everything okay?"

I had to choose my words carefully. I glanced at Parker, and he gave me a nod of affirmation. He knew me well enough to know I'd use every ounce of decorum within me in this situation.

I leaned forward and softened my voice. "Clarice, we're curious as to whether or not Jones said anything during his time you were abducted about working with someone else."

"You mean, other than that awful woman? She made us call her 'The Godmother.' Can you believe it?"

Jones had an accomplice who'd helped him on his last terror spree. She was now behind bars, though. "She was awful. But was there anyone other than her that Jones mentioned during your time around him?"

Clarice sighed, her breath ruffling the stray hairs around her face. "I don't know. It's so hard to say."

Parker rested an elbow on his knee. "Think about any conversations you might have overheard. Was Jones on the phone with anyone? Did he mention anyone else by name?"

Clarice shivered. "He was just evil. How can a person do those things to another person? I still don't understand it."

"That's the age old question that's been asked throughout time. Man's capacity for evil is . . . well, it's devastating." Not only when it came to serial killers, but there were entire villages in other countries that had been massacred. There'd been wars where brutality was king. Mother Nature herself could be a cruel enchantress.

"Think carefully, Clarice. It's important," Parker urged.

"You don't think . . .?" Her eyes widened.

"We just want to make sure there's nothing we missed," I told her.

"You don't think he'll send someone else? That one of his underlings will finish his dirty work. Do you?"

I could see the alarm beginning to spread in her. I could hear it in the rise of her voice, in the pace of her words. "It's not like that."

"If you're in any danger, the police will let you know," Parker jumped in. "I'm here right now in an unofficial capacity. We just want to make sure this is truly over."

"You think Jones or someone working for him shot Riley, don't you?" Clarice looked at me, her eyes as wide as those proverbial saucers. "You think this is all related."

"Don't read too much into this. We just need to be thorough. Is there anything you can think of?" Thankfully, Parker answered her question. I didn't think I could.

With her sleeves still pulled over her hands, she covered her mouth and stared down at the floor a minute. I didn't think she would answer. I wasn't sure she even had an answer or anything to share. Her eyes were jerky, as if replaying moments in her mind. Finally, she looked up and shook her head. "I can't think of anything. I just remember that every time I heard that front door squeak open, I felt so scared that I thought I would throw up or pass out. My entire body would start trembling."

"What would he do when he came inside?" I asked, trying to keep her thoughts focused on the facts.

"Usually, he'd mumble to The Godmother. They'd talk, like what was happening was nothing unusual. Sometimes they'd laugh over little things. I heard them talking about eating ice cream one day. It was so mundane, like our lives weren't on the line. Like everything was normal. But nothing was normal."

"They talked about ice cream, huh? Anything else mundane you heard them chatting about?" I prodded.

"I don't know." She looked in the distance and sighed again. "They did talk about some money."

Parker perked up. "What about money?"

"He was able to get his hands on some somehow. It was all confusing. I wish I could have made out more of the conversation."

"What happened to that money?" I asked Parker.

He shook his head. "I have no idea."

"If you were a serial killer, what would you do with it?" I asked him.

He thought for a moment before answering. "I'd get it in all cash. Then I'd hide it somewhere so I could go back for some dough when I needed it."

"Does what I said help at all?" Clarice asked.

I nodded. "It does. I know this wasn't easy to talk about, Clarice. Thank you."

"Whatever I can do to help."

"If you think of anything else, let me know, okay?" Parker said. "Or if you ever have questions about that degree . . ."

I turned to Parker as soon as we stepped outside. "Please tell me you're not hitting on Clarice."

His eyes widened, and he stepped back. "What are you talking about?"

"I saw the way you were offering her all of that help. I know you, Parker. I know how you operate." I didn't bother to hide the accusation in my voice.

He raised his hands. "Look, Gabby. I think you're a little emotionally charged right now. You've had a lot going on. I'm with Charlie. We have a baby. I'm not looking for a fling on the side. If I was, it wouldn't be with someone who's practically illegal."

I stared at him another moment, trying to figure out if he was telling the truth. Finally, I nodded. "I'm serious, Parker. Stay away from her. She's been through enough without adding you to her list of catastrophes."

He flinched. "Ouch. Was it that bad when we dated?"

I didn't say anything, just tilted my head farther.

He rolled his eyes and started walking to his car. "I get your point. Now, let's talk about something useful."

"Fine. What do you think about what Clarice told us?"

He jangled his keys in thought. "I was hoping for more. Ice cream and a vague mention of some money don't really do much for us."

"Has anyone talked to 'The Godmother'?" I made air quotes. The woman was in jail now, awaiting her trial date.

"She's refusing to talk to anyone. No one is getting anything out of her. She's pretty loony."

I sighed and leaned back. "So what now?"

He paused in front of his car. "Now, you keep yourself safe and let the police investigate."

"How long are they going to be able to keep Juliette's disappearance quiet? Certainly, the media's going to find out. How can they not?"

"Because right now it seems like a simple investigation of a missing person. They haven't let it leak that a photo was found at the crime scene that seems to link Juliette with Jones. If that got out, people would be in a panic again. We don't want that. Besides, they're still locating Juliette's family. They have to be informed first."

"If Milton Jones is still out there, people should be in a panic."

"Gabby, you can't let this slip. The only reason I brought it to you is because you're a friend, I knew I could trust you, and I knew you had a stake in this."

I sighed.

I climbed in his car, and we took off down the road. I didn't really know what to think or say. Instead, I distracted myself by glancing down at my cellphone. I saw my missed calls. There was another one from Teddi, two from my dad, and several from Pastor Shaggy.

One day I was going to have to return all of these calls. But I knew most of them were from people who wanted to check on me, and I didn't really want to talk about things. Talking would get me nowhere. No, I wanted to figure out who had done this. I wanted Riley to be okay. I wanted my life to go back to the way it was before all of this had happened.

"We made a pretty good team in there, Gabby."

Parker's statement pulled me out of my drowning thoughts. "What?" Certainly I hadn't heard him correctly.

He grinned. "We worked well together."

"If I remember correctly, when we worked together in the past, we got along like cats and dogs. When we dated too."

"Maybe we're both growing up, Gabby. Maybe we're both growing up."

I stared at his profile a moment. What had gotten into him?

I looked away. I didn't want to know, I decided. I just didn't want to know.

THE NEXT DAY, when the morning sun was still low in the sky and before rush hour traffic hit at full force, I stopped by the hospital. The first thing I noticed when I walked in the ICU was that Riley's gangbanger neighbor was gone. The area had been cleared, and it looked like no one had ever been there.

Nurse Kellie must have seen me staring at the empty bed. She paused beside me, a clipboard in hand.

"He was sent to the Step Down Unit last night." She nodded toward the vacant area. "Looks like he's going to be fine."

The Step Down Unit. That meant Iceman—or whatever his real name was—was getting better, that he was on the road to recovery. The good news was that the man was far away from Riley now, and all of the man's little "the gang's all here" friends wouldn't have access to the ICU anymore.

But an unexpected emotion rose in me, jetting to the surface with such force that I nearly choked. I let out a cough, trying to cover my reaction. The emotion took me a moment to identify. Was it . . . anger?

That was it. I was angry. Angry that a man who was a criminal, who'd taken the lives of others, was recovering, and my fiancé wasn't. In the very least, the man had possibly done drugs, stolen, and who knew what else?

I knew life wasn't fair. I didn't wear rose-colored glasses. But Riley was a good man, even if he was living some kind of secret life that I didn't know about.

I shook my head. No, it wasn't a secret life. But Riley had a secret named Juliette Barnes.

I remembered Parker's warning about tunnel vision. I had to keep myself in check. Certainly there were possibilities I wasn't considering.

But I couldn't think of a single one at the moment.

I nodded at the nurse, realizing I'd been scowling at the empty bed. "Any updates on Riley?" I changed the subject.

She pressed her lips together, grimness coming

over her features. "No updates. He's still hanging on."

Thanks to those machines, I thought. Without them . . . his life on this earth would be over. Too bad I didn't have the same confidence in Dr. Moreno.

"Take care, Ms. St. Claire." She hurried off.

I wanted to ask God some really hard questions. How could He heal a criminal, yet leave Riley's life on the line? Where was the fairness in that? I thought God was a God of justice. It seemed like the ultimate wrong had been done, though.

I lowered myself in the chair beside Riley, staring at that handsome face that had once been so full of life. I remembered how his blue eyes could sparkle with amusement or how they could see right into my soul. His eyes had been intelligent and compassionate and had shown so much about both his thoughts and his heart.

Riley and I had come far in our relationship. In the beginning, I'd thought that Riley was just using me to earn him points on his Sunday school records. But I'd discovered he was sincere. I'd learned the story about his past, about what he'd gone through to come back to his relationship with God. I knew his faith was more than superficial.

Riley had believed in me when other people didn't. He'd loved me in my unlovable times, sticking with me until I realized that my life without God was empty.

But suddenly, life *with* God was feeling pretty empty too. I didn't want to admit it. Did good Christians dare say or think things like that? I wasn't sure. I wanted to be stronger, just like everyone thought I was. But I wasn't.

I was mad at God. And I had no idea what to do about it.

"I could really use one of our talks right now," I mumbled, squeezing Riley's hand. My voice cracked. "You're going to come out of this. Right? You just need a little more time for things to heal inside that brain of yours."

Silence answered. Instead, I heard the beeping of the heart monitor. The sound of the breathing machine filling and expelling air. The patter of nurses in the background.

But not Riley.

I stayed with him a few more minutes. I thought I'd pulled myself together. I hadn't cried in a few days. But, as I sat beside him now, the tears wanted to fall.

I was Gabby St. Claire. I was funny and sarcastic and strong.

But right now, I felt like none of those things.

I kissed Riley's forehead and started toward the

door. I had more to do today. Even though life felt like it was on hold, some parts had to go on.

I stepped into the waiting room, half expecting to see Riley's parents . . . at least his dad. But he wasn't there. I'd heard that Mrs. Thomas was doing better and had been moved into a regular room.

I still had mixed feelings on whether or not I should check on her. On one hand, it seemed like the right thing to do. On the other hand, my presence might raise her blood pressure again. The last thing I wanted was to send her into another heart attack. Enough lives had already been destroyed throughout this tragedy. I didn't want any more grief.

As I was about to get on the elevator, my cellphone rang. I recognized the number as *America Live*, a radio talk show hosted by my neighbor Bill McCormick. Why in the world were they calling me?

Familiar anxiety began to tingle the surface of my skin. I licked my lips before answering. I fully expected to hear one of Bill's assistants. Instead, I heard Bill. That's when I knew something was wrong.

"Gabby?"

"It's me. What's going on?"

"Listen, there's something I need to tell you. Something important. You in a good place right now?"

I didn't ask him if he meant physically or

emotionally or spiritually. Instead, I said, "I'm ready." I braced myself.

"I've already talked to the police about this, just to let you know. Ever since that whole Milton Jones thing went down in the area, I've been getting phone calls from people claiming to be Jones."

Jones had left me a couple of cryptic messages over the airwaves as a means of threatening Riley and me. It didn't surprise me that there were sickos out there getting a kick out of doing the same thing. Some people were just twisted. They'd do anything for their fifteen minutes of fame.

"What's all of this have to do with me?"

"We just got another phone call from someone claiming to be Jones."

"Another fake? What did the person say this time?"

"A couple of things this caller mentioned sent up red flags. That's why I'm taking this one more seriously."

"Well, what did he say?"

"He said, 'Your time is coming.'"

Against my better instincts, I shivered. "I'm still not sure why you're calling. Why does that raise a red flag? Anyone could have gotten a quote like that from their favorite horror movie."

"Then he said you should have left a note for the owner of that black Mercedes. They're not going to be happy about what happened to their headlight in the parking garage."

I went directly from the hospital to the police station where Adams worked. The officer behind the front desk—a forty-something female with dark hair pulled back into a tight bun—might have sensed my agitation, but she still moved in slow motion. Or maybe I was impatient.

Just as she was hanging up the phone and telling me that the detective wasn't in, Adams walked in the door and I forgot about the irritating woman behind the desk.

"I need to talk to you," I started, falling into step beside him.

He glanced down at me, not slowing. "Is it Riley? Is he okay?"

His question threw me off for a minute. "He's . . . I don't know. He's not okay. He's the same. It's about something else." I tried to brush off a mix of being flustered and frustrated, a combination I affectionately called "flusterated."

He nodded toward the door in the distance. "Come to my office. I only have a few minutes, though."

"Because you're so busy with this case?" I scrambled to keep up with him.

He stopped and stared at me a moment. "I wish this was my only case, Gabby, and that I could pour all of my time into it. The reality of being a detective, and you know this, is that cases continue to get piled on you. I have no social life, and I hardly get any sleep. I still don't give each case the time I wish I could."

"I know you're working hard," I conceded. I knew that being a detective wasn't an easy life. But most of the guys who did this job lived to arrest the bad guys. Adams was no different. He worked hard, he was determined, but he was also tired and stretched too thin.

He unlocked the door by punching in some numbers on the keypad there and pointed me to his desk. I'd been here before. I knew where it was.

I'd even been here enough times that I recognized some officers and raised my chin to them in a casual hello. The fact was, I should be working with these guys. I had for a whole month before I'd lost my job with the medical examiner. Not that I was bitter or anything.

I sat across from Adams. He stared at me a moment, his eyes sagging with exhaustion. He laced his fingers together and rested them across his stomach. "What's going on, Gabby?"

"Milton Jones called *America Live* and left me another message. He's still alive." I figured Adams already knew that information, but I wanted to watch his reaction.

He stared at me another moment, said nothing, then scooted closer to his desk. "We have no proof it was Jones who called the station, Gabby."

His words were calm and even. His gaze was steady and level. But—and maybe I was imagining this—I thought I saw admiration in his gaze.

"He knew about the Mercedes in the parking garage," I insisted.

"The *shooter* knew about the car. The shooter could be pretending to be Jones. He could have called the radio station, hoping to bolster your assumptions. He could have been hoping to either feed people's fears that Jones is still alive or buy himself more time to get away by planting a red herring. Most likely, this person who shot at you yesterday is playing games."

"It's a pretty serious game they're playing."

"I won't argue with that. Shooting in a public place is serious, to say the least. Most likely, this person is the same one who shot Riley. That makes him deadly."

"But it doesn't make him Jones?" I frowned. Why did I keep coming back to Jones?

"Jones is dead. You saw it. I saw it. We both know it."

"He could have survived."

"He didn't."

"There's no body," I continued.

"I understand your apprehension. And you should be apprehensive. Someone shot at you yesterday. Someone put your fiancé in the hospital. But to think these cases are related isn't necessarily correct."

"It isn't necessarily incorrect either." I shook my head. "Okay, another question. Were there any stolen cars around the Elizabeth River around the time Jones was shot?"

He stared at me. "You think he climbed out of the river, stole a car, and drove away?"

I kept my chin up. "It's an angle that's worth considering."

"If it will make you feel better, I'll check with the Chesapeake police and see what's been reported."

"How about Garrett Mercer? Did you check him out yet?"

Adams looked away for a minute. Was that a sign that he was about to tell me a half-truth? "We talked to Mercer. I did hear that he'd confronted Riley. But we have no reason to believe he'd shoot Riley."

"I'd just met with him before I was shot at in the parking garage. He knew where I'd be."

"You need to trust me to do this job, Gabby."

I kept going. "How about the license plate I got off that car in the parking garage?"

"It was stolen. We're still trying to track down more details on who might have stolen it, but, for now, we've got nothing." He studied me for a minute before finally asking, "Are you still looking for another position in forensics, even? Or are you content with crime scene cleaning?"

I shrugged, realizing how disappointed I truly was that I hadn't been offered the job. "I had an interview. They chose someone with more education." It pained me to say the words.

He raised an eyebrow. "Maybe you should think about getting your master's then."

He had a good point, but I didn't want to acknowledge it at the moment. "Right now, I'm just thinking about Riley."

One of his eyebrows arched. "You're thinking about Jones."

"Maybe I am." I must be way too easy to read. "But I'm thinking about Jones in connection to Riley."

"Maybe you're focusing on the wrong person."

"Why do people keep saying that?" I tried to bite my tongue, but I couldn't. He was used to my candor anyway. "Maybe you're the one with the wrong focus, Detective. Maybe you're so determined that

Jones is dead, that you can't see the truth before your eyes."

"Maybe you're only seeing what you want to see," he countered.

I stared at Adams, trying to figure out how to redirect my questions. "Is there anything you want to tell me about Jones?" I waited for him to admit that he may not be dead, that he may have snatched someone else.

Instead, Adams shook his head. "No. Like I just said. He's dead."

I continued to stare. I hated the fact that I couldn't let on that I knew about Juliette Barnes. I wanted to say her name so badly. But I'd be breaking my promise to Parker if I did, and then he'd never trust me again.

Finally, I nodded and started to rise. I guessed there was nothing else I could do here.

"Since you're here, there is one more thing I can tell you, Gabby."

Hope surged in me, and I sat back down. "Okay. I'll take what I can get."

"We're closing in on a suspect in Riley's assault."

"You waited this long to tell me?"

His lip twitched. "I could hardly get a word in."

I couldn't even argue with that. "Who? Who is it?"

He shook his head. "I can't tell you yet. But the

evidence is mounting. We're hoping to go to the D.A. and present our case soon. If so, we'll make an arrest and press charges."

"Not even a hint of who this person might be?"

"I can say this. Information you gave us helped lead us to this person."

"But I haven't given you any information." Had I?

He raised an eyebrow and smiled. "Oh, but you have."

Of course, for the rest of the day, I was thinking about what kind of information I might have given Adams. I kept coming up blank.

Who could it be? Garrett Mercer? Todd Harrison? Milton Jones? Someone not even on my radar?

Though I'd been avoiding my apartment, I stopped back by there to regroup. I flipped on the news, heated up some lasagna, and poured a glass of water.

As a story about an approaching hurricane filled the airwaves, I sat down and nibbled on my food, not really having an appetite, but knowing I needed to keep my energy up.

I kept thinking about what Clarice had said. She'd overheard Jones talking about ice cream and money. I wasn't sure how far the information on ice cream would get me. Most likely nowhere.

The money, though, was bugging me. If someone had left Jones money and he still had access to it, there was no limit to what he could do.

I needed to put this theory about Jones to rest, once and for all.

I'd encountered a man named Freddy Mansfield last time I'd been investigating Jones. Freddy owned an online auction that sold memorabilia commemorating killers. It was a sick business, and I thought Freddy Mansfield was a sick man for engaging in that kind of company. But maybe Freddy had some answers for me now. He had, after all, corresponded with Jones when the man had been in prison.

What if Jones had contacted Freddy about selling some of his stuff? It could mean a major profit for both of them. I'd seen it firsthand that people were willing to pay big bucks for those types of things.

There was one other fact lingering in the back of my mind. Jones always killed his victims on the sixth day. Juliette had been taken two days ago—and that was an approximate time. Her neighbor had said he hadn't seen her in a while.

That meant my time was ticking away.

I abandoned my pasta and went to sit at my computer. I did a search on Freddy's site to see what new items he had up for auction. He had some sick stuff. He had autographed pictures, hair samples, a straw supposedly used by a serial killer. Every time I thought of his business, I felt sick to my stomach. This stuff should be illegal.

Then I saw a photo. Of Jones beside his accomplice, The Godmother. That had to be taken just in the past couple of weeks. Until then, he was in jail and would have been wearing his jail uniform. Besides, based on the wrinkles around his eyes and his thinning hair, this wasn't an old photo. Even if Jones and his accomplice had known each other before he'd been arrested, this wasn't a picture from that time.

How had Freddy Mansfield gotten ahold of that? It looked like I needed to talk to him again. I also checked the rest of his site and found a wig that he claimed was Jones'. Funny because it looked an awful lot like the wig Jones was wearing when he met me at a house, pretending to be the homeowner.

Just as I stood, a story on the news caught my ear. I turned toward the TV in time to see a bleary-eyed couple standing in front of reporters. The woman spoke first.

"My daughter, Angelina Juliette Barnes, disappeared two days ago. We're begging the public to come forward with any information that will help find my daughter."

The man stepped up to the microphone. The text

at the bottom of the screen said he was Juliette's step-dad. "Any information could help," he added. "We're offering a reward for any tip that leads to finding her. Angelina is a bright, intelligent young woman. She loves people, running on the beach, and helping others. Please help us."

Ah-ha! Her disappearance was public now. That meant I could ask Adams about her.

That also explained why her name hadn't come up when I'd searched for it. Maybe she'd only recently begun to go by Juliette instead of Angelina? I didn't know. But at least I had *something*.

I picked up the phone, not willing to waste any more time.

"I JUST SAW THE NEWS," I blathered.

"Okay . . ." Adams responded.

"Riley was representing Juliette Barnes—or, Angelina, as her parents called her. It can't be a coincidence that Riley was shot and now Juliette has disappeared."

"I've seen plenty of coincidences in my day, Gabby. Sometimes coincidences are just that—random, eerie, odd, but not related."

"She was snatched from her home, Detective. That's what her parents said. Was there a picture there?" I already knew the answer. I wanted to hear what he'd say, though.

He paused. "I can't tell you that."

But I could read into it all I wanted. "I'll take that as a yes. Jones was behind this. He didn't die."

Adams sighed. "Even if there was a picture, the picture wouldn't be the smoking gun, Gabby. The fact that Jones left photos at abduction scenes was widely reported on the news."

"If not Jones, then who?" I wasn't ready to give up.

"We're close to an arrest, Gabby. Not only for Juliette, but for Riley."

"Can't you give me anything else?"

"No. You just worry about Riley."

Didn't he know that worrying about Riley was simultaneous to finding answers?

I thanked the detective and hung up. My curiosity was burning even hotter than before. Who were the police moving in on? What information did they have that I didn't?

I sighed. Then I opened my door to leave. Maybe I'd stop by Freddy Mansfield's place again. Maybe I'd visit Juliette's pastor.

However, my own pastor was standing outside my door, poised to knock. His normal, goofy smile was absent. "Gabby. I've been trying to call."

"Pastor . . . I've been busy." It was the truth; but I'd also been avoiding him.

"I noticed you missed church on Sunday."

I shrugged, trying to act like it wasn't a big deal. "I was at the hospital with Riley."

"Can we talk for a moment?"

I wasn't ready to be confronted about anything. I was the girl who'd been a skeptic, who'd loved science, who'd denied the possibility of a loving God. When I'd had a change of heart, I'd nearly been the poster child for wham-bam conversion stories. How disappointed would people be if they knew the wham-bam new Christian was wavering? "I was just on my way out, actually."

"Can I go with you? I promise not to get in your way."

Where was I going again? My mind went blank. Either way, I had to get out of this. "I don't know if that's a good idea." Hopefully he thought it was because I was visiting a grisly crime scene, not because I was avoiding him.

"I see."

He continued to stare at me until I finally nodded. Why fight this? I just had to get the conversation over with, even if it meant disappointing people who'd had such high hopes. "Why don't you come in for a minute? I can wait a second. I just don't have much time."

"I'd appreciate it, Gabby." He stepped inside. "I've been worried about you."

"About me? What's there to worry about? I'm fine." Even though my life is falling apart around me.

Even though "fine" was a relative term. I sat on my couch and pulled a pillow in front of my chest.

The pastor sat across from me. "You've been through a lot, Gabby. It's okay to admit if you're struggling."

"Why would I be struggling? Everything works together for a higher purpose, right?" The words had a bitter edge that I hadn't expected.

"Even the people I know that have the strongest of faiths often find themselves faced with moments of doubts when tragedies of this magnitude occur. It's okay to ask God the hard questions. He can handle them. Just don't turn away from Him."

I nodded, trying to keep myself together. Who was I worried about disappointing more? God or the people who admired the 180-degree turn I'd done in my life? Why did I even have to ask that question?

I was good at sweeping up clues at crime scenes. The bad guys—and even investigators—left plenty of them behind. I thought I'd done a decent job collecting all the evidence I needed to believe that a Higher Power had created this world around me. But again, I was coming back to the question that had always bugged me. If God was a loving God, why did He allow so much evil and pain?

"Riley's a good man," I started. And I still did believe that Riley was a good man, despite his secret relationship of some sort with Juliette. "Riley's life is still on the line. Meanwhile, a gangbanger who's probably taken lives and hurt uncountable people is recovering and will probably be fine. I don't get it, Pastor."

"I don't want to give you any clichés, Gabby—"

I shook my head. "No offense, Pastor. But if you don't want to, then don't."

He pressed his lips together before finishing. "But there are certain truths in those familiar sayings. God works in mysterious ways."

"Well, I wish He'd work in practical ways that were easier to understand."

"Then our faith would be easy."

"Why shouldn't faith be easy?" My voice rose in pitch.

The pastor leaned toward me. "Faith requires us to pick up crosses and abandon the easy for the difficult."

Tears tried to push forward, but I held them back. Instead, I stood and glanced at my watch. "I wish we could talk more. But I do need to run."

"I'm worried about you, Gabby. Riley wouldn't want to see you lose your faith over this. He'd want his life—even in a time like this—to help point people to the truth of God's word."

I couldn't argue with the pastor. He was right. Riley was like that. His faith had been tested. He'd waffled around for a while, but he'd come back even stronger than before.

I hated to admit it, but my questions—the silent accusations that brewed in my mind—probably *would* let Riley down. I'd told myself that my faith wasn't because of Riley. Maybe I'd been wrong.

"I'm sorry, Pastor, but I do need to go. I'm not sure what else there is to say."

"Then how about if I just hang out? You don't have to say anything."

I turned and raised my eyebrows. "Really?"

He nodded. "Where are you headed?"

I couldn't decide if I should smirk or sigh. Instead, I announced, "You might regret this."

I didn't feel like myself as I drove down the road. It was like a gigantic weight pressed down on me. Not only my shoulders, as some liked to say. The heaviness pressed on my heart and my soul as well. Somehow, voicing those doubts aloud to the pastor had only made me feel melancholy and sorrowful. Maybe the biggest person who'd been let down by my doubts was me.

I pulled up to Lafayette Community Church. My watch showed it was just after four, but I still hoped I could catch the pastor here and ask him questions about Juliette. True to his word, Pastor Shaggy—his real name was Randy, by the way—didn't talk about spiritual matters. We talked about events coming up at the church, a new restaurant in town, and how the food in the hospital cafeteria was surprisingly good.

When I stopped in the parking lot, Pastor Shaggy sent me a look. "You trying out new churches?"

I shook my head. "I just need to talk to the pastor here. It's about a case." I said it as if I was officially investigating or something.

"I see."

We climbed from my van and tried three different doors at the traditional looking church building until we finally found an entrance that was unlocked. We stepped onto some matted red carpet, glanced down the hall and spotted what appeared to be a reception area.

Maybe it was a good thing Pastor Shaggy was with me. Maybe it would gain me more credibility or maybe the pastor here would be more prone to speak up. We'd see.

A plump secretary greeted us and a few minutes later, we were ushered into a crowded office. Books were stacked everywhere—on the shelves lining two walls, on the desk, on the floor, on a table by the window.

A man in his mid-forties with thinning brown hair sat behind the desk. Everything about him seemed ordinary, except for the trendy glasses he wore. I wondered if he wore them so he could appear to be more in touch or hip than he actually was.

He had an easy smile, one that pulled even harder across his face when he spotted Pastor Shaggy.

"If it isn't Randy Macintosh." He reached his hand across the desk, and they exchanged a hearty handshake. "Fancy seeing you here. To what do I owe this honor?"

Randy pointed at me. "This is my friend, Gabby St. Claire."

He extended his hand to me. "Gabby, I'm Micah. It's a pleasure to meet you."

"She has a few questions she was hoping you could answer," Pastor Shaggy continued.

Micah sat back down. "I'll do what I can. Fire away."

I sat in a cheap metal folding chair across from him. "Thank you for your time, and, before I start, I'd like to ask your forgiveness if I come across as hasty. Not to make excuses, but I've been under quite a bit of strain lately."

"Understood."

"I have questions about Juliette Barnes."

His grin slipped, and he shook his head solemnly. "Sweet Juliette. We're all heart broken to hear about what happened. How did you know her?"

"I didn't know her very well," I responded. "A

friend of mine did, though." For some reason, I found myself scowling at Pastor Shaggy as I wondered if he knew about Juliette. I hadn't asked him—yet.

Pastor Shaggy tilted his head, looking totally confused. I was going to have a lot of repenting to do, wasn't I? The pastor had been nothing but kind to me. I wasn't sure why I was acting so hostile. I hated when my emotions got the best of me.

Pastor Micah kept his gaze on me. "What do you need to know?"

"I'm doing a little investigating. To be truthful, it's all unofficial."

"I appreciate the honesty," Micah said. He pushed his glasses higher and waited for me.

"A neighbor of Juliette's said he hadn't seen her in a while. I was wondering if you knew where she'd been?"

He nodded. "I sure do. She went on a mission trip out in Appalachia with four other members of our congregation. She left on a Monday afternoon and returned that following Sunday."

That explained her absence. Had she heard about what happened to Riley before she departed? If they were such good friends, I had trouble seeing how she could leave in the midst of such tragedy. There were so many things I didn't understand about the woman.

"When was the last time you talked to her?" I continued.

He squinted in thought. "We spoke on Tuesday evening."

"Do you always talk to people in your congregation that often?" The question slipped out before I could stop it. I didn't dare look at Pastor Shaggy. I was sure he looked horrified.

From the way Pastor Micah winced, I'd either struck a nerve, or he was appalled by my forthrightness. He shifted in his seat. "Juliette and my wife are good friends. Plus, Juliette kept in touch here at the church office about a lot of things she was involved in. She's very active here and serves on multiple committees. We touched base about an upcoming outreach we have as an alternative to Halloween."

I licked my lips. "I'm sorry for being so blunt. I just have a lot riding on all of this."

"You won't offend me," Pastor Micah assured me. "Ask your questions. I'm a big boy."

Gratitude filled me. "Had Juliette been working since she was fired from her job at GCI?"

"She was receiving some unemployment, I believe. Plus, she filled in for us some here at the church doing administrative work. She'd sold some of her things online. She was doing what she could to make it through. She trusted that God would provide for her, and He did."

"The Lord is good like that," Pastor Shaggy added.

"That's right, brother," Pastor Micah agreed.

I ignored them. "Did she ever talk to you about the lawsuit?"

Micah clasped his hands in front of him. "Some. She was very passionate about what she believed in. Asking her not to talk about God was like discovering the cure for cancer and not telling anyone about it."

"Was she dating anyone?"

"Not that I know of. We didn't talk much about that side of her life. Really, she seemed quite content with being single. It afforded her a lot of time to do the Lord's work."

While Shaggy tried hard to appeal to people outside of the Christian subculture, it appeared that Micah was content with traditional church lingo. Neither was right or wrong, but I couldn't help but notice the differences between the two men.

"The Lord's work, huh?" Is that what she called hanging out with my fiancé?

Micah leaned closer. "You have to understand. Her brother died several years ago in a car accident. It turned her life upside down. She was changed after that. She realized just how short this life could be, and she intended on living every minute to the fullest."

I nodded, letting that sink in. "Okay."

"Anything else I can help you with?"

I shook my head. "Not right now. But thank you for your time."

"How do you know Pastor Micah?" I asked as Pastor Shaggy and I walked to the car.

"As a pastor, you get to know other pastors in the area through different events. We've talked on occasion. Gotten coffee a few times. It's really important to me that the churches in our area are united. Micah shares my vision."

We climbed into my van. "I see."

I cranked my engine and started my windshield wipers. The rain was light enough to be annoying, but not heavy enough to warrant the wipers. I put the van in drive, but then put it in park again and turned to the pastor.

"Did you know Juliette?"

He shook his head. "I did not."

"Did Riley ever talk about her to you?"

"He didn't."

"So, until today you had no idea who she was?"

"That's correct." The pastor turned toward me. "Why is this Juliette bothering you so much? I almost see fear in your gaze."

"Fear?" I scoffed. "I'm not fearful of Juliette."

"Then what are you?"

I raked a hand through my hair, trying to find the right answer. "I'm curious. Untrusting. Suspecting."

"And just what are you curious, untrusting, and suspecting about?"

I moistened my lips quickly and watched the spatters of rain on the windshield. "Riley knew her. He got together with her on more than one occasion. He was representing her in this lawsuit. Yet he never mentioned the woman. My mind jumps to the worst conclusions when I think about his reasoning. I can't think of a single good one."

"Do you trust Riley?"

"I did."

"You know Riley. Do you think he would lie to you?"

"But Juliette—"

"This isn't about Juliette. It's about Riley. Do you think he would lie to you?"

I thought about it, long and hard. I knew my answer right away; I just wanted to make sure I believed it. "No, I don't think he would."

"So you trust him?"

I didn't want to answer. So I shrugged again. "I guess."

"Rest in that, Gabby. Worrying about all of those

other questions won't do you any good right now. I'm sure Riley has an explanation."

"What if I never get it?" My voice cracked. "What if he can't talk? Or walk? Or he's in a vegetative state? There are so many unknowns."

"I don't want to sound cliché, but we just have to trust God, whatever the future holds. My story doesn't compare to your present situation. I realize that. But after college, I was actually working as an engineer over at the shipyard."

"You were an engineer?"

He nodded. "A friend brought me to church and, after that, I knew I wanted to be a minister. I wanted to reach people who were like me—skeptical, uncertain, not sold out on organized religion."

"Why have I never heard this before?"

"I've done sermons on it, but it's been a while. Maybe before you were at our church. Anyway, I quit my job. I had no money. I had no idea what I was doing. It wasn't the smartest move on my part. But I got a loan, went and got a degree in biblical studies, and I started the church I'm at now."

"Bravo to you." And I meant it. I could imagine that to be a huge leap of faith.

"Sometimes God calls us to foolish things. Sometimes people will look down on us—even fellow believers. Look at Noah. God called him to build an ark in the middle of a desert."

"So you're saying that faith can sometimes look irrational?"

"I prefer to call it radical. But yes. It's like I said earlier—if faith was easy, we'd have no cross to carry."

I was going to have to chew on his words for a while. "You ever regret your choice to walk away from one career and become a pastor?"

"No, but there were times I questioned my sanity. I wondered what I'd done, especially when I didn't have insurance and I had to go in to have an appendectomy. It took me years to pay off that bill. Even now, I depend on the graciousness of God's people in order to get paid. If offerings are low and we still have a building to rent and missionaries to support, then the cut comes from my paycheck."

"You went from stable and secure to a life of passion and . . ."

"Servanthood. I wouldn't have it any other way. All of those decisions were leaps of faith. They're scary. Unnerving. But they show us what we're made of."

"I have one more stop to make. Is that okay?"

"Sure thing, Gabby," the pastor answered.

He had no idea what he was getting himself into, I mused, as I pulled up to Freddy Mansfield's house.

Last time I'd been here, Riley had been with me. We'd worked well together and made a good team—something that had taken a lot of practice and honing. For once, we hadn't been fighting against each other. No, our efforts to find Milton Jones had brought us closer together.

When I was here two weeks ago, I would have never imagined my life would have played out as it had and brought me to this point now.

Just as I'd done the first time I'd come to Freddy's residence, I gawked at the house in front of me. It could be in the running for "Most Haunted Looking House in Norfolk." It had obviously been a beautiful old Victorian at one time. Now, it was faded and dirty with overgrown grass and butchered trees and bushes.

"Where are we?" Pastor Shaggy asked. "The place looks like something that should be on *Ghost Hunters* or something."

"You've heard of *Ghost Hunters*?" I was impressed.

"Gabby," he looked at me, dumbfounded, "I'm a pastor. I'm not a monk who's locked myself away from the rest of the world."

"Of course."

I filled the pastor in. As far as I was concerned,

Freddy Mansfield was scum. I didn't care that he looked normal. I didn't care if he claimed to simply be an entrepreneur. Profiting off of death was wretched.

I parked my van and hurried onto the porch. Pastor Shaggy followed behind me, and I was kind of glad he was here with me. Going to some of these places by myself was just never a good idea, no matter how often I tried to justify it.

Just as last time, I pressed the doorbell and strains of "The Twilight Zone" could be heard echoing inside. It wouldn't surprise me if someone like Mansfield ended up planning an entire convention around the morbid. Even sadder, it wouldn't surprise me if the event sold out.

As soon as Freddy opened his door, I assaulted him with accusations. "You sold Milton Jones mementos, didn't you? And you gave him part of the money."

He tried to shut the door, but I shoved my foot into it. The man looked so normal, it was almost scary. To see him on the street, you would never guess what he'd made a career out of. Average height, clean cut with dark hair, in his mid-twenties. "I don't know what you're talking about."

"Who contacted you?" I demanded.

"Again, I don't know what you're talking about." He pushed on the door some more.

But my foot remained wedged in place. "Don't play games. There are lives on the line."

"I don't know what you want from me. I'm trying to mind my own business over here, but you keep showing up. I'd almost rather you be some religious person trying to convert me."

"Now that you mention it, I brought my pastor with me." I nodded toward Pastor Shaggy.

Pastor Shaggy waved hello and offered a sheepish smile.

Freddy scowled at me. "You need to drive out the demons from this place or something?"

"The only demons I'm worried about are yours," I announced. "I think you're helping out Milton Jones. I want to know where he is."

His face cracked as his mouth dropped toward the ground. "You're crazy. Jones is dead. It's been all over the news."

"You sold some items for him. You gave him part of the money, and now he's using that cash to fund his murderous rampage."

Freddy raised his hands in surrender. "Wow. I don't know what you're talking about."

"I checked your website. Where did you get that picture of Jones with his sidekick?"

"I have sources."

At times like this, I wished I had a gun and wasn't afraid to use it. But I didn't. I'd had one, but I lost it while struggling with Jones in a swamp. Long story. "How about his wig? How'd you get that one? Did you steal it from police custody?"

"You don't know what you're talking about." He still pressed against the door, as if he'd slam it in my face at the first opportunity.

I pointed behind me with my thumb toward the pastor. "You wouldn't lie in front of a holy man, would you?"

He cringed and part of his lip curled up in a sneer. "Why does any of this matter?"

"What if Jones didn't die? That's why it matters."

His eyes widened—not with dread, but with excitement. "You think he took someone else?"

I shrugged. "I can't say. But I can say that I have the detective on the case on my speed dial." I held up my cell.

He scowled at me again. "You're pushy. Has anyone ever told you that?"

I considered it a compliment. "I'm going to call the detective now and explain all of this to him unless you spill everything you know. On the count of three. I'd start talking if I were you. One. Two—" I put my finger over the button, ready to dial.

"Okay, okay." Freddy raised his hands in surrender. "I'll tell you what I know. Just put the phone down."

I lowered it, but my fingers remained on the buttons, out of sight.

"Someone did contact me about selling some items regarding Milton Jones."

"When was this?"

"A couple of weeks ago." He leaned on the door.

"And you said?"

"At first, I thought it was a scam. But the more this guy talked, the more intrigued I became."

"So, in other words, you thought this guy was the real deal. You thought he was Jones. How did you get the items from him?"

"He left them in my living room. While I was sleeping." Freddy's face looked a little paler as he said the words.

A shiver ran through me. I knew what it was like to have someone sneak into your home while you slumbered. I still had nightmares about it. "You didn't hear anything?"

He shook his head.

"I saw that a couple of items sold. How'd you get Jones the money?"

"He called me again. Told me to leave the cash on my porch at night. I put the envelope together, just as he told me to do. I put it on my dining room table, went upstairs to take a shower before I went to bed. When I came back down, the money was gone. But there was a note."

"What did it say?"

"It said that if I told anybody about the 'transaction' that he'd kill my mother. Then he left my mom's name and address." He shook his head, as if disgruntled. "Are you happy now? You may have just gotten her killed."

No, I wasn't happy. I was never happy when innocent people were in the line of fire. But I still didn't trust Freddy, no matter what his story was.

"Did you ever consider going to the police with all of this?" Pastor Shaggy asked. "They could have helped. They could have maybe captured a serial killer and protected your mom at the same time."

"I didn't know it was Jones. Not for sure. It could be someone imitating him. But then he got in and out of my house so effortlessly. It spooked me, and I never get spooked."

"Yet you still didn't say anything?" I thought of all the people who could have died. It was nice that he was worried about his mom and all, but really?

He shrugged, not a hint of apology in his gaze. "I've got an image to maintain. People can't think of me, the one who sells murder mementos, as some scared little man who runs for help when the wrong people look my way."

"Well, because of your pride, more people might die. I hope you realize that." This man disgusted me. Truly.

"Think of my poor mom! What am I going to tell her?" His voice held a little too much outrage to sound sincere.

"I'm sure she's proud of you, with your successful business and all." I shouldn't have said it. Sarcasm was always my go-to weapon. Usually, it was very effective.

He raised a shoulder. "She actually doesn't know."

"I would tell her to go stay with a friend tonight. And I'd do it now." I shook my head, trying for a brief moment to think about what it would be like to have a child with this kind of involvement with a serial killer. It would be heartbreaking. "Did the caller say anything else that might give a hint as to who he was?"

"No. Nothing."

"How much money did he make?"

"Around $5000." Freddy frowned.

"That can last someone a while," Pastor Shaggy said.

Freddy let out a long sigh and gave up on pressing against the door. Instead, his shoulders sagged for a moment. "Look, this was all supposed to be innocent. No one was supposed to get hurt."

"Well, people are getting hurt. I hope you can live with yourself, knowing the role you played in all of this." With that, I turned around and stomped back to my van.

Milton Jones was alive. I was convinced of it. And he'd used that money for a deadly purpose. To get help for his gunshot wound? To buy his gun? I didn't know.

But my mission was feeling more and more urgent by the minute.

THE PHONE RANG FIRST thing the next morning. My eyes were still bleary as I grabbed my cell from the nightstand. "Hello," I mumbled, not bothering to look at the number.

"Gabby, it's Adams." His voice sounded urgent.

I quickly pulled myself up in bed. I knew if *he* was calling *me* that something big was up. "What's going on?"

"We've made an arrest. I knew you'd want to know."

"Who?" I held my breath as I waited for his answer.

"Darius Walters."

"Who's Darius Walters?" I rubbed my eyes, wishing my brain would kick into gear a little more quickly.

"You might know him by T-Bone."

I blinked, trying to grasp the gravity of his announcement. "T-Bone? A member of The Guardians?"

"Darius shot Riley. Iceman—real name Julio Preston—was the driver of the getaway car. Julio apparently dropped off T-Bone and then accidentally ran the car into an old dumpster by the railroad yard. He cut his leg up pretty bad, but waited a week to report his injuries. In the meantime, he developed gangrene, which eventually put him in the ICU. Right beside Riley."

The cases had been connected! "Did Darius confess?"

"Not yet. But we have enough to press charges."

Familiar doubt niggled its way into my mind. "What about Juliette? Are these cases connected?"

"Her disappearance is what led us to Darius. We found Darius' DNA at her house. A hair he left, to be exact."

I shook my head. "DNA never comes back that fast. She just disappeared three days ago." What wasn't adding up here?

"This case was top priority. We were able to move the evidence through quickly."

"Are you sure it was Darius?"

"DNA doesn't lie, Gabby. You know that."

"But the presence of DNA can be misleading at

times, also. Do you know where researchers got their sample that forms the base for all DNA testing?"

"Gabby—"

"From 200 FBI recruits in the 90s. Even stranger? Eighty percent of those recruits were from Salt Lake City. The sample was never random enough. DNA is not a perfect science. Don't let anyone convince you otherwise."

"We're going forward with the case, Gabby. I thought you'd be happy."

I should be happy. But the fact was, I still couldn't believe this development. Why did The Guardians pick this particular time to exact their revenge? Why did they retaliate against Riley instead of me? I was the one who'd made them mad. And, furthermore, why pull Juliette into this? The last question in particular was worth asking.

"Why Juliette? It doesn't make sense. How was she involved with The Guardians?"

"She had just left Riley's law office on the day he was shot," Adams muttered, a tone of almost apology in his voice. "We think that The Guardians suspected that Juliette had seen them and didn't want to take any chances that they'd be identified."

"Juliette was in Riley's office before he was shot?" The words did something funny to my heart. Made it squeeze, tighten, lurch, and then plummet all the way into my stomach.

"That's correct."

Did Adams also suspect that something had been going on between Riley and Juliette? Because the way his voice softened with sympathy made me believe there could be evidence of something more than simply an attorney meeting his client. "Is there something you're not telling me?"

"I'm just giving you the facts."

"Did you talk to Juliette after Riley was shot?" I held my breath, waiting for his answer.

"We did."

"What did she say?"

"You know I can't tell you that."

I sighed. "Well, this is what doesn't make sense. You're claiming The Guardians snatched Juliette so they wouldn't be discovered. Why would they go to great lengths like that, only to leave DNA?"

"Criminals aren't always as brilliant as you are, Gabby."

I heard the hidden edge in his compliment. "Did Darius tell you where he stashed Juliette so you can rescue her, at least?"

"We're still trying to get that information out of him."

"But Jones—"

"I should tell you, Gabby," he cut me off. "There's one more thing."

I braced myself. "What now?"

"A body washed up in the James River last night. We think it's Jones."

I blinked, shock ricocheting through me. "Really?"

"All the preliminary markers match. Caucasian male, same age and height. Jones is really dead, Gabby."

How could I have been so wrong? "O . . . okay," I mumbled. "Thank you."

"I need to go now. I promised you an update."

I mumbled thanks and hung up. I wanted to feel satisfied. But I didn't.

And I had no idea what to do about it.

———

Locard's Exchange Principle said that whenever two people or two environments interacted, something was exchanged.

That meant that people left trace evidence of themselves wherever they went.

If I'd shared that theory with Riley, he would have told me how there were signs of our Creator everywhere as well. He was great at turning theories into deep thoughts on God.

Right now, that wasn't what I was concerned about. I was mulling over the fact that Darius' DNA —his hair—had been found in Juliette's apartment.

If he hadn't left it, then how had it gotten there? It would have been as easy as someone getting ahold of one of his strands and making sure to leave that hair at the crime scene. That was a possibility. Whether investigators wanted to acknowledge it or not, DNA could be planted. But in this case . . . was it?

Then there was the issue of Jones' body being found. Could it really be possible? Had I been blinded by my own agenda as everyone had warned me not to be?

I really needed to think this through.

I got dressed and started down the stairs when Bill McCormick stuck his head out from his apartment. "You off so soon?"

I slowed my steps as I approached the front door of the complex. "Places to go, people to see. You know the routine."

"You talk to the police about that call to the station?" He stepped outside, totally oblivious to the fact that I was in a hurry. That was nothing new.

I remembered my phone call with Adams this morning. "Sure did. They still think Jones is dead." Now more than ever. I didn't share any more details with Bill. The last thing I wanted was to screw up their entire investigation.

"What do you think?" His hands went to his pudgy hips.

I shook my head slowly. What did I think? I knew

I couldn't always trust my gut—as much as I'd like to think I could—but something still wasn't sitting right with me. I mean, what were the odds that the hair had been found and Jones' body had washed up at the same time? It sounded like too much of a coincidence for me.

"I think he's still out there," I stated. "I think he's clever."

One of his eyebrows tugged upward. "What should I do if he calls back to the station?"

"Tell him that I'm coming for him," I blurted.

"You're not serious?"

Was I serious? I wasn't certain. The words had been spontaneous. But I nodded. "Yeah, dead serious."

Twenty minutes later, I got to the hospital. I sat with Riley for a while. I asked him why Juliette was at his office that day. I asked him his opinion on the whole case. I asked him if he still loved me.

Of course, he couldn't answer. And, of course, I kept talking still.

Finally, I stood, knowing my time was up. I didn't know what I was going to do for the rest of the day. Should I let this go? Should I trust Adams as he'd asked?

Maybe I'd see if Chad needed my help on a job. Maybe I'd just try to sleep a little bit and see if things made any more sense when I woke up. I wasn't sure.

I stepped into the waiting room and saw Riley's dad. I nodded hello.

He stood. The man had lost weight since everything happened, and he almost looked frail now. "Gabby," he started.

I swallowed the lump in my throat as I approached him. "How's your wife?"

"They're releasing her today. Overall, she's doing better."

I clasped my hands together in front of me. "I'm so glad to hear she's okay. I know this has been a lot on you."

His gaze latched on to mine, and I saw pain in the depth of his eyes—pain that I'd like to avoid. Every time I spoke to Riley's parents, things seemed to spiral into even more of a disaster.

"We need to talk, Gabby."

"About what?" Uneasiness stirred inside me. I knew exactly what he was getting at, and it was an issue I didn't want to address. I didn't want to make things worse. To be honest, I wanted the whole situation to just go away.

"About Riley." That same gaze—the one that reminded me so much of Riley—refused to break with mine.

I fidgeted. I had talked my way out of a lot of things before. Talking myself out of this one would be my hardest task yet. "Can't this wait? Your wife is in the hospital, right now. No one's thinking clearly. Especially not me."

His throat looked tight and his gaze burdened as he continued. "We've talked with our lawyers. By tomorrow, it will have been two weeks since Riley's been in a coma. His doctors have agreed that we can safely transfer him. We've arranged for it to happen on Tuesday."

My blood went ice cold. "That's only a few days away."

He nodded. "I know."

"What's the rush?"

"The sooner Dr. Moreno can start his treatments on Riley, the more effective they're supposed to be."

I raised my chin. "Mr. Thomas—Ron—I don't always use the best judgment, and I'm not always great at utilizing my people skills. I don't know how to say this without being offensive." I swallowed hard. "You should know that I'm looking for Riley's Power of Attorney documents still. I'm not going to give up. I don't believe Dr. Moreno and his treatments are the best course of action for Riley."

He nodded, not defeated but downcast all the same. "Look all you want. We'll understand if you want to slow this process down. It's very difficult for us as well. But we wanted to let you know our decision. Unfortunately, being in this state of uncertainty has been a strain for us, especially for my wife. We just feel like it's time to make a choice and stop living in wait."

Tears stung my eyes again. I wanted to get out of here before the floodgates opened again. I stood, trying to hold myself together. "I should go. Please tell Evelyn I'm thinking of her."

"Gabby . . ."

I almost turned and just started going. But something about the tone of his voice made me stay.

"I have one more thing for you."

I paused, still hesitant, still ready to flee, but curious at the same time.

Ron held out an envelope. What was this? A legal notice of his own? Heat started rising in me.

Sorrow lined his eyes. "I found this while I was going through some of Riley's things. I thought you'd want to see it."

I stared at the paper, trepidation rising in me. "What is it?"

"It's the vows Riley was writing for your wedding."

TWENTY

MY THROAT SUDDENLY BURNED. I reached forward, my lungs tightening, my eyes stinging, and my emotions going haywire. When I touched the envelope, I almost felt like the paper shocked me.

I looked up at Riley's dad and nodded. "Thank you."

He nodded back, tears in his eyes.

I took the envelope and stuck it in the back pocket of my jeans. I couldn't read the vows here. I couldn't read them now. No, I needed to lock myself in my apartment with some coffee and lots of chocolate and tissues first.

Before Riley's dad could say anything else, I waved goodbye and hurried down the hallway. I didn't want him to see any more of my tears. I didn't want to hear any more of his excuses.

I wasn't ready to lose Riley. Even if he couldn't speak back to me, I liked having him close. I wanted to come to the hospital and see him every day, even if he was hooked up to machines. Furthermore, I wasn't ready to leave his life in the hands of Dr. Moreno. Was that selfish? I wasn't sure.

In the midst of my heavy thoughts, my cellphone beeped. I almost didn't check it. I didn't feel like talking to anyone. But, when I saw it was Parker's number, I decided to pick up.

I was verbally assaulted as soon as I said hello and regretted my decision to answer.

"What were you thinking?" Parker screeched.

"What are you talking about?" Really, I had no clue at the moment. What had I done now? I was trying to be responsible and not my usual headstrong self.

"Please tell me you didn't give Bill McCormick a message to give to Milton Jones."

I vaguely remembered my conversation with Bill this morning. I *had* done that, hadn't I? "I may have said something. In anger. And bitterness too, for that matter. But I didn't mean it. I don't even remember what I said."

"Let me refresh your memory. McCormick just announced on his show, for the world to hear, that you were coming for Jones. Are you going to offer yourself as some kind of human sacrifice because you can't deal with your fiancé being in a coma?"

I bristled and quickened my pace through the sterile hallway of the hospital. "I'm not offering myself as anything. If I remember correctly, Jones is dead. They're examining his body now. So why do you sound so worried?"

Parker's voice crackled with indignation. Righteous indignation? That depended on whom you asked. "What about all of those other sickos out there, Gabby? You don't think one of them won't get any ideas from all of this? You just set yourself up for a whole lot of danger, and I'm not sure there's anything I can do about it."

"I didn't ask you to do anything, much less to try and protect me. Why don't you just worry about yourself?" My words left a bitter taste in my mouth. What was wrong with me? What had happened to the girl with so much hope? The one grateful for a clean slate?

"Everyone has said you're pushing away from them." Parker's voice took on a new tone, a solemn one.

The switch in the conversation even made me more angry. I could handle his self-righteousness much better than I could handle his compassion.

"Everyone? Since when have you talked to everyone?" The last I heard, when Parker and I had broken up, he hadn't continued to stay in touch with my friends. What . . . had he been investigating my social life?

"I talked to Sierra. She said you're avoiding her."

Had I been? I couldn't remember. I just remembered being focused.

Before I could retort, a man in the distance caught my eye. Why did he look familiar? He pushed a maintenance cart and wore coveralls with the hospital's name on the front.

Had I been at the hospital so often that I was starting to recognize the maintenance workers? That was one sure sign that I'd been here too much.

The maintenance man rounded the corner. I wasn't sure what I was doing, but I followed him.

He almost looked like . . . I shook my head. No, it couldn't be.

"Are you there, Gabby?"

What had Parker said before that? Something about Sierra? "For the record—not that it's any of your business—I'm not avoiding Sierra. She's a newlywed. I'm giving her space."

"The pastor at your church said you weren't returning his calls."

"You talked to him too?" I nearly screeched. "What are you doing? Investigating *me*?"

"No, Gabby." He sighed in that ridiculing way I'd become accustomed to from him. "I ran into Sierra when I stopped by the apartment looking for you the other day. I talked to the pastor because I had to ask him a question for this investigation."

"A question about Riley." I filled in the blanks. Did Parker know that Riley may have been cheating on me? Maybe I'd told him. I couldn't keep anything straight right now. Knowing Parker, he'd discovered that on his own, and it was just one more reason he was feeling sorry for me. My ex feeling sorry for me was the last thing I wanted.

"I even heard a rumor that you've been listening to piano ballads. That's a sure sign of depression."

I ignored Parker this time. Instead, I focused on the maintenance man in front of me. He kept walking, whistling as he did. I stayed a good distance behind him, not wanting to clue him in to my presence.

I wasn't even sure why I was following the man, except for the fact that he looked vaguely familiar. I had to *know* that the man wasn't someone who should be on my radar. If I simply let him go, the question of who he was would bug me for the rest of the day . . . the rest of my life even.

"Are you still there, Gabby?"

"I'm here," I said more quietly than before.

"Look, I'm not trying to make you mad. I'm just worried. A lot of people are."

I hardly heard him. Maybe I didn't want to hear

him. Instead, I turned another corner, cutting through the maternity unit. "I can take care of myself."

"Now you're sounding like the Gabby I first met. Too headstrong for your own good."

"I really don't want to talk to you anymore."

"Where are you anyway?"

I decided to confess what I was doing. Someone needed to know . . . just in case, well, you know. Parker seemed the easiest choice at the moment. "Parker, you're going to think I'm losing my mind."

"I've thought that for a long time."

"Ha ha. So funny you are." I watched as the man walked past the nursery. I hurried past a young couple staring with googly eyes at the babies on the other side of the glass.

"What are you doing right now that might only increase that opinion, Yoda?"

I hesitated, but only for a second, before blurting the truth. "I think I see Milton Jones."

"Gabby . . ." There was a definite undertone of warning in his voice.

"What's the big deal? You said he's dead." How many times could I play that card? You'd better believe I was going to keep using it for as long as I could.

"Have you lost your mind?" he screamed. "Stop following him. Now."

"I'm keeping my distance. I don't want to

confront him. I just want to know if it's him. If it's him, I want to see where he's going."

"I'm headed to the hospital now, Gabby. Don't do anything stupid."

The man pushed through the doors and out of the maternity ward. Then he started toward the staircase. The staircase? No. It would be incredibly hard to follow him there without being seen or heard. But what other choice did I have?

"You're being quiet. That's not a good sign."

"He went in the staircase, Parker." I kept walking, kept following him.

"Don't go in the staircase."

Maybe I'd wait a few minutes. Then I'd step inside. I'd listen for footsteps. Determine if the man was headed up or down. And then I'd slowly follow.

I'd be subtle, something I was never very good at doing.

"Why do you think it's him, Gabby? Tell me what you're thinking."

"It's the way he moves."

"Same height?"

"Same height, same frame. He must be wearing a wig because he's got a ponytail. He's wearing a base-ball hat as well."

"I'm alerting security at the hospital. I want you to stand down."

I paused outside of the staircase. How long had it

been since the man went in there? It felt like hours. In reality? It had probably been a few seconds.

"Did you hear me, Gabby?"

"I don't work for you, Parker." Certainly it had been thirty seconds, at least. I had to go in now. "If I'm not talking, it's because I have to be quiet. I just wanted to let you know."

"Gabby!"

Before I could hear anything else, I turned down the volume on my phone. Parker was so loud that everyone around could hear him, and he wasn't even on speaker.

I licked my lips before opening the door to the staircase. I listened for a minute, trying to hear something other than my heart pounding in my ears. It was quiet.

My hands were shaking as I pushed open the door farther. Slowly, I slid inside. My senses were on alert, my skin felt alive with anticipation, my throat was dry.

"Gabby?" Parker's tiny voice rang out from the phone below.

I didn't respond. I didn't want to signal anyone to my presence. I listened again. The footsteps were going down.

With a moment of hesitancy, I let the door close behind me.

Silence surrounded me. Had the man left the staircase? On what floor? Had I lost him?

I slipped my flip-flops off, not willing to take the risk of them plopping against the floor. I'd take my chances barefoot.

I peered around the corner. Saw nothing. No one.

So I started down.

I moved slowly.

"Gabby! What are you doing?" Parker growled into the phone.

I ignored him.

I reached the first landing. I still saw no one. I crept down another flight of stairs and paused by the door leading to the first floor. There was one more level down, into the dungeon of the hospital, I supposed.

Had the man exited here? Or perhaps he worked down on the next floor. I weighed my options.

Then I turned to go down one more flight.

Before I realized what was happening, the door behind me flew open. I raised my hands, ready to fight.

Before I could, something zapped me.

A Taser, I realized.

My body stiffened. I lost control of my limbs until I fell on the floor. My body went rigid, yet I remained cognizant of everything going on.

"Gabby? Gabby, what just happened?" I heard Parker yelling on the phone.

I looked up. The man I'd been following sneered down at me.

It was Jones, I realized.

He *was* alive.

And I was about to die.

CHAPTER
TWENTY-ONE

I TRIED TO THINK. I tried to remember everything that had happened through the haze of being tasered.

I lay on the cool cement floor, unable to move. Unable to scream. Unable to make my muscles do as I wanted. Instead, they twitched and stuttered and flinched.

Jones only smiled. "It's your time, Gabby. I'm glad you accepted my challenge. I've always found you a worthy opponent."

He pulled out an oversized bag and began dragging me until half of my body was enclosed. He kept working, kept tugging and pulling and rearranging until I was totally in the cloth sack. Then he pulled out some duct tape and smacked it over my mouth.

"Just in case you regain use of your lip muscles."

With that, he heaved me on his shoulder, stepped out the door, and stuffed me into a linen cart.

Then slowly, without any hint of nervous anxiety, he began pushing the cart, whistling as he went.

Where were we? Which direction were we going? I had to pay attention to details. They could save my life.

Then I remembered Parker. I'd dropped my phone. But he'd known I was here at the hospital. He'd alerted security. There was no way Jones was getting out of this hospital.

"How are you today?" someone called.

"Couldn't be better," Jones responded, warmth saturating his voice.

Psycho.

That's what the man was. He had no conscience.

I wished I could move. I wished I could kick or scream or climb my way out of this. Truth was, even if I hadn't been tasered, it would be hard for me to maneuver out of this sack, out of this cart.

The material swallowed me. Wrapped around my legs. Pressed against my face. Made it hard to breath.

The cart bumped and jerked and jarred me. If it wasn't for my body weight pressing downward, I wouldn't know which way was up.

Jones began whistling again. What was that song?

My thoughts still felt muddled. My body still

rebelled from being tasered. Nothing felt right at the moment.

"Mr. Jones," I realized. By Counting Crows.

Great. He wanted to be a rock star so everyone could love him. Wasn't that what the song was about? And Jones was becoming a rock star to an entire army of sick, twisted individuals who glorified murder.

The cart hit another bump. Something squeaked. The air seemed to brighten around me, despite the dark bag.

He'd managed to get me outside, I realized.

A car squealed in the distance. Suddenly, someone jerked me from the cart. My knee hit the edge and pain jarred through me again.

I felt someone running, my body bouncing with each step. Heard him breathing heavy. Heard another voice. A male I didn't recognize. Or did I?

Then my body hit something. A door slammed. Another door slammed.

And we were moving.

I'd been put into the trunk of a car and we were leaving the hospital, I realized.

I continued to try and pay attention. We turned left—probably onto the highway, if I was envisioning this correctly. I tried to keep track of everything. I tried to remember every turn and bump and noise.

I heard traffic. I felt juts in the road. I sensed the grates of a bridge beneath us.

The more we drove, the quieter it became outside.

Inside the car I heard no radio. I heard no talking.

Panic rose in me. I would never admit this, but I should have listened to Parker. I shouldn't have been so stubborn and determined. Especially not now of all times.

I had to stick around. I had to make sure that Riley's parents didn't let Dr. Moreno subject Riley to his from-freezing-cold-to-nearly-electrocuted experiments. That was going to be hard to do, based on my present circumstances.

This wasn't good. It wasn't good at all.

So I began praying. This is where it had all started with me and God. In my desperate moments, I'd cried out to Him. I'd made promises.

And now here I was again.

Full of doubts. But certain that the outcome of this was beyond my scope.

Finally, the car came to a halt. A moment later, the trunk was opened. Two hands grabbed me and jerked me out. I hit the ground.

Someone rustled around with the bag. Finally, I was dragged out by my feet. I laid on the rocky ground, coughing up the dust that swirled in the air. A gravel driveway, I noted. Lots of trees around me.

And a familiar smell.

The smell of the swamp.

The light, however dim, hit my pupils, and I squinted up.

Jones' leering face came into view.

"Welcome home, Gabby St. Claire. Your final home, for that matter. This place is the last one you'll ever have a memory of."

Then he rammed something across my head.

Everything went black.

———

I opened my eyes. Blinked several times. Tried to see through the darkness around me.

Everything flashed back to me.

Jones.

The hospital.

The drive here.

His threat that I'd die.

Then there was Riley, the fact that his parents were indeed blinded by their own bias toward this doctor, and I might not be there to stop them.

The police thought Jones was dead. Knowing Jones, he'd left no evidence behind at the hospital. No one would find me here.

A cry escaped—the sound desperate, almost hollow.

"It's going to be okay," someone said above me.

I tensed. That voice wasn't Jones. But whose was it? It was a woman . . .

Slowly, a face came into focus.

I pulled myself up, ignoring the grit under my fingers as they touched the floor, and gaped at . . . Juliette Barnes.

I licked my lips. They felt dry and cracked. The duct tape was gone and had apparently taken off a couple layers of skin.

"I'd say don't be scared, but I think both of us know that's impossible right now."

My gaze darted through the room. It was dark. How long had I been out?

There were no windows, I realized. No closets. Just a dirty tile floor. A couple of blankets and a pillow were lumped in one corner.

"Where are we?" I whispered.

Juliette shook her head. "I have no idea. In the middle of nowhere. I haven't seen daylight in days."

I pulled my knees to my chest, my mind still groggy. "I'm Gabby."

Juliette nodded. "I know. You're engaged to Riley."

"And you're Juliette, the secret woman in his life."

Juliette's eyes widened. "Oh, Gabby. I have so much to tell you."

Before she could say anything else, footsteps pounded outside the door. I braced myself for what was to come next.

THE DOOR swung open and Jones stood there, an evil glimmer in his eyes. He stepped inside. He wore muddy boots, a flannel shirt over his undershirt, and jeans that sagged at his hips.

"You're awake." He nodded down at me, for a moment, sounding like a doctor checking on a patient. "I see the two of you have met. Cozy, huh?" He grinned.

I scowled back at him.

"Don't get too chummy," he continued. "Your days are numbered."

"You're the one who should be worried, if you ask me." I don't know where my words had come from, nor did I know how much trouble they were going to get me in. But seeing Jones had reignited the fight in me.

We'd battled before. I wasn't about to let him win here. Not without a fight.

He leaned down and smoothed my hair, which I could only assume was a frizzy mess right now. "Oh, Gabby. So brave. So strong. So admired."

I tried to jerk away from him, but his hand reached down. His fingers wrapped around my throat. My airway constricted. Slowly, he pulled me to my feet, still choking me.

I gasped for air. I tried to claw at him. Tried to pry his hands from around my neck.

He lifted me off my feet. I kicked, but he pressed me against the wall. My head hit the plaster behind me with a dull thud.

I didn't want to show my fear. But I didn't know how to hide it. Tears pooled in my eyes as my lungs screamed for oxygen.

"I will break you," he snarled.

He sneered at me, those soulless eyes of his glaring up at me with satisfaction. He lived for this, I realized. He lived to show others the power he could have in their lives.

I wanted to show defiance, but my life force was fading. I wanted to spit in his face or kick him hard or claw out his eyeballs. I could do nothing but silently beg for air.

My hands tugged at his hand as it encircled my throat. Where did he get this strength? Torturing others seemed to give him bursts of adrenaline that allowed him to do the unthinkable.

My brain kicked into gear, for just a moment. I had to try one last thing before my last breath left me.

I tried to raise my knee, to push Jones away.

Instead, my leg fell limply below me, like a ragdoll. My body had taken over. Primal instinct kicked in. I fought for air, to do whatever was necessary to stay alive and right now that meant I had to breathe.

The last thing I remembered before I passed out was the smile on Jones' face.

I woke up to cold water splashing me in the face. I sputtered, gasped, tried to pull myself back.

A bucket came into view. Jones pushed my head inside. I gulped water into my windpipe before he finally pulled me back up.

I tried to take a breath, but couldn't. Instead, I sputtered, choked, gurgled.

"Maybe you'll learn not to be so mouthy now." He shoved me into the bucket one last time before taking a step away. "Hope you enjoyed that water. That's all you'll be getting for a while."

I continued to cough the water out of my lungs as Jones left the room. I heard the lock click in place.

More water burbled out of me as my face pressed against the ground.

I braced my palms on the floor on both sides of me, trying to regain control of my body. I managed to push myself two inches up from the ground before collapsing again.

As soon as he was gone, Juliette scooted over to me. "We can't talk back. He gets mad. Just act compliant."

"Easier said than done," I croaked, still breathing deeply, trying to get a good dose of air into my lungs.

"He'll force it from you. You might as well just do it."

I glanced up at her, still gulping in deep breaths. "That doesn't sound like the fighter everyone described you as."

She shrugged. "This is the first time I've ever had to fight for my life."

That's when I noticed the bruises on her face. Her busted lip. The way she cradled her arm.

"How'd he get you?" I finally pushed myself upright and wiped my face with the edge of my T-shirt.

She cringed and pulled her knees up closer to her chest. "He snuck into my apartment while I was sleeping. I think he got the key from the superintendent somehow. I didn't even hear a thing."

"He never leaves any evidence as to how he got in."

"He tasered me, knocked me out, and I woke up here." She shivered. "How'd he get you?"

"Similar, only I was in the hospital. Not as a patient. Visiting Riley." I crawled back to the wall and leaned against it, my throat still burning. Drops of water still gurgled in my throat with every breath.

I paused, listening. I heard a car start and then tires against gravel. "He's leaving."

"He'll be back."

"Who's he working with?"

She shook her head. "I didn't know he was working with anyone."

"You haven't seen anyone else here?"

She shook her head again.

"But someone else was driving the car when I was abducted."

"I haven't seen anyone."

I stood, my legs feeling weak. "Have you checked this room? Is there a way out?"

"No windows and only one door. You tell me."

I shook the door.

"It's tight. I tried that already. Besides, it doesn't matter. Jones said that even if I were to escape, the swamp would kill me."

"I think I'd take my chances." I rattled the door

again. It was definitely locked. I might be able to pick it, if I had some sort of tool to use.

I turned and surveyed the room. It was probably eight feet by eight feet. But no windows? No closets? Where were we?

I remembered the other cabin, the one where Riley and I had found Jones a couple of weeks ago. I remembered that the women had been kept in the attic. There'd been no AC, and outside had been extremely hot.

I didn't think this was an attic. The roof wasn't angled enough. The floor felt solid, like concrete was beneath it. I felt certain we were on the first floor.

My gaze rested on the bucket. I bent down and worked the handle. If I could get it off, I might be able to use the thin metal to unlock the door. In the least, I could use it as a weapon.

"There's a storm coming, you know," I told Juliette. "The swamp isn't exactly where I want to be when a hurricane comes through. Too many trees. Too much water."

"When's the storm supposed to hit?"

I shrugged, still wrestling with the metal. "I should have paid more attention to the news. I had other things on my mind. I think it's on Monday, though."

"That's only two days."

"Yeah, I know." One side of the handle broke free.

I worked carefully, not wanting to spill any water. I didn't know how clean the liquid was or where it had come from. But I also didn't know when Jones would be back. If worst came to worst, we might have to drink from this bucket. Our lives could depend on it.

Finally, the other side of the handle broke free. I didn't want to waste any time. Using the edge of the bucket, I bent back the loops at the end of the handle. At last, one end was straight enough that it might work in the lock. I hurried toward the metal and inserted the makeshift key.

I turned it, trying to find that magic spot that would make the lock click and the door open. Juliette crawled beside me and watched.

I twisted the metal, lifted it up and then down, moved it from side to side. Nothing.

"Do you want me to try?" Juliette asked.

I nodded. "Have at it."

I sat back, wishing I'd taken locksmith classes somewhere along the way.

Juliette tried but gave up after several minutes. "That's harder than they make it look on TV."

I nodded. "Those aren't ordinary bedroom door locks either. I used to be able to pick the locks in my brother's bedroom using the metal twist tool off the processed meat can."

Juliette smiled. "I remember those. I used to save

them, pretend like they were keys." Her smile quickly slipped. "What now?"

I nibbled on my bottom lip and tasted blood there. "I'm not sure. I'll try the lock again in a minute. Otherwise, we think of a plan."

"I'm going to keep praying," Juliette announced.

I nodded. "Do that. I will too. We're going to need all the help we can get right now."

Juliette stared at me from the adjacent wall. She looked haggard. Her hair was stringy, her face was dirty, her clothes soiled.

"How is he?" she whispered. "I haven't heard any updates since I was abducted."

"Riley?" I questioned.

She nodded. "Yeah, Riley."

"It's a mess." I didn't know how much to say. I mean, I still wasn't sure who Juliette had been to Riley. There was a part of me that wasn't sure I wanted to know. "He's still in a medically induced coma."

"I can't believe this happened to him."

"Me neither. I need to be there to speak for him, to watch out for him." I let my hands fall to the side, signifying the futility of the mess around me, of being locked in a shack in the swamp with a serial killer as my only lifeline. "And then this. What a mess."

"I've been praying. It's all I've been doing."

I raised an eyebrow. "Trying to convert Jones?"

She gave me a questioning look.

"Your reputation precedes you."

"I told him I was praying for his soul. He slapped me and told me he didn't have a soul."

I shuddered. "I believe him."

Juliette watched me for long enough that I fidgeted. "You're just like I thought you'd be."

"What do you mean?"

"You're spunky and pretty and smart. Just like Riley said."

This time, at the mention of Riley, I scowled. She was talking about him like they were such good friends. I knew I should dive in and ask her all of the hard questions. But I'd already suffered a lot of tragedies recently. Did I really want to add a new one to my list?

"Why didn't Riley ever mention you?" I asked.

She frowned. "I don't know for sure why Riley never brought me up. I can only guess."

"Yeah, me too."

"It wasn't like that, Gabby."

My throat burned. This time, it wasn't because Jones had tried to crush my windpipe. No, this time it was because my emotions felt more powerful than my willpower. "What was it like then?"

Her gaze lingered on her hands, which rested on her knees in front of her. "We go way back. He was friends with my brother."

"Who was your brother?"

"His name was Scoggins."

Understanding washed over me with enough force that I sucked in a deep breath. Scoggins had been killed in a drunk driving accident. Riley had been in the car with him—not driving, but Riley had still felt responsible, like he should have stopped his friend from getting behind the wheel.

"I was Scoggins' little sister. He was my hero. Riley too. I had a rough time after my brother died."

"I'm sorry." Some of the details started falling in place.

She shook her head. "I actually tried to commit suicide a couple of times in the aftermath of my brother's death." She didn't say it with shame, nor did she say it with pride. She spoke matter-of-factly.

I blinked. I never imagined those words coming out of her mouth. In my mind, she'd been the perfect Christian. More and more, I was starting to realize that there wasn't such a thing as a perfect Christian, no matter how much I kept assuming there was.

"It's true. My parents were drunks—very classy drunks, but drunks all the same. They were never around. As soon as I left for college, they divorced. My mom got remarried and started a new family. My dad moved to Dubai, of all places. He's been climbing the corporate ladder since then. I felt like they both moved on without me. Scoggins was all I had."

"I'm sorry," I repeated.

"My life spiraled out of control. I was taking prescription drugs like they were candy, doing anything to numb the pain. Riley and I lost touch. He was dealing with his grief in his own way too, I guess. I think every time he saw me, he remembered his failures. In his mind, at least."

"What changed? How long have you guys been in touch?"

"He sent me a letter a year or so after the accident. He said he was trying to turn his life around. He apologized again for the accident and for my loss. I thought that would be the end of it."

"But . . ."

"Then almost a year ago, I got a job out here. When I almost died from one of those drug overdoses, I had a huge wake up call. I turned my life around, so much that I started calling myself Juliette instead of Angie."

"Kind of like from Saul to Paul?"

She nodded. "Yeah, exactly like that. I had a new start and a new outlook. After I moved here, I found

Riley's email address and let him know I was in town. We met for coffee. He told me that being around you had made him think of me."

I frowned, unsure of the meaning of those words.

She shook her head. "No, not like that. It's just that I had a bad family life. I was struggling. He said he'd seen you struggling with your mom's death and your dad's bad decisions. It made him realize that he should have tried harder to be there for me. He didn't know about my suicide attempts."

"But you told him?"

"I'd never told any of my friends. It was my dirty little secret, you know? Everyone thought I had it together. Finally, things really were getting better. I had my new job. I started going to church, and I really started turning around, you know?" She frowned. "Then I got fired from GCI. I decided to fight for what I believed in."

"What did Riley say about that?"

"He said he wasn't sure I had a case. He agreed to take it on, I think, just because it was me. Maybe he'd started feeling guilty, like he owed me something."

Maybe that's where Riley had thought of me. Wasn't that my life story? Feeling guilty and trying to make up for not only my own mistakes, but the mistakes of others?

"I still don't understand why Riley didn't tell me about you. It doesn't make sense to me. I thought we shared everything." I hated how hurt had crept into my voice.

"Scoggins' death was a very painful part of Riley's life. I reminded him of that. You've got to believe me, Gabby. Riley is like my big brother. That's all we were. Friends."

I shook my head. "If you were just friends, he would have told me about you."

"I can't speak for him or his actions, but no lines were ever crossed. I promise you, Gabby."

TWENTY-THREE

SOMEHOW, I'd fallen asleep. I don't know when it happened or how it happened. But I woke up with a cold sweat across my brow.

The room came into focus. It was even darker than it had been earlier.

Juliette slept with her head against the wall in a corner. She'd pulled a blanket over her legs.

It was eerily still in the house, and I wondered if Jones had returned.

I didn't remember hearing anything, and I felt like I would have woken up to the rumble of car tires on the gravel or to the slamming front door or to the man's boots plodding across the floor.

If he wasn't here, then where would he have gone? What was he up to? Was he searching for his next victim? Maybe he was busy planting clues that would lead the police astray.

If only I hadn't dropped my phone. If only there was some way I could contact the outside world. But there wasn't. No matter how hard I tried to make that happen, it wouldn't, so I needed to look at other possibilities.

But I couldn't think of a single other thing I could do to get out of here.

I hated feeling helpless, and that's exactly what I felt now.

The skin was tender around my throat. I had a knot on the back of my head from one of the times I'd fallen to the ground. My elbow ached. Without food, my energy would start depleting.

I mentally exhausted all of the possibilities of escape.

So my thoughts turned to Juliette. She seemed like a sweet girl, really. I almost hated to admit it.

What I didn't understand still was why Riley hadn't told me. The one person who could clear up that mystery was in a coma and unable to communicate.

I had to think this through. It had only been a month ago that Riley had finally told me the whole story about what had happened with Scoggins. That part of his life was so gut wrenching for him that he didn't share it often.

It wasn't that he'd wanted to maintain that image of being perfect. It was just that he didn't like talking about that portion of his past, not even with me. I figured with time, that might change and he might be more open. His wounds were obviously still healing.

Maybe there were things about Riley that I just didn't understand. As much as I felt like we were soul mates, he still hadn't trusted me enough to tell me everything about his life. That thought broke my heart.

Everyone had secrets, though . . . right? Maybe I even had secrets. Were there things I hadn't told Riley?

I bristled. I heard something. A sound.

For the last couple of hours, I'd heard the wind hitting the shabby sides of the house. I'd heard a spattering of rain. But this sound was different.

It was a car coming up the driveway.

Was it Jones . . . or was it help?

I crawled across the floor and shook Juliette. Her eyes slowly pulled open. "Riley?"

"Riley?" I nearly barked. "What? I'm not . . ." I cut myself off. Had Juliette been dreaming about my fiancé? I wasn't even going to go there right now. "No, it's Gabby. Someone's coming."

"It's probably just Jones. Who knows what he'll do now."

I could sense a change in her. Maybe it was the

lack of food. Maybe Jones was wearing her down. But she almost sounded defeated.

We'd never win this war if we thought we were going to lose. At least, that sounded like a spiffy little saying that I'd heard somewhere before.

"We've got to do this together, okay?"

"I'm ready to be with Jesus," she mumbled. Her head flopped to the side and hung there as she stared vacantly at the floor.

"Juliette, you've got to be strong. We need to fight this."

"I'm not afraid of dying, Gabby." Her eyes looked glazed. "I've had a lot of time to think about this."

I turned her head toward me. "Listen to me, Juliette. You almost killed yourself twice. I'm not going to let you hand your life over to Jones just so you don't have to face reality anymore. Understand? You talk about Jesus. Jesus is your hope. He has a plan for your life. You've got to take this Garrett Mercer to court."

She shook her head. "If I get out of here, I'm dropping the lawsuit."

"Juliette, what is wrong with you?" Her eyes didn't even look right.

She shrugged. "I'm just tired."

I glanced around. She had a blanket at her feet, so she'd obviously stayed awake longer than me. What else had she done?

I eyed that bucket of water. It was the only other thing in the room. "Did you drink out of that?"

She nodded. "Just a few sips. I was so thirsty, Gabby. So thirsty."

Jones had put something in that water. I'd swallowed some when he'd dunked my face into it. But I'd bet she'd swallowed a whole lot more.

I patted Juliette's knee. Only in my life would I have to save a woman who'd been secretly hanging out with my fiancé. "It's going to be okay."

I heard the front door open. I heard the familiar sound of boots pounding across the floor. With each step, my anxiety grew to nauseating levels.

Just then, the lock to our room jangled. A moment later, Jones stood there, that same glimmer in his gaze. I quickly grabbed the handle I'd pried off the bucket and slid it behind me.

I knew Jones' M.O. He only kept his victims alive for six days. Juliette had been snatched . . . four days ago, maybe? Her time was limited. Mine was quickly slipping away as well.

"Still awake, are we?" He sneered. "I thought you'd both be sound asleep."

I glared at him a moment. Billy Bob Thornton. That's who he reminded me of. "What do you want, Jones?" A quiver in my voice betrayed me.

"I'm just checking on my girls. Making sure you're ready for our big day that's coming up. You know me well enough to know what I'm talking about, don't you?"

"I know you a lot better than I ever wanted to."

He smiled sardonically. "Sweetest words you've ever said to me, Gabby."

"Why don't we stop playing this game? You know the police are going to find you."

"The police think I'm dead."

"You probably put that body in the water your-self, didn't you? You knew the police would be looking for confirmation that you died. Who'd you kill in order to throw the police off your trail?"

"Just a bystander. No big deal. No one will miss him."

"That's not your M.O., Jones. You're supposed to only kill women."

He grinned again. "Investigators have only begun to touch on the scope of what I've done. Do you know how many unsolved murders there are of people that I had to kill off? No, they weren't my joy killings. Like you will be. But they were people that got in the way. A few I had to practice on."

"You're sick."

"Why, thank you."

"It wasn't a compliment." I glared up at him. "How'd you survive the fall off the bridge anyway? That along with the gunshot wound? You shouldn't be here."

"It's like I told you before. People underestimate me. People underestimate what sheer willpower can do. I did swim for my college. I'm not sure if you knew that. I was an endurance swimmer. And I could hold my breath for more than five minutes. Besides, I had a bulletproof vest under my shirt. The bullet just grazed my shoulder. Really, the wound looked much worse than it actually was. Even with that little boo boo, I was able to swim over to the bank of the river before they ever got the police boats in the water. I stole a car and found this old cabin."

"Then you started planning on how you could shoot Riley. You didn't do it yourself. You got one of your followers to do it."

"My followers?" He chuckled. "Now, I don't know if I'd call them followers. In fact, this time I hired someone to do my dirty work."

"You hired The Guardians." Things began clicking in my mind.

"Perfect choice, huh?"

"You got money from Freddy."

"It was more fun to do it that way, more fun than stealing."

"Then you convinced 'The Godmother' to give you all of her money before the police arrested her. You could afford to hire someone to be your hit man, especially since you couldn't do it yourself, not with your injury. That's where The Guardians came in.

You're a smart guy. You knew they already had a vendetta against me."

"Very good. I've always said you were a worthy adversary. I did have a hefty sum of money that was gifted to me. I buried it, of course. It was the only way to keep it safe."

"Again, you used more people. Sounds just like something you'd do. You go around thinking everyone else is evil, when the truth is that you're the one who's messed up."

He scowled and rotated his shoulder, as if remembering the bullet he took there. "I've seen you, you know. I've heard you arguing with police. You insisted I wasn't dead. You believed in me, Gabby."

"Unlike your sister." I needed to turn this conversation around and play mind games with Jones now. When no physical weapons were available, you used what you had.

His grin slipped. "She was a conniving little . . ." He shook his head, not finishing his sentence. I could fill in the blanks.

"Keep me alive, and I'll make sure people keep believing in you."

"Shut up," he sputtered. His nostrils flared.

I'd pushed him past his limit. Now he was starting to lose it. I gripped the bucket handle, knowing it was my only chance of winning this fight.

Jones had a good fifty pounds on me, mostly lean muscles.

He leaned down to grab me. That's when I lunged at him. I went straight for his eyes. The metal jabbed at him in the eye socket.

He howled in pain and grasped his face. Then, in one motion, he threw me back. My head cracked against the wall, and I sank to the floor.

When I looked back up at him, I knew I was in trouble.

I braced myself for a fight.

CHAPTER
TWENTY-FOUR

"YOU'RE REALLY BANGED UP. You shouldn't have done that. I told you. Be compliant." Juliette whispered, peering at me. She started to touch my injured cheek, but I swatted her hand away.

"Compliant is not in my vocabulary. I'm a fighter." I could barely say the words. My entire mouth was swollen from where Jones had punched me repeatedly. I could taste blood. My ribs ached from his kicks.

When he'd finished beating me up, he'd done his little "choke me until I pass out and then stick my head in a bucket of water" trick.

Then he'd left.

Meanwhile, the drugs Juliette had apparently taken had worn off. She leaned over me now, trying to make me feel better.

"Fighting doesn't always help you to survive, you know."

"Fighting is the only way to survive right now. I've seen pictures of what Jones does to his victims."

Juliette grimaced. "We just have to pray for the best. That's all I can do."

I turned, causing pain to rip through my ribcage.

"He really got you good."

I shrugged. "I'd like to think I got him good too." I remembered how he'd howled in pain. I didn't feel satisfied, but if I died, at least I'd know I went down fighting.

Silence fell between us a moment. "I've been thinking about why Riley may not have told you about his relationship with me," Juliette started.

"Okay . . ." Did I want to hear this? I wasn't sure.

"As much as Riley tried, I think he always felt responsible for Scoggins' death. He felt guilty that Scoggins died and that he didn't."

"I thought he let go of that guilt when he turned back to Jesus."

"I think you and I both know it isn't that easy."

I shifted, an ache in my heart. "I thought it was just me."

She shook her head. "Those emotions can be powerful. It's kind of like a person with a drinking problem who's trying to recover from addiction. You take it one day at a time. You do your best. But there are days when that beast of addiction or guilt or whatever your demon is will rear its ugly head and you have to make a decision. You have to fight it or let it win."

"Those are pretty wise words from someone who thinks I should be compliant now."

"You're right." She let out a weak laugh. "I'm a work in progress. What can I say?"

"You know what I think is weird? I think it's weird that tragedies can pull some people closer to Jesus and push other people far away." Tragedies seemed to do both for me. Maybe I was an enigma.

"We all have natural inclinations that we fall back on. That's why faith can't be just an inclination. It has to be a choice. I chose all the time to embrace everything that God had for me in life. I continue to choose it every day, even when I don't feel like it."

Funny, I mused silently. Adams and Parker had both mentioned bias and tunnel vision while investigating. People could have those same hang-ups when it came to their faith. My natural tilt was toward independence and doing things my way. When the going got tough, I tended to want to cling to what I'd known for my entire life. My upbringing and life experiences, in many ways, were ingrained into me.

Juliette was right, though. Faith was about choosing to follow Christ. About picking up our cross. It wasn't always easy, and it didn't always feel natural. But that's what made it so rewarding.

I rested my head against the wall, listening to the rain spatter on the roof and letting those thoughts sink in. "So, you were really going to sue Garrett Mercer?"

"Riley didn't think I should."

"But you thought it was a good idea?"

She shook her head. "Not really. I mean, at first I did. I was angry. I couldn't believe that Garrett couldn't see the importance of what I was doing."

"You defied his rules."

She sighed. "It's like this. You're in a burning building. You've got to get out. You know the exit. Wouldn't you feel this urgent need to tell everyone else where it was before the fire consumed them?"

"So life on earth is the burning building?"

"We don't know how long we have on this earth. We could have years left or we could have mere hours."

"Don't I know that?" I looked at the room that could potentially become my grave.

"Exactly. No one thinks their life is going to end unexpectedly. I'm going to hold myself personally responsible for the people I could have told about eternal life but didn't."

"You're really on fire, aren't you?"

"What's it mean to be a Christian if you're not

consumed by God's love, if you're not living a life of transformation?"

Her words stuck with me, and I chewed on their meaning. I remembered Pastor Shaggy talking about appearing foolish, about not being afraid to be radical.

Somehow, in the midst of those thoughts, I drifted to sleep.

———

I couldn't be certain, but it seemed like a good twenty-four to thirty-six hours had passed. Time seemed to be at a standstill inside this little room with no windows. The minutes crawled by. With each second that passed, I thought about Riley, about how he was doing, about whether or not his parents were still making plans to have him transferred up to that hospital in D.C.

Outside, the rain continued to beat harder against the house. The hurricane was coming, I realized. We were in this shack, in the middle of a lowland area that was already saturated with water. Trees here didn't have deep root systems, and we were surrounded by massive, giant-sized oaks that could take down this shack.

If we were still here when the hurricane hit, there

was a good chance the storm might finish us off before Jones could.

Jones had returned twice since I'd jammed the metal wire into his eye. He wore a homemade gauze and medical tape patch over his wound now, which made me feel a niggle of satisfaction. The emotion was short lived. The first time he'd come back, he'd taken Juliette out of the room. They'd been gone a while. When Juliette returned, half of her face was swollen, her shirt was ripped and bloody, and she was crying.

Jones had left me alone—this time, he'd warned. He'd be back for more.

I'd tried to comfort Juliette, but eventually she'd fallen asleep crying.

Now, I couldn't sleep. I could feel my soul wearing thin—right along with my physical strength. I'd wracked my brain, trying to figure out how to get out of here. I had no answers. I had no suggestions. With my energy depleting, I didn't know how I could fight Jones anymore.

I had nothing.

I reached into my pocket, hoping to find something. I felt . . . Riley's vows. With everything that had happened, I'd nearly forgotten they were there.

Juliette was still sleeping, and I hadn't heard anything from Jones in a while. Though the light in the room was dim, I pulled out the envelope. Slowly, quietly, I pulled open the seal.

I momentarily closed my eyes, praying for comfort and self-control, before unfolding the paper. I lowered the sheet to the floor, letting the light from beneath the door flood onto it. Slowly, the words came into focus.

From the way lines were scribbled, I could tell Riley wasn't finished with them yet. Things were scratched out, there were arrows, and sentences squeezed on top of other sentences. It took a moment for me to know where to start.

If I were to quote Westside Story, I'd say we have "One Hand, One Heart."

If Carousel were to inspire me, I'd burst into, "If I Loved You."

If I were to get sappy, I might say this was "Some Enchanted Evening."

The first tears pricked my eyes. Riley had been trying to touch on my love of musicals. Only someone who truly loved me and understood me would begin a task like that.

He continued:

• • •

I promise to give you my all —
 A shoulder to cry on,
 A hand to hold,
 An ear to listen,
 A heart to love.
 Oh, and I promise to make you coffee every morning.

I chuckled. I'd been badgering Riley for a couple of weeks before his assault about adding that "coffee clause" to our vows. He'd been listening. Sweet Riley. My sweet, sweet Riley.

You're my partner,
 My friend,
 The love of my life,
 The one God has intended for me.
 And I can't wait to spend forever with you.

He had loved me. Despite all of my doubts and fears and misgivings, Riley's heart had always been with me. For me. And I knew that my heart would always be his.

I wiped away the tears on my cheeks and rested my head against the wall.

I'd been wrong. I'd been distrusting about everything that mattered, acting as my own worst enemy at times. But now, when everything else was stripped out of the way and my life was on the line, I realized that Riley still loved me. Even more importantly, God still loved me.

My heart lurched when I realized that I'd put more faith in the belief that Jones was still alive than I had put in both Riley or God's faithfulness to me.

Please, forgive me, I prayed silently. *I didn't fully realize what I was doing or how I was acting. I want to make things right.*

As I closed my eyes, trying to get some sleep, my heart felt more at rest than it had in nearly two weeks.

But, any time now, Riley's parents were going to move him. Some quack doctor would play with his life. I had to make things right between his parents and me.

And I had to do it in a way that ensured only the best for Riley's future.

TWENTY-FIVE

WHEN I AWOKE, Juliette was staring at me. She had a dazed look about her. She was fading quickly, I realized.

Hopelessness tried to bob to the surface of my mind, but I refused to let it. My resistance to the emotion was becoming weaker, though. As if to remind me, my stomach grumbled. When had I eaten last? I couldn't even remember. Eating hadn't seemed all that important with Riley in the hospital. But now, without the means for food, I wanted it more than ever.

"I wish he'd just kill me," Juliette whispered.

"Don't talk like that." I tried to hush her.

"We're going to die here."

"Maybe we could both take him," I mumbled.

"I'm feeling so weak . . . he'd just throw me off of

him like a wet blanket. Then he'd make me pay for trying."

"There's got to be something." My gaze scanned the room as it had so many times since I'd been here. It stopped at the wall across from me. "Juliette, why does the paint on that wall look fresh?"

Juliette blinked at me. "What are you talking about?"

I nodded toward the wall across from the door. "The rest of the walls in this room look grungy. That one is beige, and the paint is fresh. Why?" And why hadn't I noticed that fact before? Sure, the room was dim, but there was definitely something different about that wall.

"I have no idea."

I pulled myself to my feet. My entire body protested. I winced with pain as I put weight onto my ankle. I glanced around, knowing there was nothing with a sharp edge in the room. But I needed something other than my fingers.

"I need something hard, something solid, with an edge."

"We've got nothing in here," Juliette said.

There had to be something! Just then, my engagement ring caught my eye. No . . . but yes. What other choice did I have? I slowly pulled it off my finger. "This will do."

"Gabby . . ."

"Don't worry. I won't be attacking Jones with it."
I had no energy left to fight him right now.

I leaned against the wall and began scraping the ring into the plaster.

"What in the world are you doing?"

She thought I'd lost my mind. Maybe I had. "Following a hunch."

Finally, the ring caught in a groove, an area where the drywall was softer than the rest of the wall. I began digging out as much of the plaster as I could.

"I really don't know what you're doing."

"We've got to work quickly. Please. Help me pull away some of the wall after I run my ring through it."

She looked at me like I was crazy again, but she did as I asked. I moved to the other side of the wall and searched until I found another groove where the drywall was softer. We worked and worked until I had a square dug out in the center of the wall.

"Now do you want to tell me what you're doing?"

I slipped the ring back on and dug my fingers into the wall. "There was a window here."

"What?"

I nodded. "Houses like this one don't have interior rooms without windows. He put drywall over the window and then plastered over it so we wouldn't know."

"Really?"

"Yeah, and he could have only found this place right before he snatched you. It's been wet outside. I doubt this drywall and plaster had time to dry sufficiently. That's the only reason I was able to dig into it like this."

"Are you for real?"

"I hope. Because, if I'm right, this is our chance to get out of here. Help me."

We both burrowed our fingers into the wall and pulled and tugged. Nothing happened. But I could see the drywall tape. I knew my theory was worth following.

"This is useless," Juliette muttered. "What if he walks in and finds us like this?" Panic began to stretch through her voice.

"That's why we have no time to lose. Let's keep going."

We dug our fingers into the ditches we'd formed. On the count of three, we tugged at the wall again. Finally, the section of drywall popped out. We nearly toppled with it but we caught ourselves in time. We lowered it to the floor.

A window stared at us.

Juliette and I both looked at each other with wide eyes. Triumphant grins spread across our faces. We were finally one step ahead of Jones.

"We did it," Juliette squeaked.

I hadn't really thought about what to do after the piece of drywall came out. But I knew I didn't have time to ponder it for too long. We had to move—now.

Using the heels of my hands, I pushed the screen out. Rain from the hurricane spattered inside. Beyond the walls of this prison, it was dark and the wind howled and the torrent of water from the sky looked merciless.

"We need to go. We don't have much time." Riley didn't have much time. I had to stop his parents before they moved him.

Despite my protesting body, I climbed out. The rain hit me harder as I landed with a splash onto the soggy ground below. I raised my face to the storm for a moment, drinking in the fat drops of water. Juliette tumbled outside a moment later. She could barely pull herself to her feet. The woman was fading, and fast.

I nodded toward the woods surrounding us. "We're going to have to run through the swamp."

Juliette blanched, wisps of her hair clinging to her cheeks and forehead. "The swamp?"

"The road is too dangerous. He might see us." Just as I said the words, a cypress tree in the distance cracked. It hit the ground with a loud crash, making our surroundings tremble. The vibration went from my feet all the way up to my heart. I wouldn't let it seize me, though.

"But, it's not safe—" Juliette started.

I grabbed her hand. "It's safer than Jones. Come on. Let's go."

We could parallel the road, I reasoned. Just stay out of sight. Maybe that would lead us to help eventually. I prayed it would.

The rain and wind picked up. It was just a matter of time before Jones realized we were gone. The noise of the storm had covered up our escape so far. But we had no time to waste.

I took my first step into the swamp. I sank into water and mud up to my ankles. I pushed away thoughts of leeches and bears and snakes and other critters I'd rather not think about.

I kept my hand fastened on Juliette's. We had to stick together out here. Otherwise, we'd both be goners. This landscape had claimed more than one life before. Of course, this swamp had also shielded runaway slaves. That's how I had to think of the area —as a fortress, not as a death sentence.

I heard a sound in the distance. A shout maybe. I couldn't be sure as the storm roared around us.

As lightning flashed, I looked back and saw Jones on the porch. At least, that's who I thought I saw. It was a blurred figure, but the rain made it impossible to be sure of his identity.

"We've got to hurry."

"I'm not sure I can do this." Juliette paused against a tree, sagging there and gulping in air.

"We've got to. There will be time for rest later. Now we've got to move."

Through the storm, I heard gunfire.

Jones was shooting at us, I realized.

He wasn't willing to let us get away.

The noise seemed to kick our adrenaline into overdrive. I pulled Juliette deeper into the woods, into the swamp. The rain pelted us. The puddles nearly swallowed us. Underbrush slapped us.

But we kept moving.

The rain disguised any hints that Jones was getting closer. The one thing I knew for sure was that I'd hurt his eye. I doubted he could see well. His eye might even be infected by now, and that could slow him down even more.

"Gabby, I can't." Juliette jerked me back. Her face was scrunched with pain, and she leaned down on her knees. "I can't go any more."

"Yes, you can." Panic threatened to rise in me.

"I'm so tired."

"Juliette, you're the one who talks about doing everything through Christ's strength. I'm praying that He's going to give you that strength now. We've got to move."

She stared at me a moment before nodding. "Okay. I'll try."

Just then, a gust of wind blew through. Something cracked. Juliette screamed as another tree crashed in front of us.

My heart was racing. That had been close. Too close.

I craned my neck behind me. Where was Jones? Where had he gone?

I wiped the water from my eyes, wishing I knew if we were running deeper into the swamp or toward safety. I thought we were following the road, but the darkness made it hard to know for sure.

Just then, someone grabbed my arm. I snapped to a stop, my shoulder aching at the intensity.

I looked up. Jones. It was Jones.

Juliette's eyes widened, and she screamed, backing away.

"Run!" I shouted to Juliette. "Get help!"

She stared at me a moment. Then she looked at Jones. Back at me.

Finally, she took off.

Jones sneered at me. "You didn't think you'd get away that easily, did you?"

"A girl's gotta try." I had to admit, I was trembling. Maybe it was the rain that soaked me to the bone. Maybe it was the murky swamp water that suctioned my feet to the ground. Maybe it was simply Jones and my primal reactions as I remembered what he'd done to me. I wasn't sure.

But I was going to have to draw on every ounce of my strength and my faith to get through this.

"I'm going to kill you right here, right now." He stepped closer. "You're going to wish I was easy on you. You're going to wish I killed you the way I killed those other girls. That's how bad this is going to be."

I glanced behind him. Was it my imagination, or had that tree moved? I glanced down at the roots. The ground here was saturated, which would make the root systems more compromised. Hurricanes were known for taking down trees, roots and all.

"When I'm done, the swamp is going to help finish you off," he shouted. "The creatures here will feed on the remains of your body until it's gone. The police will never find you. You started as no one, and you'll finish life as no one."

Jones had abandoned his gun for a knife. He grabbed my hand, twisted until it was palm up, and then he smiled as he raised the weapon. "Nice, isn't it?"

I tried to jerk back, but I couldn't escape Jones' grasp. He lowered the knife slowly, running the blade down my palm. The razor sharp edge pierced my flesh. He prodded deeper until I cried out with pain. "How's that feel?"

I closed my eyes, remembering Riley. I had to fight for him. When I opened my eyes again, I felt a new fire inside me. "You can destroy my flesh, but you can't destroy my spirit."

He spit on me.

The rain washed it away.

I glanced back at that tree again. It wasn't my imagination. The old oak was teetering and about to fall as the wind prodded it.

And Jones was standing right beneath it. Thanks to his bloody eye, he couldn't see it out of his peripheral vision.

"Prepare to die, Gabby." He lunged at me with the knife.

With everything in me, I pushed him back. The knife caught my arm. Pain screamed from my bicep.

Jones fell backward just as a gust of wind swept the landscape. He landed in a deep puddle and tried to pull himself upright, but the mud was like quicksand.

I turned, started to run, started to flee.

But then I saw the tree sway again. I heard a crack.

Then the whole mighty oak crashed onto him.

I held my breath. Waited. Wondered. Dared to hope.

Jones had disappeared beneath the tree. It was like the swamp had swallowed him. The darkness and rain and wind did nothing to help my investigation.

Was Jones dead? Was he really dead?

I walked closer, each step tentative and filled with a touch of apprehension and anxiety. I half expected to see Jones rise from the dead like one of those madmen from a horror movie. I half expected that he'd somehow avoided the tree and survived. I braced myself to see him again, to feel his grip on my arm, to see that deadly glimmer in his eyes.

I inched closer, lifting up prayers. I could get through this. I had to get through this.

Finally, I spotted Jones' feet. They stuck out from beneath the tree like the Wicked Witch of the East in *The Wizard of Oz*.

I lifted my face to the rain. *Thank you, Jesus. Thank you, Jesus.*

Now I just hoped that Juliette had managed to find help. Otherwise, I might have survived Jones, but this swamp and storm were going to take me down.

CHAPTER
TWENTY-SIX

AN HOUR LATER, help arrived. Local police found me, cordoned off Jones' body, and led me to an ambulance. I'd lost a lot of blood, apparently. The EMTs kept saying something to that extent, at least.

Juliette—against all odds—had found help. There had been a house located not too far from the swampy area. The homeowners had called 911, and now here we all were.

I'd been admitted as a patient at the hospital. Right now, I was lying in my little room, when Parker and Adams walked in.

Parker blanched when he saw me. "You look awful." He waved his hand in front of his face. "You smell awful too."

Using my last ounce of energy, I punched him in the shoulder and muttered, "Shut up."

Parker glanced at Adams. "She's going to be just fine."

"Good work out there, Gabby."

"Or dumb luck. It just depends on how you look at it."

Adams shook his head. "You followed your instincts. You never stopped arguing that Jones could be alive, and you were right. I just wish you hadn't almost died in the process."

"I told you not to follow him," Parker added with a scowl. "This could have turned out much differently."

I nodded. "Believe me. I know. I didn't want to lose sight of Jones when I saw him in the hospital. I knew if I did that it would be too late. We might not find him again."

"The good news is that, since you were foolhardy and didn't listen to me, Juliette is alive. I credit that to you."

"And people told me that being brash would only hinder me in life. They were wrong."

Parker and Adams chuckled.

My smile didn't last long. "How is Juliette?"

"She's going to be fine," Adams said. "Her physical wounds will heal much more quickly than her emotional ones. The same for you."

I didn't want to think about that now. I'd have time to deal with my emotional scars later. "I'm glad she's doing okay."

"I wanted to let you know that we found some papers in Jones' shack," Adams continued. "From what we can tell, he had his next victim already picked out. We found photos, and feel like it was just a matter of time before he struck again."

My throat tightened. "Who?"

"Riley's mom. In fact, that may have been one reason why he was in the hospital when you spotted him."

I shivered at the thought. The woman had just had a heart attack. She wouldn't have survived being snatched by Jones. "At least we all finally know that Jones is dead. Really dead. He won't be hurting anyone else."

"You can say that again." Parker nodded. "We're also investigating some other unsolved murders that we think Jones can be tied to, both here and in California. I have a feeling that his list of victims is going to keep growing."

I frowned and shook my head. People like Freddy Mansfield would find out things like that and only admire Jones more. Speaking of which . . . I glanced at Adams. "You should really check out this guy named Freddy Mansfield."

"Freddy Mansfield? Funny you said his name. We've already arrested him. He was the person driving the getaway car when Jones snatched you at the hospital."

"He was?" I'd had no idea his involvement would run that deep.

"He claims his mother's life was being threatened. We're looking into it."

"Good."

Adams shifted. "I've gotta say, Jones was pretty clever paying The Guardians to help him. They already didn't like you, so when they saw the opportunity to make your life even more miserable, they jumped on it."

"Nothing like having several enemies bond together to plot your demise." The smile quickly faded from my lips. "Do you know when I can get out of here?"

"The doctors want to run a few more tests," Parker said.

"Riley . . ." my voice faded. Today was the day they wanted to transfer him. I was in another hospital in a neighboring city. I might have been rescued in time to save myself, but had I been rescued in time to stop Riley's parents from transferring him? Would my abduction slow them down any?

"Actually, you have some people outside who want to see you. Mary Lou, while not family, seems to have something very urgent she wants to say.

Would you like for me to send her in?" Adams asked.

I nodded. What in the world could be that urgent? I braced myself, unsure if this would be good or bad news. I prayed it was good.

The two men stepped out of the room, and Mary Lou stepped in. She rushed to my bed and patted my hand. "I was so worried," she started.

"Me too," I admitted. "But thankfully I'm still here."

Her smile slipped. "I have some news for you."

"Bad news?" I questioned. A million scenarios, all including Riley, swept through my mind.

She frowned. "I'll let you decide that. I was cleaning out Riley's office, and I just happened to find these hollow books on one of his shelves. I had no idea they were there even."

"Hollow books?" I let out an airy laugh. "I'd forgotten about those. I gave them to Riley as a joke."

She swallowed, though her throat looked tight and uncomfortable. "He had put his Power of Attorney documents in the book, Gabby."

I tensed. "Oh?" That was all I could say. I didn't want to ask any more questions.

Mary Lou nodded. "What his parents have been telling you is true, Gabby. His dad has durable Power of Attorney over him."

"I see."

"I'm sorry."

I thought tears would wet my eyes again. But maybe my tears had dried up. I nodded. "Okay. If that's what Riley wanted. I can't exactly argue with his written words, can I?"

"There's one other thing I thought you should know. His parents, and Riley's doctor, decided to take Riley out of his medically induced coma before transferring him."

"When?"

She shook her head. "I don't know. Today originally. I'm not sure if anything has changed or not."

"I've got to get to the hospital, Mary Lou."

She nodded. "I thought you'd say that. Do you want me to send the doctor in so you can plead your case?"

"Plead my case? No, I'm checking myself out."

An hour later, I sat in a wheelchair in the entry to the hospital where Riley was a patient. It had taken a lot of talking and insisting and threatening, but they'd finally discharged me. I was achy, dehydrated, battling chills, and even though I'd cleaned up, I still smelled like the swamp.

But I was here.

I'd brought my entourage with me. Teddi and my

dad. Chad and Sierra. Mary Lou. Even Parker had shown up.

But I knew when I went into Riley's room, I'd be without any of them. No, I'd have to face Riley's parents, knowing they'd been right. Feeling like they were making a bad choice, but being powerless to stop them.

Plus, my own partiality was getting in my way. Not in my investigations, but in my decisions. My bias told me what was best for Riley was staying here. But that hospital up near D.C. did have a great brain injury staff. I'd still fight against Dr. Moreno. But I had to let go of what was best for me or what was best for Riley's parents, and I had to think about what was best for Riley.

Even if it killed me to do it.

Apparently, my doctor had called this hospital and explained things to them. I had to promise I would let them admit me here when I discharged myself at the other hospital. Doctors still needed to monitor me or something. I didn't even care at the moment. I only cared about seeing Riley.

I waved bye to my friends, grateful that they'd all come out to show their support, especially since I had pushed most of them away. I hadn't really meant to. I was just trying to process everything.

My dad squeezed my hand. "I love you, Gabby."

I nodded toward him. "Thanks, Dad."

I had nothing to say as the nurse pushed me down the hallway, onto the elevator, and up three levels. My anxiety seemed to grow with every minute.

I met Riley's mom and dad at the door to the ICU. To their credit, they didn't flinch when they saw me. In fact, Evelyn gave me a quick hug. "I'm so glad you're okay. We were so worried."

"She's right. We've had enough excitement lately to last a lifetime." He leaned closer. "And, between you and me, I'm glad you got your guy, Gabby. My soul can rest now that I know the person who did this to Riley won't be hurting anyone else. Especially not my Evelyn."

I was pretty sure that was the first compliment Riley's dad had ever given me. I'd take it. "Thank you."

I glanced at my hands before meeting Mr. Thomas' gaze again. "Look, I really need to say that I'm sorry for the way I acted. There were better ways I could have handled things, and better ways I could have treated you. I'm definitely a work in progress, and sometimes I feel like I fail more than I succeed, especially when I let my emotions get in the way. Please accept my apology."

Riley's parents both hugged me.

"Of course we do," Evelyn whispered. "Forgive us for not consulting with you more before we made our announcement. There's room for forgiveness all the way around. We know you love our son."

"Thank you," I whispered.

We all exchanged glances.

"We can reschedule this," Mr. Thomas said.

I shook my head. "No, I'm here now."

"You sure you're ready for this?" Mr. Thomas watched me carefully before his gaze flicked up to his wife.

Evelyn and I nodded slowly. I felt so uncertain, yet hopeful, yet fearful. Emotions were rarely as easy and simple as I'd like them to be.

Together we went into Riley's room. They'd already taken him off the ventilator and he was breathing on his own. That was a good sign.

As I watched Riley's chest rise and fall, I realized there were no words for the moment. Nothing anyone said could make me feel better or worse. I just wanted to get this over with.

The doctor stepped in. He flinched when he saw me, but quickly gained his composure. "No one can predict how this will go," he started. "We've seen some positive progress. I think taking him out of this coma before he's transferred is the best idea. I think he's ready. We just don't know exactly what to expect."

The reality remained that Milton Jones had ripped too many lives apart. Innocent people had suffered.

In fact, this world was filled with suffering; no one could escape its clutch, it seemed.

And, all of that, had brought us to this moment.

Despite the bandage on my hand and how my palm ached every time I moved it, I grabbed Riley's hand as the doctor walked to the other side of the bed. I was surprised when Riley's mom reached down and grabbed my other hand.

Tears glistened in her eyes. This was hard for them. I could tell that it was. If anyone understood the enormity of this moment, it was Riley's parents. Maybe I should have given them the benefit of the doubt a little more.

The doctor told us what he was going to do. How he'd unplug the machines. How he'd disconnect Riley from the medical equipment keeping him in this comatose state. And then we'd all wait and see.

I braced myself. *Lord, watch over him. Help him to come out of this.*

Was it selfish to want him to be like he was? To pray that he could still walk and talk and do what he used to? I mean, on one hand, I was happy he was just alive. Maybe I was praying for too much.

That didn't change my prayers, though.

The doctor adjusted something on Riley's IV. Probably the medication they'd used to sedate him. "It will take a few minutes for this to wear off."

I held his hand. I waited. I watched for a sign that he'd be okay. For him to open his eyes.

I don't know what I was expecting. I knew he wouldn't instantly sit up and return to normal.

But the minutes just dragged on and there were no changes. No signs of hope.

An hour later, the doctor announced, "He doesn't appear ready to come out of his coma yet. We have to give him time."

A tear rolled down Evelyn's cheek. Ron hung his head down toward his chest. I'm not sure what I was doing, until I realized I'd laid my cheek against Riley's hand.

Did this mean he was in a coma? Not a medically induced one this time? Was I jumping to conclusions too early?

"Riley, you're still in there, right?"

"His brain still has significant function," the doctor said. "If he had brain death, we would have recommended taking him off this medical equipment much sooner. We just have to give it time."

I remembered the vows Riley had written for me. I raised my head and began to hum, "If I Loved You."

Riley's mom and dad looked at each other like I was crazy. I didn't care. I continued to hum until my hum turned into soft singing. I continued to sing softly until my soft singing turned into louder singing.

Tears wet my cheeks, but I continued. I didn't care how crazy I looked or sounded.

I just wanted Riley to hear me.

As I finished the last note, my voice cracking, I lowered my forehead back down to his hand.

When this was over, the nurses were going to bypass my regular room and take me up to the psych ward instead.

"Gabby?" Evelyn asked.

Slowly, I raised my head. "I just love him. I do."

Just then, I felt pressure on my hand. My gaze darted down to where my hand met Riley's.

I felt it again.

A squeeze.

Riley squeezed my hand!

"What is it?" Evelyn asked.

"He's responding. He's responding!"

Who would have ever thought something so little, something as small as a squeeze of the hand, could bring so much joy?

But, that motion had brought me hope.

And sometimes hope was all a girl had to hold on to.

Two weeks later, my body was still healing. I had bruised ribs and a sprained ankle. But I was at home, busy with paperwork for Trauma Care. I did what I could on the job sites, but Clarice was continuing to fill in for me.

My cellphone rang. I saw the number and recognized the first three digits as the hospital's. I braced myself for this call.

"This is Gabby."

"Gabby, it's Evelyn." Her voice sounded charged.

"What's going on?"

"You've got to come down to the hospital now. Riley woke up. Please, come now!"

I nearly fell over myself as I hurried to the hospital. I was breathless by the time I reached his room. His parents stood at his bedside when I walked in. A new light glimmered in their eyes.

I paused, my heart in my throat when I looked at Riley. He was sitting up in bed, his eyes fastened on me. He looked pale and swollen and bandaged. But he was awake!

I took a step closer, unsure what to say, how to act. I'd dreamed about this moment, but now that it was here, I tried to be cautious.

I swallowed, licked my lips, and then grabbed his hand.

"Hey, Riley," I told him softly.

I resisted the urge to throw myself in his arms and sob about how much I loved him and missed him.

He peered at me, a blank look in his eyes. "Do I know you?"

I gasped. Looked at his parents a moment. They had strange expressions—concern and . . . something else.

Why hadn't they told me he couldn't remember me? Why would they withhold news like that? I opened my mouth, but no words came out.

"Riley Thomas," I heard Evelyn mutter. Was that reprimand in her voice?

A wide smile spread across Riley's face as his gaze met mine. "Just kidding."

My head snapped back toward him in a double take. I couldn't have just heard him right. What was going on here? "What?"

He smiled again and squeezed my hand. "I'm just kidding. Of course I know who you are. Gabby. My fiancée. The love of my life."

I nearly melted with relief. My hand went over my heart. Emotions ping-ponged inside me. Irritation. Relief. Love. Hope. Aggravation.

I narrowed my eyes at Riley, making sure I kept my tone light. "I . . . you . . . that wasn't funny."

He grinned again. "I couldn't resist."

I sat beside him and ran my fingers across his

cheek. "Be glad you just came out of a coma, or you'd be in big trouble right now."

"It's good to see you, Gabby." His smile faded. "You're okay, right?"

"Why would you think otherwise?"

He faltered. "Because . . ."

His eyes went from my bruised jaw to my busted lip to my black eye. "Yes?"

"You look wonderful, yet not that great."

"Have you taken a look at yourself yet?" I teased.

"I don't want to see. For a long time." He squeezed my hand. "My parents were telling me about everything you did for me. Thank you."

"It's nothing you wouldn't have done for me. And your parents were pretty great. I'm glad we've gotten to know each other better." And we had. We'd had dinner together several times and didn't have a single disagreement. I was so thankful we'd moved beyond our differences.

"I've talked with my doctor, and I've decided to stay here for my recovery." He glanced at his parents. "My mom and dad said they understand."

Relief nearly crushed my heart and broke me into a million pieces. Which was weird considering my spirit soared higher than it had in a long time. The relief was just so strong that it felt palpable. "I like that decision."

He pulled my hand up to his lips and kissed it. "I love you, Gabby."

Joy spread through me. "I love you too, Riley. Welcome back. I've missed you more than you imagine."

~~~

Thank you so much for reading *To Love, Honor, and Perish*. If you enjoyed this book, please consider leaving a review!

Keep reading for a preview of *Mucky Streak*.
~~~

NOW AVAILABLE

MUCKY STREAK: CHAPTER ONE

I brushed away my discomfort, instead trying to appear sophisticated and coolly in control. I felt neither of those things. My life at the moment felt about as frazzled as my curly red hair.

I brushed a piece of the thus stated hair behind my ear, sucked in a measured breath, and extended my hand. "Mr. Mercer."

"Ms. St. Claire. I'm glad you could meet with me." Garrett Mercer grinned, the ever-present sparkle still in his eyes as he circled from behind his desk and took my hand. His grip lingered a little too long.

As I pulled my hand back, his eyes remained smiling in a way that made me think he was more Irish than British. The man liked getting a reaction from me. I knew that much from my last encounter with him.

Garrett owned a company called Global Coffee Initiative that not only sold organic, free trade coffee, but also donated a good portion of the proceeds to build water wells for the less fortunate around the world. He was a textbook entrepreneur/prodigy, and he had a killer accent.

I lowered myself into the chair across from him and crossed my legs, trying to maintain an aura of professionalism. Lack of sleep and stress made common courtesies feel a little more challenging. I wished for a moment that I had the unruffled composure of the woman who'd just deposited me in Garrett's office. I was pretty sure she was Garrett's assistant—a neat and prim little blonde named Lyndsey. She probably wasn't just his assistant, if I had to guess based on the glance they'd exchanged. Then again, all of Garrett's employees looked like they'd just stepped out of an Abercrombie & Fitch catalog.

I cleared my throat. "Your phone call certainly made me curious."

He'd left a message two days ago, asking me to call him about a possible job. I had no idea what kind of job someone like the wealthy, world changer Garrett Mercer might want to hire a crime scene cleaner like me for.

I didn't know the man that well, other than the

fact I'd met him during my last investigation. One of his employees had been a suspect, and Garrett and I had chatted a couple of times. After the case was closed, I figured Garrett would be gone from my life for good. Yet, here I sat.

Garrett leaned against his desk, his ankles crossed and his arms now resting to his side. "Anything I can do to get you thinking about me."

He winked. The man was charming. I'd give him that. Probably one of the many qualities that helped him build his successful enterprise in the coffee world, and landed him on several "most desired," "most beautiful," "most interesting" and any-other-positive-superlative-you-might-want-to-include lists. He had this certain kind of demeanor that made women clamor for a chance to be around him. That made employees eager to please him. That made the media swoon.

But not me. I was immune to the man's charms. I was . . . wait for it . . . I was all professional.

Barely holding it together was more like it.

What I really wanted to do was take a nap. Maybe escape to the Bahamas for a while. Maybe lose myself in a musical. None of those things were an option.

Instead, in the overhead music of my mind, I continued to blare "Stronger" by Kelly Clarkson. That's right—I was determined that all these hard times were just going to make me more of a fighter.

Garrett studied me for a minute, not even trying to hide his curiosity. "You look tired. Can I get you some coffee? Maybe one of our new flavors like maple bacon or autumn harvest?"

Normally, I might refuse. But I could really use some coffee to chase away my chills and my crankiness. Escaping the man's scrutiny for a moment also sounded delightful. "Actually, that sounds great. Just regular coffee, please. Two sugars and one cream."

"I've got it."

I should look tired. I'd been working myself to the bone. When I wasn't working, I was taking Riley, my fiancé, to therapy as he tried to recover from a brain injury. I had to admit that everything—being abducted by a serial killer and almost dying, my busy schedule, the stress, the shock of life's unexpected curveball—was catching up with me. I was just plain exhausted. My joy was slipping away, and life was beginning to feel like a chore.

It's just a phase, I reminded myself. I could get through this. As long as I had God and Riley by my side, I could handle anything. In theory, I easily believed that. It was much more difficult to put into practice, though.

I glanced around the office as I sat there waiting for Garrett to return. Garrett's company headquarters was located in an old warehouse turned office space. The floors were still cement, only sealed and polished. Open space, windows, and skylights made the area feel big and exuded a very urban, modern, and repurposed vibe.

Very much like Garrett.

Tall, sturdy, and stylishly underdressed, the man was considerate of the environment, responsible, and wealthy. Apparently, he'd nearly flunked out of college, only to turn his life around and create the successful business he had today. That's what my best friend Sierra had told me, at least. I tried not to ask too many questions or appear too interested when Garrett and I spoke.

I glanced around at his office. Minimalist decorations. Large picture windows. An enormous aquarium with crazy looking fish inside. Pictures of him surrounded by kids with dirty faces but big smiles and barren landscapes behind them.

Gerard Butler, I decided. That's who the man reminded me of.

A moment later, I heard him in the hallway. He murmured something and a woman giggled incessantly. I glanced behind me. Lyndsey. His "assistant."

He handed me a cup, made from recycled paper —of course. Our hands brushed, and I'd bet anything it was no accident. Garrett was a touchy feely kind of guy. He liked getting what he wanted.

"So, I'm sure you're wondering why I asked you to meet with me." He settled back in his normal position, leaning against his desk like he was posing for some random *GQ* photographer. He wore jeans that probably cost more than I made at one job site and a lush beige sweater that zipped up to his neck.

I took a sip of my coffee and let the warmth spread through me. "I am curious as to why you wanted to meet with me."

"I'll get right to the point, then. I heard about your work in the Milton Jones case. By all accounts, you were brilliant and brave. Your work helped to take a serial killer off the streets, and we're all safer because of it."

"What can I say? It's all in a day's work." I didn't mention that I'd almost died and that I was still having nightmares—night terrors were more like it— about the ordeal. I cringed whenever I saw a swamp or an old cabin or when thunder shook the walls of my apartment. Each caused strong memories to swell so fiercely that I could hardly breathe.

Milton Jones had probably made some lists himself—as one of the most horrific serial killers that America had seen this decade. Maybe in the past two decades. I wasn't sure. Thankfully, he wouldn't be a problem for anyone else anymore.

"I understand that you worked for the medical examiner for a while." He took a sip of his coffee, but his eyes stayed on me, watching my every expression.

"You've done your research."

"I'm nothing if not thorough." That smirk—it was becoming all too familiar—tugged at his lips.

I had no doubt that the man was as smart as a whip . . . or as sly as a fox. I wasn't sure which one yet. "What's all of that have to do with this meeting? You want details on how I tracked Jones down? Because, honestly, I have a million other things I need to be doing. No offense."

Reporters had been knocking down my door, trying to get the inside scoop. Even a few national broadcasts had contacted me. I had mixed feelings on sharing my side of the story . . . mostly because my side of the story included almost losing the love of my life. I was so grateful Riley was alive, but so much had changed since he'd suffered from a gunshot wound to the head.

Though the doctors expected a full recovery for Riley, I was trying to accept the fact that things would never be the same. I was trying to be okay with that. It was easier said than done, though.

Like most things in life.

"No offense taken." Garrett leaned closer. "No, I didn't bring you here to waste your time. I want to hire you, actually."

I raised an eyebrow. "Hire me? You have a crime scene you want me to clean? Something you want to tell me? Let me guess: Entrepreneur by day, serial killer by night?" I wouldn't have said it so lightly except I knew it wasn't true. Well, I was pretty sure it wasn't.

"No, I don't need you to clean for me." His grin slipped some, and he straightened the sleeves of his sweater. "I'd like to hire you as a P.I., Gabby."

This was a new one for me. Sure, I'd solved a few crimes. But no one had ever *hired* me to do that. No, it was just because I was nosy and pushy and loved justice too much for my own good. "A private investigator?"

"Yes. A private investigator. Just one more confirmation that you're good. Nothing gets past you." He winked.

I scowled again. "Funny."

"All right, enough playing, right? Yes, I want to hire you to look into a case. Law enforcement would call it a cold case. It will require some travel, but I promise to compensate you well."

Compensation sounded good. Especially since I'd just overdrawn my checking account by more than three hundred dollars. "I'm listening."

He stiffened and rubbed his chin. Instead of gushing out some story in the gregarious way I'd become accustomed to when it came to Garrett, he stood. He went to the other side of his desk and sat, a somber new expression on his face.

"There's a part of my life that most people don't

know about. I try to keep it quiet because, quite frankly, it's painful."

He had my attention now. I supposed in my mind I pictured people like Garrett to have everything handed to them on a silver platter; to live charmed lives void of pain and heartache. I should know better than that by now.

"My family moved here from England when I was fourteen. My dad worked for a consumer products company, then moved on to a start-up before being offered a job with a pharmacy company in Washington, D.C. My mum and sister and I came along for the ride. Begrudgingly, I might add."

I shifted, intrigued by his story already. "Okay."

"We moved again three years later when a pharmaceutical company in Cincinnati offered my father an even more prestigious position. When I was 19, I came home from college for the weekend. I was late arriving. I'd decided to stay for a party the night before, so I came home on Saturday instead of Friday night as planned."

I waited to hear what happened next.

His face tensed, as if the memories were painful. "Quite truthfully, my mum and dad had been quite argumentative the past several times I'd seen them, and I would have rather not been around them. They insisted they had something to speak with me about, however."

"Go on."

"When I walked into my house that morning, I found my family." He paused and rubbed his throat. "They'd all been shot in the head execution style."

I sucked in a deep breath, the horror of the event washing over me. "That's terrible."

"To say the least. My life changed from that day forward. Tragedy does that to you." He shifted, tugging at his pant leg now, a small tell as to how painful this was to him. "This is where I would like for you to come in. You see, the police never found the person responsible for my family's death. I won't have a moment of peace in my life until the person who murdered them is behind bars."

"Where are the police at with this? Have they completely given up?"

"They say that they've followed every lead, and that every lead has dried up. They've got nothing."

"I know it's hard to get closure without all of the answers. Any of the answers, for that matter."

"You've got that right." He held up a folder stuffed with papers. "I was able to get my hands on the police reports. I have all the information on who they interviewed, who their suspects were, what evidence they found."

I stared at the papers like a kid salivating for cotton candy at the circus. I wasn't delighting in his pain; I was salivating at the chance for justice to be served, for answers to be found, for lives to be restored.

He pressed his lips together. "Are you interested in taking this on?"

I paused, trying to think through my response. Putting my brain into gear before my mouth engaged was my new resolution, and no, it wasn't New Year's. Big life changes could cause a person to rethink things. "What makes you think I can figure this out if seasoned investigators can't?"

"Something tells me you're different, Gabby. You're spunky and determined. I have a feeling people open up to you more easily than they'd ever open up to one of those crusty old detectives."

"I'm flattered." I actually *was* flattered, despite how sarcastic my words might have sounded.

"I'm serious." Garrett's eyes met mine, all teasing gone. "What do you think?"

The offer was tempting. Very tempting. But I didn't know if I could take it on right now. I had my hands full with my crime scene cleaning business and trying to help my fiancé. Taking Riley back and forth to therapy as he recovered from his brain injury seemed like a full-time job. Plus, I was cooking for him, cleaning his apartment, buying his groceries, and even doing his laundry. Small, mole-hill-sized tasks had turned into giant mountains for him.

"I'm not sure what to say," I finally said. "To be honest, I have a lot going on in my life right now."

He nodded toward my engagement ring. "When's the wedding?"

I realized I'd been absently twisting and turning the jewelry on my finger, remembering the events that had played out over the past couple of months. I frowned. "I'm not sure."

Garrett quirked an eyebrow and tilted his head compassionately. "That doesn't sound good."

My heart squeezed at his words. I wouldn't let Garrett Mercer get the best of me. Things were fine between Riley and me. "It's a long story."

He stared at me again, and I wondered what was going on behind those green eyes. "I see. I won't pry. Just promise me you'll think about taking this job. Take these files. They contain the basic information. Look them through."

"I will. I'll be in touch." I glanced at my watch. "But I should run now. I have another appointment."

"I understand. But you should know that I'm not a very patient man." He leveled his gaze. "I need an answer in a week."

"I can do that." I took the file from him, and something stirred inside me. Something I hadn't felt in the last couple of months. Something I hadn't felt since Milton Jones.

The longing to find answers. The excitement of a

new mystery. The adrenaline surge of facing an engaging challenge.

Garrett stood to walk me to the door. His hand went to my lower back to guide me across the room and, just as it happened last time, a jolt of electricity shot through me. I wasn't sure why the man had this effect on me, but he did. And the fact had me steamed.

He seemed to realize this, too, based on the sparkle in his eyes. Maybe he could feel my skin tighten. Maybe he could hear the quick intake of my breath. I wasn't sure.

But I didn't like that, either.

"Good day, Gabby. Help yourself to another cup of coffee on the way out."

I walked toward the reception area, hating the uncertain feeling in my gut. I hated the pull between two opposing desires: investigating an intriguing case or being a good, responsible fiancé. It appeared I couldn't be or do both.

It didn't matter right now, though. I had to pick up Riley from therapy.

Click here to continue reading.

ALSO BY CHRISTY BARRITT:

BOOKS IN THE SQUEAKY CLEAN UNIVERSE

On her way to completing a degree in forensic science, Gabby St. Claire drops out of school and starts her own crime-scene cleaning business. When a routine cleaning job uncovers a murder weapon the police overlooked, she realizes that the wrong person is in jail. She also realizes that crime scene cleaning might be the perfect career for utilizing her investigative skills.

SQUEAKY CLEAN MYSTERIES
#1 Hazardous Duty
Half Witted (Squeaky Clean In Between Mysteries
Book 1, novella)
#2 Suspicious Minds
#2.5 It Came Upon a Midnight Crime (novella)
#3 Organized Grime

<u>#4 Dirty Deeds</u>
<u>#5 The Scum of All Fears</u>
<u>#6 To Love, Honor and Perish</u>
<u>#7 Mucky Streak</u>
<u>#8 Foul Play</u>
<u>#9 Broom & Gloom</u>
<u>#10 Dust and Obey</u>
<u>#11 Thrill Squeaker</u>
<u>#11.5 Swept Away (novella)</u>
<u>#12 Cunning Attractions</u>
<u>#13 Cold Case: Clean Getaway</u>
<u>#14 Cold Case: Clean Sweep</u>
<u>#15 Cold Case: Clean Break</u>
<u>#16 Cleans to an End</u>
<u>While You Were Sweeping, A Riley Thomas Spinoff</u>

SQUEAKY CLEAN IN BETWEEN MYSTERIES
Half Witted
Half Truth

THE SIERRA FILES
#1 Pounced
#2 Hunted
#3 Pranced
#4 Rattled
#5 Caged (coming soon)

ABOUT THE AUTHOR

USA Today has called Christy Barritt's books "scary, funny, passionate, and quirky."

Christy writes both mystery and romantic suspense novels that are clean with underlying messages of faith. Her books have sold more than four million copies and have won the Daphne du Maurier Award for Excellence in Suspense and Mystery, have been twice nominated for the Romantic Times Reviewers' Choice Award, and have finaled for both a Carol Award and Foreword Magazine's Book of the Year.

She is married to her Prince Charming, a man who thinks she's hilarious—but only when she's not trying to be. Christy is a self-proclaimed klutz, an avid music lover who's known for spontaneously bursting into song, and a road trip aficionado.

When she's not working or spending time with her family, she enjoys singing, playing the guitar, and exploring small, unsuspecting towns where people have no idea how accident-prone she is.

Find Christy online at:
www.christybarritt.com
www.facebook.com/christybarritt
www.twitter.com/cbarritt

Sign up for Christy's newsletter to get information on all of her latest releases here: **www.christybarritt. com/newsletter-sign-up/**

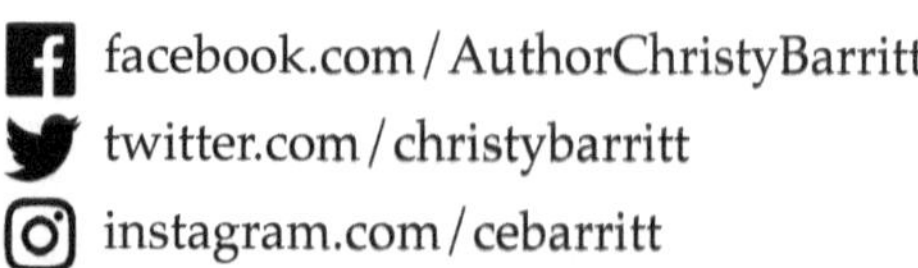

www.ingramcontent.com/pod-product-compliance
Lightning Source LLC
Chambersburg PA
CBHW031438160726
47994CB00005B/1786